Praise for Howard Means

"Finally, the cliché is peeled away, and the essence of this utterly American character is so revealing. John Chapman comes alive here, and it is a thrilling experience to escape the specific gravity of the decades of myth."

—Ken Burns, writing about *Johnny Appleseed: The Man, the Myth, the American Story*

"In Howard Means's fine hands, we discern how the terrible events at Kent State unfolded — relentlessly, ineluctably — like a Greek tragedy."

—Hampton Sides, author of *Kingdom of Ice*, writing about *67 Shots: Kent State and the End of American Innocence*

"In this gracefully written and well-informed narrative, Howard Means supplies a critical missing piece in the making of the United States ... Anyone curious about how this country came to represent the best and worst of human nature will find surprising revelations in this book."

—Noah Andre Trudeau, author of *Out of the Storm*, writing about *The Avenger Takes His Place: Andrew Johnson and the 45 Days That Changed the Nation*

"An exuberant and sweeping cultural history of the sport and a thoughtful meditation on its possible origins and humankind's relationship to water itself."

—Julie Checkoway, author of *The Three-Year Swim Club*, writing about *Splash! 10,000 Years of Swimming*

"*Splash!* is an incredible book — the most amazing stories of anything and everything you wanted to know about the world and culture of swimming and its history. I loved every page."
—Rowdy Gaines, three-time Olympic gold medalist

Also by Howard Means

Splash

67 Shots

Johnny Appleseed

The Avenger Takes His Place

More Books from The Sager Group

Chains of Nobility: Brotherhood of the Mamluks (Books 1-3)
by Brad Graft

The Deadliest Man Alive: Count Dante, The Mob and the War for American Martial Arts by Benji Feldheim

Death Came Swiftly: A Novel About the Tay Bridge Disaster of 1879
by Bill Abrams

Sing Sing Follies (A Maximum-Security Comedy): And Other True Stories
by John H. Richardson

Going Home to Die No More: A True Kentucky Story about a Train Robbery and a Hanging after the Civil War
by Russ Witcher

Who She Was: My Search for My Mother's Life
by Samuel G. Freedman

On the Run with Mad Bombers, Outlaw Lovers & Movie Stars: True Stories
by Daniel Voll

Lifeboat No. 8: Surviving the Titanic by Elizabeth Kaye

Hunting Marlon Brando: A True Story by Mike Sager

Miss Havilland: A Novel by Gay Daly

Saloon Man: A German Immigrant Battles the Limits of Liberty, 1870 to 1915 by Robert Mugge

See our entire library at TheSagerGroup.net

Almost Home

A Novel of
the *Sultana* and
the Last Great Tragedy
of the Civil War

Howard Means

Almost Home

A Novel of
the *Sultana* and
the Last Great Tragedy
of the Civil War

Howard Means

This is a work of fiction built on a framework of solid fact. The Confederate prison at Cahaba, Alabama, has been nearly forgotten. The fate of the *Sultana* and its passengers on that last voyage up the Mississippi is a minor footnote in the bloody history of the Civil War. Both — the prison camp and the soldiers who survived it only to meet even worse horror on their voyage home — deserve a better place in American memory.

For BPL

Main Characters

The Muncie Men

George Ethridge, husband of Eliza, father of George Jr., Eben, and Madeleine.

Ephraim Ethridge, George's younger brother.

Henry Wellington, Ephraim's contemporary and best friend.

Jake, uncle to George and Ephraim and brother to their mother.

Boy, unofficially adopted by the Muncie men and of uncertain origins.

Prison Commanders

Howard Andrew Millet Henderson, first commander of the Confederacy's Cahaba Federal Prison in Alabama and later instrumental in the founding of Camp Fisk near Vicksburg, Mississippi, the last stop for Union prisoners returning home. A Methodist minister by training, Rev. Henderson officiated in 1883 at the funeral of Ulysses S. Grant's mother, Hannah, with the former Union Army commander standing by his side.

Lt. Col. Sam Jones, in charge of Cahaba's prison guard force, acting commander of the prison during H.A.M. Henderson's many prolonged absences, and Henderson's polar opposite. A native of New Orleans, Jones disappeared at war's end.

Sultana

Union Army Capt. Frederick Speed, who oversaw the loading of passengers on to the Sultana as it sat at dock on April 24, 1865, in Vicksburg.

Nathan Wintringer, the Sultana's chief mechanic.

The Confederate Cahaba Federal Prison in Alabama

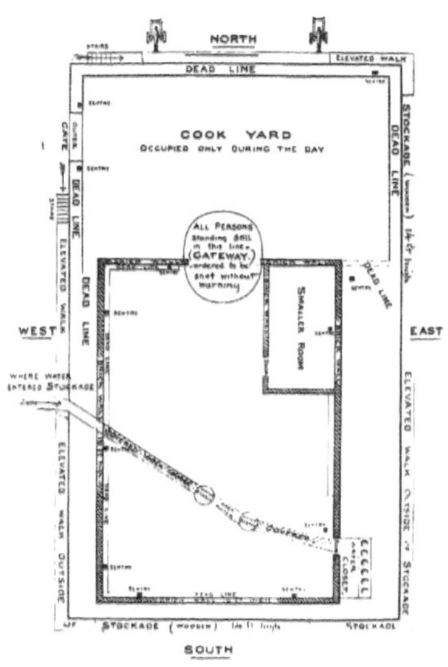

The Only Known Photograph
of the *Sultana's* Last Voyage

1

Cahaba Prison, Alabama, April 1865

Finally, you learn to wait.

You learn to wait while the rain falls for four days and nights; wait as the rivers rise over their banks, carrying with them the town shit and your own; wait as this new sewer-lake begins seeping into the cotton warehouse that is now a prison, your home. And then you learn to wait in your skin and bones: wait as the sewer-lake-pond-river consumes your toes, your feet, your ankles — assuming you have no boots, and almost no one does; wait as it crawls up your shins and over your knees; wait until your balls and prick are sodden; and then wait some more because when you are standing in a flood and not allowed to leave (few bullets left anywhere, but maybe one for you?) there is nothing else to do.

George was six feet, tall by any standard: the water crested at his navel. Jake was shorter, squarer — even after a year of eating almost nothing still miraculously built like a boiler. (Or maybe not so miraculously since boilers were what Jake had built for twenty years before marching off to war one beautiful morning in that dire and losing summer of 1862.) On Jake, the water crested near to armpit high.

"You think it's going to get any higher?" he had asked, tiptoe on his old bum of an ankle. "It's going to be a mite uncomfortable underwater."

"Oh, hell, Jake, comes to that, we'll just fit a sail to you and ride you on out of here." That was Ephraim, who had never sailed a thing in his life, not even a paper boat. George thought of telling Ephraim to watch his tongue — once an older brother, always one — but held back. The circumstances were extraordinary.

"Our own ironclad," Henry chipped in, chest high in the flood like Ephraim, the two of them Romulus and Remus, all but suckled at the same teat.

There'd been other floods. There had to be. The warehouse sat on a point of land where two rivers that couldn't stay within themselves met a railroad that wasn't anymore almost in the center of a town that had been resurrected from the dead and was soon to die again. Flooding is what Cahaba did best —its own art form. But whenever the rivers had overflowed their banks before, the men had been able to take to whatever high roosts and perches the warehouse afforded: the tiers of hammered-together bunk beds stuck off in one corner, the railings that surrounded the wood crib, the wood pile itself. The Muncie Men — George, Jake, Ephraim, and Henry — had slept one night like barn cats, strewn all over a pile of scraggly green logs.

This time was different. This time the water kept rising and raising everything with it. An artesian spring ran through the prison, filling three huge vats that had been sunk into the ground: one for drinking water, one for the men to wash in (though never anything like soap), one for washing clothes (though by then clothes were hardly that). From the vats, the spring ran beneath a water closet with six crappers, carrying the waste away to the river beyond. The flood slopped over the vats, adding their stale water to its own mix. It pushed through the crapper holes so that any man who had been allowed to use one — none were — would have found himself taking a shit underwater.

This time, too, Col. Jones was in charge of the prison, not Capt. Henderson, and Col. Jones as always had a bug up his ass. The men finally sent a delegation to him on Day Three: stood just inside the dead-man line that marked the warehouse door (any man crossing that, or even lingering there, to be shot without warning), screamed through the clattering rain for permission to advance, were so granted, and waded through the prison yard until they were standing beneath the walkway that ran along the stockade fence that surrounded the warehouse prison that was the men's confinement and home.

Their request had the virtue of simplicity. High ground stood not far beyond the stockade. If the colonel would grant the prisoners permission to move en masse to said promontory until the rain had ceased and the rivers returned however temporarily to their banks, the prisoners would upon their troth and sacred honor vow not to attempt escape or any other matter of rebellion upon Col. Jones, his corps of guards, Cahaba Prison, the good citizenry of Alabama, or the sovereign nation (if that's what it was) of the Confederate States of America. (The promise backed up by practicality, too: Not one man in fifty among them with the strength to slog through sodden fields much of anywhere, much less to Union lines, wherever in God's name they might be.)

Regal upon that walkway, staring down at the soaked Federals below him up to their emaciated bellies and beyond in water, flanked on either side by his own armed cadres, Col. Jones barked out his answer loud enough for even the men in the back of the warehouse to hear:

"No! Not if every damned Yankee drowns!"

And so they stood, and stood some more. Maybe two, three thousand prisoners in all. No one bothered to count. There was no point. Suffice it to say: a vast, reeking lake-forest of skin and bone washed in this sewage-drenched and outsized confluence of the Alabama and Cahaba rivers.

There was food for the water men: a cracker a day, doled out from a rowboat moored to the warehouse door, and even that the weak lost to the strong unless they had the wherewithal to cram the cracker into their mouths the moment they received it, and the tenacity to keep their jaws clamped tight until the cracker was soft enough to chew and the cracker-mush finally soft enough to swallow. Humanity, small gestures of decency, flourished everywhere amidst their travail, but survival flourished, too. The wounded, the puny, the ones who couldn't or wouldn't make friends were cut from the pack, set upon, whittled down until only splinters survived. The Muncie Men covered each other's back. Always.

On the third day, shortly after the delegation had visited him, Col. Jones ordered rations increased to a quarter cup of cornmeal a man — a barbed generosity that spoke to the man's whole character. There was, of course, no way to cook the meal, and no way not to eat it, so the men held it in their mouth, mixed it with saliva and the filthy water that surrounded them, swallowed, and prayed to God for release. And God must have listened, for inside each of them, the cornmeal warmed, soaked in the stomach juices, swelled, bloated, turned digestive tracts into boilers, and finally exited in an explosion that would have been far worse had it not been so commonplace and had they not already sunk so far below the baselines of human decency.

A Congregational minister tried leading them in song the second day: "Lord hear us when we cry to thee, for those in peril on the sea." A joke! Almost the rarest thing to be found in their confinement, much less among this Biblical deluge. Though only a corporal, the minister was said to be a college man, some school up in Maine state, a wild-eyed abolitionist who couldn't wait to trade his surplice for the

Union blue. If it was true, if ministers were college men and this infantryman was the minister he claimed to be, then George reckoned he might be the only educated man in the entire prison who still cared deeply about what he had set out to do. If the months upon months of prison hadn't already leached them of conviction, the water finally did.

In the South, so George had been told, no man whatever his station could get out of fighting. The womenfolk wouldn't allow it. George used to imagine prison camps back north where the Reb officers gathered in the evening to sip sweet French wines and talk in ancient Greek and Latin. Up Muncie way, his home, the gung-hos had come storming out back in the summer of '61 when Jervis opened a recruiting office down at his supply store and began forming up companies. The Johnny Rebs had stunned the Union at Bull Run; time to teach the seceshes a lesson in return. Besides, it was only nine months — a chance to escape the Indiana winter. Everyone would be home for spring planting.

A year later, when Father Abraham issued his call for 300,000 new men good and true to join the cause, fervor had sunk among the would-be warriors of eastern Indiana. McClellan had failed at Richmond; Lee was driving the Federals before him, back across the Rappahannock. One more river to go, and he'd be in Washington City. Too many of those blithe spirits who had crowded around Jervis and his fellow graying patriots twelve months earlier had come home trimmed by the surgeon's saw, or had been left swelling under the sun on the field of honor. Too many of the women who had cheered their sweethearts off were left to wait a widow's pension, uncertain in the best of times.

George didn't know of a single high-born man who had joined up that second time around. The one exception: old Effing the Banker's son. The boy had taken a mule kick in the head when he was little and hadn't made a lick of sense since.

High-born wasn't George's problem. He'd stood his ground a year earlier because, having almost never seen a Negro in his life and caring less for or against states' rights than he cared for purgatives, he saw no advantage in it. This time, he put down his name and took the hundred-dollar bonus. That and the $11 a month he was to be paid for his three-year tour would keep a roof over Eliza and the children. So long as his Papa farmed and the soil wasn't salted, there would always be food.

Besides, conscription was coming. That was plain as day. The rich would be able to buy their way out. The poor, the farmers, the mechanics, the mousy shop-clerks, the drovers and haulers and cartmen — those are the ones who would be ordered to fight, who would be marched into cannon fire. Better to go in on his own, George reasoned, when he could still command a price. Footloose and fancy-free, Ephraim and Henry had followed on a lark, the lark now long flown away. Jake had come in at the last minute — "to see the world a bit," as he put it, and for "the hard specie," but more so, George was certain, to keep a watch on his oldest sister's two boys, now old enough themselves to kill and be killed.

Of course, not everyone stood four days in that deepening baptism of water. Not everyone could. It began before the start of the second day. Some wag would shout out "Timmmmmber!" and if you were close enough, you could hear the splash, a startled shout, maybe even the thrashing of someone staggering back to his feet. The men roared each time it happened, and they roared when one of the guards sent to stand upon the railing that surrounded the wood pen and fire upon anyone who attempted to clamber out of the water himself fell asleep and plunged forward face first into what had by then become a septic tank.

They laughed harder still when a Grayback cavalry colonel no one had ever seen before came prancing in imperiously a little after dawn on Day Three; shouted out, "Well, hello, boys. Y'all about through with your baths?"; and rode his dappled gray right into the sunken tub where non-existent laundry had only four days earlier been given non-existent soakings. By the time he scrambled back on his floundering steed and turned for the warehouse door, a little ball of shit had attached itself to his little ball of a goatee. The most farcical English comedy could not have been more funny.

The jokes had lost their luster by the end of that third day, after the fallen trees stopped righting themselves. Why? Why should it kill a man to stand in water? Because these weren't whole men. No. No. If food was air, they all would have suffocated. George knew as little about medicine, he supposed, as any man alive could know, but what a lesson in breaking bodies they all received every blessed day of their confinement and never more so than when they were called to be water-men.

The prisoners would float the bodies that couldn't right themselves toward the front of the warehouse — a natural current ran that way — and the ones at the front would push them over the deadman's line (that threat, at least, muted for the floaters), out into the yard. There, guards in rowboats would pull the ex-prisoners in with long-handled gaffs, tie some more or less permanent part of them to the stern, and row them through the front gate to the high ground where living Federals were not allowed to assemble. Later, after the water had finally agreed to go down, some raggedy-ass group of survivors would be sent out to the meadow past the paling, over the river, to dig the shallow ditches to bury the men who had died because, while they had been deemed well enough to fight on land, they couldn't stand in water.

Years later, former dwellers of the former Cahaba would claim that the prisoners dropped down among them like an unwanted load of something dire and contagious had actually enjoyed the Great Flood. "Why," they would say, "we could hear them singing and laughing — roaring even — while we were still cooped up in the second floor! Yankees just strange, we figured."

Strange, perhaps, but were the people who said such things mad? Deranged? Delusional? Had they tripped delicately down their soaked stairways, stepped ever so carefully across their submerged drawing rooms, set out perhaps in a rowboat or canoe of their own to the higher ground where it was possible to see inside the stockade, and had a look at the pathetic scene inside? Memory is the biggest liar of all.

The rivers did recede. They always do — even the Great Flood went down. By noon of Day Three the water was halfway down George's hips; by midnight, to his shin bones. Before the fourth day was over, it disappeared altogether, and George and Jake, Ephraim and Henry — who had managed little catnaps by leaning in against each other like stacked bean poles — flopped down in the wet mud, curled themselves around one another for warmth in that March Alabama chill, and slept the sleep of the nearly dead. When they awoke, George and Ephraim's hair was matted together, held in joint tenancy by large drying clots of that clay left by the decaying Appalachians, brother bound by mud to brother. And still Col. Jones was there — Jones and his command staff, Jones and his riflemen (the rifles still plentiful, even when ammunition was nearly gone), Jones and his guards, standing on that walkway at the top of the stockade fence, staring in at his charges, unwilling yet to walk among the pigs in their wallow.

2

Water! It was the curse of the place and its cause, its reason and its ruination. The Alabama River curls its way for more than 300 miles south-southwest from the center of the state almost clear to Mobile Bay. The Cahaba, its chief tributary, winds down from the north, supplying drinking water to Birmingham, which didn't exist at the time of the Civil War. Where the two join and the Cahaba becomes the Alabama, the state raised its first capital, all the way back in eighteen-hundred-and-nineteen. Mobile Bay had been under Spanish rule only six years earlier. The rest of the territory had been wrested from the Creek Indians about the same time by none other than Andy Jackson, Old Hickory. (And the Creeks themselves marched on to Oklahoma, 700 and more miles from any place they had ever known as home.)

A year passed before there was anything like a capitol to meet in. The first legislature convened in Huntsville, north almost to the Tennessee line. But build a statehouse they did in Cahaba and a town to go with it, filled with all the ambitions of a raw frontier. Giddy with the future and their stolen land, the new lawmakers passed a resolution on Christmas Eve, 1824, praising the French hero of the Revolutionary War, Marquis de Lafayette, and inviting him to the capital for a visit. Flattered, maybe just curious, Lafayette agreed. He entered the state from Georgia and traveled under armed escort through the remnants of the Creek kingdom until he struck the federal road, then proceeded grandly on to Cahaba. To celebrate the great man's presence, the Lafayette Committee was awarded a budget of $17,000, more than the annual budget of the state itself. (Cost overruns added another $4,000 to the tab when the bills were finally settled. There's nothing new in the world.) The highlight of it all, undoubtedly, was the banquet thrown at the Bell Tavern Hotel in January of 1825. Lafayette to dinner? Who next? What more? The sky was the limit! But it was water, not sky, that won.

One year later, floods devastated the place. Within weeks, what was to become apparent almost four decades further on to thousands of forlorn Union prisoners of war became inescapable to the citizenry of Cahaba and to Alabama at large: The site chosen for a state capital was in the floodplain of two rivers, neither of which showed any allegiance to its own banks. Cahaba, in short, was unfit for human habitation or much else living other than the legions of biting insects that spawned in its watery residues and the needle-fanged snakes that prowled its rivers and dozed lazily among the grasses.

Soaked and mildewed, dispirited from their scant half dozen years at Cahaba, legislators removed to Tuscaloosa, seventy miles or so northwest, on higher ground, which meant drier ground, which anyone sane would have wanted. Within a month, the old capital, still echoing with the tinkle of hundreds of glasses toasting the Marquis de Lafayette, was all but abandoned. Within a year, it was a ghost town. But progress of a sort intervened. The timberland of central Alabama was cleared; its black soil, tilled; black slave labor, brought in to work the land — to plant it and harvest it, to bleed on it and for it and of it. God was in His heaven. Cotton was King. Alabama's "Black Belt" sat at the right hand of the Maker's Throne. And all of its fruits — the bales and bales of what numbed and gnarled and raw fingers had pulled from the unforgiving cotton bolls — all of it got floated down the Alabama River, and from there to the docks of Mobile and the ports of New England, old England, and more.

Who could resist? The geological consequence that had created the first Cahaba — water flowing into water, the waters flowing to the sea — created a second one, but this time a railroad was added to the mix: the Cahaba, Marion, and Greensborough line, and a large brick warehouse, right where the two rivers and the railroad met: a place cotton could be stored waiting shipment. Work began on the warehouse in 1859 and was suspended in April 1861. War had come on. Worse, the bumper cotton harvest of 1860 had left English warehouses crammed with bales awaiting processing at the nation's textile mills. Worst of all was the Union naval blockade. Even had there been a market in England for Confederate cotton, ships couldn't get there. Growing the stuff played out the fields and left nothing to eat — an acceptable trade in peacetime but a disastrous one in war. Sometime in the spring of 1863, the warehouse meant to hold agricultural products began to hold human ones instead. By then, the railroad that fed the warehouse that fed the steamboats on the Alabama was all but gone, too: cannibalized to extend the Alabama & Mississippi Rivers line westward from central Alabama through Meridian, Mississippi, to Vicksburg and the great river itself. Again, as always, war had imposed its own priorities.

A June 25, 1862, communication from Special Agent A. S. Gaines in Demopolis, Alabama, to Secretary of War G.W. Randolph in Richmond particularizes the demise of the Cahaba, Marion, and Greensborough Railroad. 55,367 pounds spikes, 3,810 pounds bolts and nuts, 17,636 pounds fish bars, 1,276 bars of railroad iron had already been delivered to the Alabama & Mississippi, Gaines writes. Some 300 to 400 more bars of iron were yet to be obtained.

Still, Cahaba endured. By the fall of 1864, the writing was on the wall, but fortunes could turn. Lee could escape Richmond. Johnston could rise up in North Carolina. Nathan Bedford Forrest could rescue his beloved Alabama. Jeff Davis, genius or fool, might yet have one last trick up his sleeve, and he needed it for the economy was all but gone, too. Confederate currency was ridiculous, bonds and notes worthless. Once the war had turned, though, England would come in and the blockade be cleared by Her Majesty's Navy. Surely, the textile mills of Liverpool were starving for cotton now. Accomplish that, and the warehouse that dominated the town could be a cotton warehouse once again, not a human one. Andersonville over in Georgia was built for the latter purpose; it could handle Cahaba's load. Then came the floods, and everyone who knew anything knew that Cahaba was no more.

Within a year of the war's end, the place had pretty much emptied out. Freedmen squatted there, broke down the old prison walls for shelter of their own, farmed what had once been town streets; but the floods defeated even them: people for whom there was no rock-bottom to life. Cahaba became a ghost town once more, slid backwards through history past what it had been to what God had meant it to be, disappeared until even its footprint was hard to discern. By century's end, hunters squatted where Lafayette might once have held a scented handkerchief to his powdered brow. By the start of World War I, even that faint emanation was gone.

Finally, it all came down to water, to rivers, to geological flow, none of which would have surprised in the least those men who stood so long that early March of 1865 in what twice had destroyed the place. But if they survived to tell the tale, it was not the Alabama and Cahaba rivers about which they would have done most of the talking. Water was not through with them yet, not by a long shot.

3

How long ago had it been since the Great Flood? George pinched his eyelids tighter still, saw the score marks he had been making on the warehouse wall these many months gone by, and began calculating: five plus five plus five to what? Six weeks? Which made this the very opening of April 15 in the Year of our Inattentive Lord 1865.

They had left Muncie thirty-one months ago almost to the minute: at daybreak the 15th of August, eighteen hundred and sixty-two. A farmer's cart had hauled them to New Albany, where the 66th Indiana was being organized. (Drummers and pitchmen had been dispatched statewide to dangle patriotism and coin, the failure to take Richmond stinging like lye in the Union wounds.) On the 19th, the Regiment was mustered in and set out for another Richmond, this one in Kentucky, where they arrived just in time to have their ranks picked apart by rifle shot, then blown to Kingdom Come by artillery fire. Two boys who had hitched a ride on the same farmer's cart with them were mowed down by a single cannon ball, the front one splattered into the back one so hard that it was near impossible to tell which was which.

"Ain't no need to see that," Jake had said, shepherding his small flock away, green at the gills himself, while rifle balls crackled the leaves around them.

Most of those who weren't killed were captured, only to be paroled and sent back to New Albany, tails between their legs. The ones who escaped death and capture — the Muncie boys among them — were marched back to New Albany all the same. They had been in the war less than a month and hadn't netted a single mile.

Maybe, so George had allowed himself to think, his war was over, but no such thing, no such luck. On the 18th of November, they were moved on to Indianapolis, too briefly to send for Eliza and the children, and from there to Corinth, in the northeastern corner of Mississippi. Six weeks earlier, some 22,000 Confederate troops under Generals Van Dorn and Price had attacked the Union base there, pushing the Federals back almost two miles before being shredded on Day Two and retreating to the south. Now, there was mostly sickness to fight: The place had been a sump of disease ever since Beauregard had massed 70,000 Rebs there the previous spring, only to cede it without a fight in the face of Halleck's greater force and resources. Four long months, the Muncie men sat on garrison duty. Then, in mid-April 1863, they joined General Grenville Dodge's expedition into Northern Alabama — battle at last, although in the way of armies, not quite.

The 66th had no sooner marched out of Corinth than George, Jake, Ephraim, and Henry found themselves among two companies sent on ahead to Nashville to join the Indiana 51st under Abel Streight, the extra hands being necessary to drive into Alabama the pack animals that were to carry the ammunition that would blow up the railroads that would isolate the Alabama Graybacks from the Confederate armies to the West. Abel Streight might even have achieved his mission had the 250 mules he encountered in Nashville not been, on the one hand, sickly and mange-ridden and, on the other, unshod, unbroken, unusable. Once all the culling was done, what he had left to load on to the rafts waiting to carry his four-legged force across the Tennessee into enemy territory was hardly worth the casting off. Which is how on the evening of April 24, 1863, the four Muncie men found themselves a few miles west of Tuscumbia, Alabama, foraging not for food to feed their growling stomachs but for pack animals to please Gen. Dodge — a reversal of priorities that, as George had noted, went against the rules of nature and of mankind.

"That recruiter fellow in New Albany didn't say nothing about being a mule-herd," Jake allowed, stepping out of his boots stuck inches deep in the fresh russet mud.

There was no element of surprise. Everywhere they went, the farmers had freed their pack animals, driven them into secret hollows, down into riverbeds, caverns, and declivities known only to them, it being better to lose an animal altogether than to have it fall even half dead into Federal hands. Now with the rain pouring down upon them, the Muncie men had finally cornered a stray Jenny — like them, up to its withers in mire. Nearly two full days into their foraging, this counted a victory.

"Well, it is a girl, Jake," Ephraim noted as they leaned their rifles against a cottonwood tree and set out with rope to haul the miserable beast to higher ground. "Might be the closest you been to one in some time."

"Like twenty years," Henry added.

"Har, har, har!" The laughter not quite right, nor the direction it came from. "Yankee boy in loooooooove!"

"Least we know how to shave," Henry opined as the four of them slogged back to the tiny knoll they had set out from. (Little choice: The Rebs were armed by then with their own rifles, in command of the high ground; and molasses in January moved faster than they could have even if they had wanted to try to escape.) The Muncie men could see it now: They had gone and gotten themselves captured by a band of boys in Rebel uniforms, the oldest looking among them covered in peach fuzz and suppurating pustules.

"I'll shave *you* a new face," he announced to Henry, drawing his bayonet with a flourish while the others set out to string the Yankees into a trap-line. But, hell, they were boys, as excited as if they had turned over a rock and found a full-blown rattler wintering below. What's more, being boys, they were no more capable of sustaining anger than they were of sustaining anything else that didn't involve an excess of sexual energy. Soon, their captors were clapping the Muncie crew on the back and recounting tales of farm animal couplings that George even in his worst need had never imagined. The rain soon made the jokes depressing — that and the marching. Seeing Jake's boots sticking out of a fat boy's knapsack didn't help either. Still, the Junior Rebs hadn't shot them. Between dead and captive, no choice at all.

The four Muncie men had been in uniform for 969 days, George calculated, and prisoners for all but 247 of them. One other thing prison taught: counting.

Where did the war stand? He'd heard everything: that Davis was in chains, that Lee had ridden Traveler through the front door of the White House and left through the back with the Railsplitter split wide on the point of his sword. Johnston was marching. Sherman was burning. Philadelphia had fallen to the Confederates. Richmond to the Yankees. The Mississippi ran red with everyone's blood: Reb and Federal, South and North, secesh and Unionist. The Potomac, too. England had committed to the Confederacy. And France. The French fleet was sailing on New Orleans, had broken the blockade at Wilmington and sunk the Union fleet at Hampton Roads. Russia, wherever in creation that was, would send reinforcements. So would Canada and Mexico.

"They're closin' in on ole Grant, Yankee boy," the wall-eyed guard had shouted down to George and Henry the other afternoon as they paced the yard. "Got them pincers working from all sides. This here *tac-ti-cal* warfare! Gonna squash that nigger-lover like a melon," the guard's own bony hand squashing the air as he talked.

"You reckon?" Henry asked when they were out of earshot.

George shook his head. He accepted not a word of it, accepted not a word of anything and least of all from the disgraced Wall-Eye. Everything with him was discounted since the day (and night and day) of his undoing. Rumor — that was the third thing prison was good for: A new one spread like prairie-fire every morning, it seemed.

Morning. George had no sooner thought the word than he felt the first hint of light on his face, saw the world go minutely orange beyond his eyelids. It was the moment he disliked more than any other: this waking up to a new day that would drag on as every day did until the light at last died again and he could be reborn into the forgetfulness of night. George scrunched his body down into itself; prayed for more sleep; told himself that he was nestled in that tall river grass just where the East Fork turns through Muncie, the taste of Eliza still on his lips; gave up immediately (too dangerous, that route); and popped an eye open. A rat sat no more than a half dozen feet from where he lay, square on top of Captain Downey's chest.

A surprise! The deluge had driven the rats out, sent them scurrying before the rising water on their rat legs, flooding into the yard and from there to who knows what burrows and holes. George hadn't seen one since.

Maybe they had come back weeks ago. Maybe somewhere in the warehouse-prison, men were eating them, wringing little rat necks, ripping away rat skins, sinking teeth into warm rat flesh. George had no idea, and no censure for anyone who might have done so. This was a prison. You did what you did to survive. He simply had not moved down that rung on the ladder of humanity — or perhaps moved up it. If humans were nothing more than animals who could reason and talk, if we had no soul inside us, no residue of God (and where was that residue in war? where?), then rat-eaters were one step closer to superiority than he had allowed himself to become. He said it again, silent as a dream: This is a prison. I am a prisoner. I will survive. He could still taste the corn-meal mush they had cooked up two days ago. On the whole, he thought he preferred mush to rat flanks, but who knew? Who was to say?

George felt in the dirt, found a pebble big as his thumb-nail and round, raised himself up slowly on his side, and let it fly — a sweeping, low motion as if he were skipping stones across a pond. The pebble hit the rat square in its snout. It stayed there a moment longer, sniffed the air as if checking to see if that sense still worked (or marking George for revenge some night when he was deep in slumber), then skittered off into the dust and dark corner, while George crawled toward the captain, belly to the earth, as if he were creeping up on an enemy line. Which in a sense he was.

"Captain?" he whispered, not quite with urgency, the former presence on his chest being all but sufficient to the answer. "Captain?"

George listened by his nostrils, raised an eyelid, stared at the white that met his gaze, noted the subtle pallor of the skin — a first, small flush of gray upon the stubbly pink of his face — and thought two words: Good. Riddance.

Captain Downey had been mean and fractious, insis-tent upon these five feet between himself and all the non-commissioned men: a "cordon sanitaire" he called it, as if French could excuse bad manners. Just as the Congregational minister had been the sole self-professed man of the cloth at Cahaba prison, Captain Downey was for sure the only officer who remained within its walls, or the only one who would admit to his sin. The other captured officers, maybe ten in all, had been paroled into the town upon their vow not to attempt escape. They lived among their enemy, rented rooms from them, took their meals at boarding houses and hotels.

Such was the power of an officer's word, even when brother was slaughtering brother, countrymen mowing down one another. All, that is, but Captain Downey.

"I got a theory," George said one afternoon as the Muncie group stood in the yard, watching the captain smoke, his invisible wall of privacy ringed by fellow prisoners wistful for the aroma. (The tobacco a dollar a plug from the sutler just beyond the prison gate. Coin was another thing the captain wouldn't share, nor the staples it purchased.) "Either that man just wants to lord it over us, or he's sitting on some secret."

"Two," Jake interrupted.

"Two what?"

"You got two theories, not just one."

"Two then, two theories, and I'm favoring the second. I think the captain turned tail in battle. If he lived in town with the other officers, they'd smell it on him the way a dog sniffs a badger down its hole."

"Better to hide among the lepers than feast with the Pharisees," Ephraim added. The phrase summoned forth the spirit of his and George's poetry-loving mother so powerfully that all four men — sons, brother, surrogate offspring — found themselves suddenly short of breath, as if her spirit had descended upon them and pulled the air from their lungs. For months thereafter, they had called themselves lepers; the officers, pharisees; and Capt. Downey their Judas Iscariot. The metaphor didn't parse, but the sense conveyed. That was all that mattered.

Now George leaned over that stone heart, talked into those deaf ears. "Perhaps, dear Judas, I might borrow a bit of stationery?" He stuffed his hand into the captain's saddlebags, always by his person even now that he had no person, and drew out the writing kit. "That is, dear sir, if you have no further use of it."

Twice within the last five months he had asked the captain for a single sheet, one envelope, a moment's use of his pen and inkwell. Twice the captain had looked at him as if he asked to borrow his member to make a cuckold of him. So be it. The captain had joined the corporals and the privates who were never going home, the water-men who couldn't right themselves, the starved-to-death and dispirited-to-death and the just plain dead. Demotion by other means. How could it matter what tore the stripes and stars away?

George tucked the writing kit beneath the tail of his shirt, looked quickly to either side, then skittered in a low crouch over to the wall, lit by a first weak beam of morning light breaking in through the warehouse roof. The kit felt soft in his hands, like baby skin. He ran his thumb over the monogram: "PCD, 1861." Phillip Downey — George knew that much although it was always "Captain, Captain, Captain." A flap inside the kit covered a pocket. Inside the pocket, a daguerreotype. George pulled it out, studied the silvery face: all bunched, what seemed to be a large wart or mole prominent on the right cheek, and turned it over. "To my dear son, Phillip," written on the back. "To keep close until you come home to me." A mama's boy, George thought, another piece of the puzzle, the stink of cowardice now all over the man.

He pulled out a small crystal inkwell, lifted the stopper, saw the last dregs of ink slop across the bottom as he tilted it this way and that. A pen, nib in tact. A sheet of the linen paper that, in life, the captain would never have surrendered. George opened the kit across his knees just as he had seen the captain do — it made a sort of soft, portable desk — dipped the nib in the ink, gave it a gentle shake, and began.

4

My dearest Eliza,

What I would give to be back in Muncie with you and the children just now — the stars, the moon, everything I might ever own. I've dreamt so many times that I'm waking up in our bed. I can hear little George shuffling around in the kitchen, getting the fire going. Eben is trailing behind him. Madeleine, bless her, barely makes a sound in her crib. And your body, oh, your body, Eliza, is pressed against mine. And then I realize, it's just a dream; only rags where you had been so warm just moments before; Jake or Henry or Ephraim or one of the others yawning or worse. Too long I've been in here. Too long. Why Madeleine must be doing her letters, and Eben his chores! O Lord, Lord, Eliza, I am weary of the company of men.

George stared off into the distance, men sleeping, groaning, life leaking away by the spoonful as far as the eye could see, a haze of dust settled over everything. What did Eliza know, he wondered? When she went to bed at night, closed her own eyes, felt for him as he felt for her in the small dark hours (she did, she did), what image did she conjure up of him, his days, his life, the years now (always shocking to realize) he had spent apart from her? Did she even know if he was alive? Did she care? (Again, that lizard voice, louder: She *did*. She *did*.)

It had been six months since he last wrote Eliza; last had the paper to write her on, last had a pen to write her with, last had anything worthwhile to trade the guards for posting the letter; longer than that since he had heard from her and that a hurried note, scribbled down to hand to a passing relation, who had volunteered to post it from Cairo, over in Illinois. Nothing moved through enemy lines more efficiently than the Mississippi, than rivers, than water.

The most recent correspondence from Muncie had come from his mother, written on Christmas Day 1864 to them all. A goose was roasting, snow falling lightly, everyone soon to arrive for dinner. She wrote little of particulars, guessing correctly that too rich a picture would be too painful for those who had so little. (There wasn't a man among them who couldn't taste that goose, who couldn't feel its melted fat rolling down his chin.) Of the war news, she wrote nothing at all, knowing her letter would be read by the guards before it was ever passed on. The crops had come in abundantly, everyone was well, love to all. Locusts could have descended upon the land, their sting as the sting of scorpions, and she never would have mentioned it: She was no woman to inflict her problems on others. Instead, she closed with a quote from Wordsworth: "Trailing clouds of glory do we come / From God who is our home." Improbably, the letter had arrived only a few days after the new year. Even in the despair and destitution of a civil war stretched way too long, mail sent from one combatant nation to another sometimes managed to seep through.

In truth, Cahaba had seemed almost a relief at first. After Tuscumbia, they had been marched here, marched there, twice almost forgotten in the rush to a hasty retreat or a sudden advantage, passed from the boys to men, from men to the infirm. Together — wounded captors and hobbled captives — they had limped half a day to get here, not a moment too soon. Cahaba meant they could stop walking, be unleashed from one another, and the place was in its infancy then; the guards, giddy with relief at having been pulled off the front lines and put in charge of prisoners who controlled neither cannon nor rifle.

"Choose your bunk, gentlemen," cried the sergeant who greeted them, a red-haired drink of water with buckteeth that seemed to explode out of his face. "Private Napps here will take your dinner order. Oysters on the half shell special tonight. Full linens and petit-fours. Cee-gars and brandy, we regret to say, are extra, but if you want, I'll come by for free, tuck you in, and kiss you goodnight once you've said your prayers." The thought of those teeth digging into his flesh haunted George still.

The brick walls of the warehouse had been completed, but the place was less than half roofed. Its long side, nearly 200 feet, ran almost due north-south along the Alabama River, inland from its west bank maybe twenty-five feet. The building was 116 feet across, one story high, just shy of 22,400 square feet in all. George had counted it all, paced it off, estimated where he couldn't get to, multiplied it out. Numbers kept you sane.

Around the warehouse, tight against its south and west sides, slightly looser against the east one, ran a wooden stockade fourteen feet high. For nearly all of its length, the stockade was topped by a walkway used by the guards. At the north end, across a cook and exercise yard seventy-five feet deep and 140 feet wide, two cannon sat trained on the warehouse gateway, a reminder that it held prisoners, not cotton now.

To convert the building from agricultural to human needs, a bunk room sixty by forty feet had been set off by wooden walls, just to the east of the warehouse entrance. Inside the room, two rows of plank bunks climbed three tiers high, space for 800 men. At the very back left of the building a hole had been punched in the brick and the water closet attached over the channeled artesian spring. You could hear it gurgling below. A heavy sunken grate of metal and wood bisected the channel as it left the crappers, a discouragement to men who wanted to follow their shit to the river, the bay, the sea, to home.

Dead lines were everywhere: five feet from the interior walls of the warehouse, with eight sentries posted inside to enforce it; ten feet from the stockade, with whole companies of guards waiting overhead to fire. The space between the long eastern face of the warehouse and the stockade was all a dead zone: Cross into any portion of it, and you might as well run a bayonet through your own viscera. So was the area around the gateway to the warehouse. Any man standing still for a space of twelve feet just inside the warehouse and ten feet just outside it could and would be shot on sight. Even the lame, the halt, the nearly dead sprinted as best they could in and out of the building. It was said that any guard killing a delinquent prisoner was rewarded with a three-month furlough. True or not, the possibility concentrated the men's attention. The day ended at nine sharp every evening. Violate that, keep a card game going toward the wee hours, plot some escape deep into the night, and a bullet waited, too.

Subtract all the dead lines and forbidden zones (and George had), and the men had roughly 15,000 square feet inside to themselves and 6,000 square feet of yard. Had all 800 bunks been full and no more, each man could have claimed something like 19 square feet for himself within the warehouse — a space less than five feet by four feet — and another seven and a half square feet in the cook yard, about enough space to turn around in. But war is a hard mistress on planning, and numbers on paper are meaningless. Existing inside them is what gives the numbers texture, dimension, life.

There were no linens, of course, nor even hay to sleep on. The Muncie men claimed four bunks side by side on the second tier — off the ground enough to catch a breeze, they hoped; near enough to the door to find one; and far enough away from the sentry posted inside the bunk room so they couldn't have to smell his rifle oil at night. For bedding, they had the rags from their own knapsacks: shreds of shirt, a change of underwear, no cloth needed now to keep their own rifles clean.

Nor was that first dinner oysters and brandy, for all the bucktoothed redhead's crowing. Rations were raw: a quart of meal a day, half a pound of cured beef, maybe some beans or field peas and those maybe edible. Jake pulled some dry branches from the wood bin that first evening, built a fire in the cook yard, and used a pot left hanging on the warehouse wall. They all watched as he stirred the cornmeal in, waited for it thicken, then tore off bits and pieces of the beef for a little flavor. It was no roast goose, but it was a meal, better than anything they had eaten since leaving Corinth, and the planks for sleeping improved upon the wet earth they had lain on for nearly three weeks.

A gate had been set into the stockade near the north end of the west side. As they squatted by Jake's cook pot, they saw the gate open. Beyond it sat tended fields, even a milk cow grazing — promises of plenty to come. Not that it mattered: They were passing through, sure to be paroled, repatriated and sent north in exchange for some similar passel of prisoners sent south, each granted safe passage to his own front lines. Cahaba was a train depot, George decided, nothing more. The Muncie men would sit back and wait for the whistle to blow.

They had burned their bedding planks by mid-winter, anything for warmth and this was Alabama, Dixie. The bedding rags were tinder, something satisfying in the sizzle of the lice and other vermin that nattered at their sleep. To compensate, the Muncie men dug out burrows in the earth of the main part of the warehouse, as close to one of the open fire beds as they could clamber. They could practically watch the heat disappearing through the half-open roof of the place.

The red-haired sergeant, no thicker than a blue heron, who had welcomed them so enthusiastically to Cahaba Federal Prison, clutched his chest one bitter damp morning in March of 1864, was heard to cry "Excelsior!" (or perhaps "Elixir!" or "Egad!" or "Ai, God, help me!" — the story never told the same way twice), and pitched face-forward flat on to the trestle table where rations were measured out. For months thereafter, as they gathered their uncooked meal, the prisoners would stroke the two small gash marks left by his front teeth for luck in the poker contests and other games of chance that by then were all the entertainment they could muster, card packs as frayed as their clothes. A fourth thing prison taught: superstition.

As April dawned and 1864 ripened into spring, one thing was clear: The paroles, the repatriations, the exchanges were over. The Muncie men weren't going home, weren't going anywhere. Nor was anyone else. Captive or captor, everyone grew morose, trapped in a marriage no one would have chosen for himself. The "why" another of those abiding mysteries.

By that summer, dry wood for cooking had become as valuable as gold and nearly as hard to find. The men divided themselves into companies of 100 each; the companies, into units of ten. Each unit was allowed to send one man out to scavenge for wood every eight to ten days. Each scavenger was allowed to haul back what he "could carry on one arm" — a stupid regulation, idiocy itself, but this was war when idiocy is always ascendant.

Throughout most of the Muncie men's first year in captivity, fall wood abounded, dried hardwoods easy to split and eager to burst into flame. By the summer of 1864, anything dry and fallen had long since disappeared. Scavenger parties and their guards ranged farther and farther into the surrounding woodlands. Worn men with dulled axes were felling green trees, sectioning them, splitting what they could, hauling back what they could carry — wet wood always twice the weight of dry. At night, when each unit built its cook fire out in the yard, the wood had to be coaxed into flame with tinder that barely existed — a tuft of dead grass, some shred of stolen paper, a shirt corner, a last letter from home. Once lit, the pall of smoke from all that green wood clutched at lungs, grew choking, seemed worse than the hunger but not nearly so insistent.

Perry S. Summerville, Company K, Second Indiana Cavalry, broke his leg when he was captured near Stilesboro, Georgia, in the late summer of 1864 — a wagon wheel rolled over it as he was trying to escape — and was sent to the prison hospital for two months. On November 14, fitted with two good wooden crutches, Perry Summerville took his place among the Cahaba men. Soon, he was using a knife he made from a piece of iron palmed in the hospital to shave kindling bits off one of his crutches. When the first crutch disappeared, he started shaving down the second one. It wasn't much more than a large splinter when even that was stolen from under Summerville's head as he slept one night. You did what you needed to. You learned to hop everywhere on your one good leg. You survived.

Only one thing was rarer than the wood to cook food with: the food itself. The milk cow disappeared after the first summer, a promise never delivered. George dreamed of udders almost as often as he dreamed of breasts, until even that faint emanation of hope went away. The tended fields disappeared, too, unless you counted one small patch of cotton, and just try eating cotton bolls or the husks they spring out of. (A thought that seemed to occur to the cotton farmer, too, since he — she? — left the bolls to rot in the fall rains.)

Beans, field peas, crowder peas appeared upon the trestle table from time to time, but they were all string, all rot. The men took the pods, then left them to dry in the sun so they could use the seeds inside for poker chips: a penny for the crowders, a nickel for a field pea; pole bean seeds cost a dime to play. Fortunes were won. Fortunes were lost, all tradable in legumes. No one ever collected.

The quart of cornmeal a day, the half pound of cured beef became a cup of cornmeal, a corner of bacon or beef, but by the Muncie men's second autumn, even that meal had been halved and the beef / bacon / pork mostly forgotten. At first, there wasn't salt enough to cure the meat that was available. At the start of the war, saltworks in New York, Ohio, and Pennsylvania alone yielded nearly five times the quantity of salt produced in the entire Confederate States of America. Within two years, a concentrated Union naval assault on the salt-works in Virginia, Florida, and Texas had reduced already meager Reb supplies to a trickle, and a dear one at that. A 200-pound sack of salt that was selling for a half buck in New Orleans in April 1861 was selling for fifty times that in Savannah by January 1863. Soon enough, the salt itself would become academic: There was little meat left to preserve by any means, for any purpose.

Henry, of all people, became a French chef of cornmeal. He could brown it for coffee; steep it in water for beer; turn it into pone or dodgers, mush or cakes or, with an edible bean or two on hand, something faintly akin to hoppin' john. George thought him a magician. Jake worried that he was possessed. Ephraim just gawked at his old friend's hidden skills. You never knew someone until you knew him in duress. They would watch Henry circulating among the units at mess time, comparing recipes, trading a handful of filched cress for another handful of dandelion greens, spring pokeweed, anything for some flavor.

Whenever a load of bread was delivered to the prison, the guards fell on it first. What passed down to the men was blue with mold and alive with weevils. They picked and ate. They learned to accept tastes that once might have choked them. They threw *nothing* away unless it wouldn't stand still as they raised it to their mouths. Undulation: That was the culinary baseline. If it didn't move, wave, keen, sigh, it was headed down the trap. They'd shit the worst out, or throw it up, or let it worm its way around their bowels. Their stomachs never shut up: *Feed me! Feed me! Feed me!*

The November before the Great Flood, the adjutant commander's horse dropped dead underneath him just at the gate. The next morning when the men went out into the yard, the horse was stripped to its skeleton. A week later, what remained turned up with their Thanksgiving Day rations, the last meat anyone would see for more than a month, though by then "meat" seemed too kind for it. Henry covered the unit's chunk in coals for hours until the green of the meat had been charred through and through. It was, at least, something hard to chew on, though that presented its own set of problems.

George had a rule he was always glad to pass on to new arrivals: "If you can stand to smell it, you can put it in your mouth. If you can stand to put it in your mouth, you can take one swallow. If you can take one swallow and not retch, you can take another." He'd always had an iron stomach.

What was anyone to do? They were a city of enemy human flesh, forced upon an unwelcoming host who had barely more to eat than they did. And that was just the white folk.

"See 'em?" Henry asked one sweltering morning in September of 1864.

Enraged at some slight to its long-eared dignity, a mule the evening before had kicked a hole in the eastern side of the stockade large enough for a boy, maybe even a man to crawl through. The Muncie men were standing as close to the opening as they dared, back a good five feet extra from the dead line. The guard duty overhead had been doubled. Even for this rare gift of a look into the world beyond their confinement, no one wanted to risk a lead ball through the top of his skull.

"See what?" George assumed Henry was talking about the weeds and grasses growing along the banks of the Alabama — some clump of witch-hazel he wanted to turn into a Sunday salad, bullrushes to be dried for smoking. It never ceased to astound him what lore Henry had picked during his long days in the woods tracking squirrel and coon, escaping his stepfather's ministrations.

"Them." Henry was pointing with his chin toward a large clump of reeds on the far side of the river.

"I don't see nothing" — Ephraim speaking for Jake and George, all three squinting into the morning sun.

"What are we supposed to be looking for?"

"Don't look for nothing, Jake. That's the point. Just look and see what you see."

They tried it, shifting from foot to foot, coughing, doing all they could to look as if they were doing something else — another prison habit — and slowly something did begin to emerge: a patch of black that became a head, specks of white that were eyes, stick arms, stick legs.

"Coloreds," George said. "Must be a dozen in there."

"I make it closer to two dozen," Henry corrected.

"What are they doing?" Ephraim, wanting to know.

"Just being still, by the looks of it"

"Still? For what?"

The Negroes had gone away by that afternoon, or hid themselves better. By that evening, the broken palings had been pulled off, replaced by new ones. But the question gnawed at them all through that fall and into their second winter. For what?

Fall of that year found the prison stuffed tight as a sausage. It had to be: Cahaba had an entrance but no exit unless, like Captain Downey, you left into the waiting earth. There had been no more than a hundred men at Cahaba when George, Jake, Ephraim, and Henry first arrived. The place felt spacious. By that fall, the hundred had become four hundred, by the dead of winter, eight hundred, and still the prisoners came and came and came. Most, it seemed, were captured while foraging for food to feed a company, a regiment, a division, perhaps only themselves — impossible on the face of it whatever the dimension. The war had been carried to the South, to Georgia and Alabama, and Georgia and Alabama were starving. But at least the men had tasted hunger before it became their daily feast.

Col. D. T. Chandler, an inspector general with the Confederate army, arrived at Cahaba in early October 1864 to have a look at conditions. On the 16th of that same month, he filed his report with Richmond. Cahaba Federal Prison, he wrote, had been intended for 500 men. Bunks had been provided for eight hundred. The prison now held 2,151 men, including sixty-nine then in the prison hospital and another seventy-five who should be there. (What criterion he could have possibly used for the latter calculation is anyone's guess.) Cooking utensils were insufficient. Axes to chop the firewood were laughable. A multitude of cooking fires — more than 200 of them — in a confined yard created a daily miasma that threatened the health of guards and prisoners. Open fires for heat on the floor of the partially enclosed warehouse did the same. (Chandler didn't mention the green wood, but surely he noticed it.) The guards, the inspector general noted, received rice daily. Prisoners never did. Common vinegar, the indispensable all-purpose medicine, good for intestinal woes, fever, pains and sores, was warehoused in Mobile, an easy steamboat ride away, yet it had never been requested for distribution to inmates.

"Great suffering and much sickness will necessarily occur among the prisoners during this winter from the impracticality of making fires inside the building and the inability to furnish them with proper clothing and bedding," Chandler predicted.

Worse the combination of overcrowding and an inadequate, undertrained guard staff might easily lead to mutiny, rebellion, mass escape. The cannon trained on the warehouse entrance could kill only so many. The rest could crash the gate, roam free, raise havoc among the thinly protected populace. Desperate men, Col. Chandler knew, were capable of desperate acts. Sometimes the act even succeeded.

Chandler had more than criticism. He had a solution, too: Move the prison a mile south to the plantation of Joel E. Mathews. There, a stockade of up to twenty-five acres could be built on higher ground, with good water and timber, where the flooding Alabama and Cahaba rivers had yet to reach. The prisoners had already cleared part of the site by felling its trees. They could fell more and provide themselves not just with cooking and heating wood but with a shelter, roofed and walled, some place that might retain heat for at least a few hours after the embers burned out. Idle hands were the devil's playthings, an idle mind the devil's workshop. Set to the challenge of bettering their lot, the prisoners would no more be idle. The devil, as he should, would have to take the hindmost.

Failing that, Chandler wrote, the existing prison needed to be enlarged: a cookhouse and bakery added, three more tiers of bunks, sinks added on to the crappers, the stockade walls pushed out another dozen yards to the north so the men would have room to move during their days in the yard.

Col. Chandler directed his report to the hawk-faced James Alexander Seddon, the fourth Confederate Secretary of War in a scant three-plus years. (Jeff Davis, as everyone knew, was his own War secretary.) Seddon's office sent the report on to L. B. Northrop, the army's commissary general. On November 5, less than three weeks after submitting his evaluation and recommendations, Chandler had his reply:

"The means of obtaining supplies afforded this Bureau in officers, men, and money are entirely insufficient to enable it to provide for the large number of troops in the field more than the actual necessities of life, and it cannot be expected that the prisoners shall fare better than our own men."

In short, go eff yourself. A South that had neglected to notice, in the first flush of those cannons firing on Ft. Sumter, that it had inadequate supply lines, that it had almost no pre-existing means of production of war materiel, that it lacked sufficient bodies (Negroes excluded) to wage a long war and sufficient salt to preserve the food that might feed them wasn't about to concern itself with prisoners now that its oversights had come home to roost. The prisoners weren't the mice scurrying behind the baseboards; they were the dried stacks of mouse shit left behind by the hidden scurrying mice.

Instead, Cahaba was simply closed down. Improbably, a hundred of the most desperately ill men were sent east to Savannah, to be exchanged for imprisoned Graybacks. Another 1,500 were packed off to Andersonville, over in Georgia. The Muncie men were among four hundred sent on to Meridian, just over the state line in Mississippi. They marched on foot eight winding miles north along the western shore of the Alabama to Selma and went from there, by rail, to Meridian: seats, not freight cars; a loaf of bread to share among them; pails of clean water to dip from. In truth, it seemed like a dream.

"That place yonder," Ephraim said, staring out the window at some vast, gabled plantation house. "I got me a girl there, name of Lorena, just like in the song." And with that, he began to sing in that beautiful Irish tenor of his, a voice his Mama claimed was more of God than man.

The years creep slowly by, Lorena
The snow is on the grass again
The sun's low down the sky, Lorena
The frost gleams where the flowers have been
But the heart throbs on as warmly now
As when the summer days were nigh
Oh, the sun can never dip so low
A-down affection's cloudless sky.

A hundred months have passed, Lorena
Since last I held that hand in mine
And felt the pulse beat fast, Lorena
Though mine beat faster far than thine
A hundred months...'twas flowery May
When up the hilly slope we climbed
To watch the dying of the day
And hear the distant church bells chime.

They were halfway between Demopolis and Meridian, inching along on tracks that seemed to be held together with baling wire.

"What color's her hair?" Henry asked when Ephraim was finally through.

"Raven. Black as midnight, with eyes like glowing embers."

"Figured as much." Henry favored blondes, with flaming redheads a close second. This was familiar territory for the two of them.

"What in the hell does that matter?" Jake chimed in. He was forty-some years a bachelor. Women's hair, much less its color, was a deadline of its own for him: Cross it, and who knew *what* might happen?

George kept his peace. Eliza's hair was a rich brown, almost chestnut. When it wasn't hidden under a bonnet, she liked to pile it up on top of her head with pins every which way. It smelled of pine tar and lye-soap and rose-water, too. Dear God. Dear God.

The track cleared off after Ephraim's solo; the train picked up speed; the future seemed to be racing at them. Yet when they finally got to the compound in Meridian not long after dusk, the Muncie men felt as if they had come no distance at all. The huts were full. New men slept outside on the ground. There was no more nor better wood to burn on that side of the Alabama-Mississippi line than there had been on their own. Less than a month later, they were back in Cahaba, the grand experiment abandoned, the place more crowded now than ever it had been, and food even less abundant. They returned by rail again, standing this time crammed into a few passenger cars. It was almost midnight when they covered the first stretch eastward to Demopolis. Ephraim waved drowsily as they passed by where he thought the gabled plantation mansion might be: "Night, Lorena, honey. Sleep tight." Beyond the train windows, the dark seemed almost liquid.

To feed the prisoners, the government in Richmond had imposed a tithe on nearby farms and plantations: meal, pork, bacon, beef to sustain this alien population. For a time — when there were only six- to eight-hundred prisoners and the fields and granaries and livestock pens still had some bounty to them — the tithe even made some sense. Sacrifice in a time of crisis shouldn't fall just to those who shoulder a rifle and walk boldly into the breach. By late 1864, though, the tithe had become yet another of those grim running jokes of war. The same quantities were being requisitioned for more than two thousand men that had first been asked for less than a quarter that many, and they were being drawn from fields and silos and slaughterhouses that were as leached of surplus as the people who worked them.

Did anyone notice? Of course! Prisoner or planta-tion manager, it slapped you in the face each waking day.

Everything was growing larger and smaller at the same time, a physical impossibility that became a daily reality. By the end of 1864, the prison had the largest population it had ever held, and the men had the least food they had ever been allotted and the least space to themselves they or almost anyone else could ever imagine. Jesse Hawes, Ninth Illinois Cavalry, wrote afterwards that he and his fellow prisoners had, by early 1865, six square feet of space to themselves. Calculate that: two feet by three feet. Lay it out on the floor. The absence of food shrunk most men down to lesser dimensions, but still the average inmate couldn't have done a pirouette on little ballerina toes without slamming shoulders into the soldier next to him. Privacy vanished utterly. One man was always abutting another, on his toes, mouth next to mouth, nose next to nose. Disease barely had to work at all to leap from prisoner to prisoner.

At first, the men made room inside by sliding closer and closer together until they were sleeping against one another, half sitting up or with their heads in each other's laps, almost comforting. They were about to start sleeping in shifts, half at day, half at night, when the flood came. The waters thinned their ranks. The typhus, the dysentery that followed the flood thinned them more. And, too, they learned to adjust. They made their peace with dignity. They found what amusement they could.

The yard had been expanded while the prison was vacated: That much of the battle Col. Chandler had won. The stockade now pushed nearly into the center of town. The flood hadn't been down a week when the men decided to hold a dance at the new dead-man's line. Ephraim and others sang. A boy from Kentucky fiddled with new strings torn from a cat who had made the mistake of wondering in to the prison in search of its own meal, its own little rat snack. George had been a famous leaper in his youth, known throughout Muncie for his ability to vault tall fences, hop on to table tops in a single bound, pick up a fiddler's crescendo and follow it into the night sky. (It was during one such soaring moment that Eliza McCorkle's heart had first fixed on the Ethridge boy. Silhouetted against the night sky, he looked like some Roman deity come down to earth!)

George's youth was not so far behind him, but he was surprised to find any spring at all left in his legs. It was, though, and leap he did, it seemed, half the night long. But it wasn't just the able who joined in. Men who could barely stand, men with only fragments of clothes left to them linked arms and reeled, do-si-do'ed, stomped their feet. Inside the warehouse, the too-sick, the dying tapped against the packed earthen floor or sang along in little last whispers of breath:

> *De Camptown ladies sing this song,*
> *Doo-da, Doo-da,*
> *De Camptown racetrack's two miles long,*
> *Oh, de doo-da day.*

Not a man among them knew that Stephen Foster, who had written those lyrics, had died fourteen months earlier after a fall in a Bowery hotel in New York City — depressed, drunk, with 38 cents to his name; maybe the most popular songwriter in the world and no better off at the end it seems than the least among Cahaba's inmates.

Softened by who knows what, Col. Jones let the revelry go on till nearly midnight: an unheard-of dispensation. Then he had a rifle volley fired so close to the tops of the dancing men's head that it seemed to split their hair right in half. With that, Jones turned on his heel and disappeared from the walkway. There was no need for further instruction. The men were locked inside their warehouse within five minutes time, as fast as so many could push through the entrance, each man on the back end expecting to be the one shot to drive home the lesson that Col. Jones had preached in so many ways, on so many occasions: *You live or die at my pleasure.*

Did they think in town that this, too, was merriment — a festive round of gunfire to bring the dead-line dance to an exclamatory close? Did they take it as more evidence that the prison was joviality itself? Did they have any idea what it was like to be locked inside that warehouse, locked inside that stockade? Any idea what it was like to wake up every morning knowing that nothing about your life would be different — unless, of course, you managed to die or get shot that day? Whether it was the screams of his wife or the bellow of a mare with a foal turned backwards inside her, childbirth was the worst sound George knew, and Eliza had gone through it three times. (Another miracle, all three children alive and well, Eliza too. So far as he knew.) But childbirth ended, in life or in death. This never seemed to. How to tell her about it all? Like his mother, George kept misery to himself.

5

I don't know what the newspapers up there might be writing these days about this prison or the others like it, but it's not all bad. They make sure we got decent bedding, and they feed us when they can. And now that no more prisoners seem to be coming in to replace the ones who get carried out, we're getting more room to ourselves each day. And, Eliza, we all look out for each other. Why this stationery I'm writing you on was giving to me by Capt. Downey. He's about the only officer in here. The rest got paroled into town like Chinese kings, but Capt. Downey told the Rebs that he'd led his men into battle and by golly, he was not going to leave them now. The Capt. said just this morning that he was giving me his saddlebags when we finally get free. He said he wouldn't have hands enough left to carry all the things he wanted to take with him. I like the life out of him.

George heard a sound like a black snake in a corn silo, looked up, and saw a wraith half human sidling toward the captain. Pennsylvania 14th, George thought; captured a few months after his group and marched southwest from Gadsden with a bullet in his left jaw. The bullet was still there, now with less flesh around it so it pushed out like some sort of minor third ear not far below a real one.

A nice enough fellow, not given to tomfoolery like so many. A year earlier, maybe more, back when it was yet possible to believe that things might get better, he had shared his chunk of bread with Jake — a gesture. He was lonely, separated from his company, far from home on foreign ground. He wanted a knot of friends to walk the yard with, to while away the evening at cards, for protection, too, from the prison gangs. He'd swing it, he said: come up with some way to trade places with one of the men in their unit. He'd cook with the Muncie men, eat with them, walk with them, become one of them. How about it? No, George had told him. No.

The Muncie men shared their food; they pooled their water. No one of them went without if any one of them had a thing to eat or drink. To steal from one was to steal from all; to insult one was to insult four. That's what it meant to be family, or nearly so in Henry's case. You couldn't just let a stranger into the middle of that.

Millbank — that was his name! George laid his writing kit carefully to the side and made a small click with his tongue. *Click, click. Click, click.* When Millbank gazed his way, George bared his teeth, let out a low animal growl, and made to lunge toward him. Pain and ruin in his eyes, Millbank leapt up like a startled pig, then turned and skittered whence he had come. Now that he was dead, the captain was George's territory. He settled again with his back to the warehouse wall and spread the writing kit across his legs.

6

Ephraim hit a rough patch not long back, but he gets stronger every day, better. You tell Mama that Jake and me are doing everything we can to keep him and Henry out of trouble down here. It's not easy, mind you. Those boys would find mischief in a pulpit, but we're going to bring Ephraim home safe and sound. Mama and Papa can count on that. Capt. Henderson's been gone more than two months now. This ain't the same place without him.

George took his pen, dipped the nib in what little ink remained in the crystal well, and drew a line through the last two sentences. Then he dipped the pen again and scratched them out until there was nothing left at all but a solid black band. The letter was never going to be sent. No censor would ever have to read it because George had nothing to trade for postage, no favors left to call in from anyone. Still, what had he been thinking? It took so little to end up on Col. Jones's wrong side. Once there, you never got right again.

The prison had two commanders — a formula for disaster. And it was two different prisons depending on who was in charge. Capt. Howard Andrew Millett Henderson, nominally in command of Cahaba Federal Prison, was by consent of just about all the inmates under his authority a gentleman, a saint, almost a savior. It sounds insane — men were starving under his command — but the prisoners adored him. His own father had hailed from New Hampshire, a graduate of Phillip Exeter Academy and Yale University. In Paris, where he had gone to oversee a college for women, the older Henderson met and married one of his students, Jane Elizabeth Moore. Their son graduated from Ohio Wesleyan University, studied law in Cincinnati, then was ordained a Methodist minister and assigned to Demopolis, in Alabama, not half a day's ride from Cahaba. He was said to have argued brilliantly there on behalf of states' rights before the war of secession began. What he thought of a state's particular right to enforce the enslavement of fellow members of the species goes unrecorded — maybe it was a hole in his character. Everyone has them. When the prison was established at Cahaba some two years into the war, Reverend Henderson seemed a natural choice to run it.

Henderson was a short and unassuming man: no more than five feet six, with a kind of squinchy and benign face. Far more important, he seemed inclined, always, to treat the men under his authority with dignity. In the early months, before the numbers overwhelmed everything and everyone at the prison, he would sometimes mount the walkway himself and read aloud the newspapers that came on the morning steamboat packet. Lincoln was, of course, beyond despicable, and the turncoat Andrew Johnson — now serving as military governor of Eastern Tennessee — was not far behind him, but at least it was word of the outside world. Mail got through, too, in both directions.

With Henderson's approval, perhaps even his urging, two local ladies — Amanda Gardner and her daughter, Belle — opened what was in effect a public lending library for the men. Guards would carry requests into town, to the Gardners' door, and one of the ladies would fill it as best she could from their own bulging book shelves. (The guards always hoped it was Belle, who lived up to her name though still a girl.) George, who read the best of any of the Muncie men, went through nearly all of the *Leatherstocking Tales* during the first year of their confinement: aloud. Ephraim and Henry grew weary of Natty Bumpo — who wouldn't? — but not Jake. He sat wide-eyed as any schoolboy while his oldest nephew read on, shushing Ephraim and Henry when they wouldn't shush themselves. The point is, it passed the time. The few prisoners transferred on from other camps never failed to remark upon it. The only books available to them before had been Bibles. How much betterment can a man take?

Everyone who visited the prison remarked, too, upon how Henderson had caused the old Bell Tavern Hotel, scene of the great Lafayette banquet, to be turned into a hospital for his charges, along with the townspeople and whatever Confederate soldiers could get there. Nothing was perfect. There was never enough medicine. The absence of vinegar seems to have been another hole in Henderson's character, or knowledge. (Or perhaps he simply didn't believe in vinegar's healing properties.) But everyone knew: He tried, and trying made a difference. At Andersonville over in Georgia people were dying wholesale of gangrene, of scurvy, of killing epidemics. The unfortunate 1,500 Cahaba men who got transferred over there in the fall of 1864 might just as well have thrown themselves through some rift in the earth into the fiery bowels of the planet. Cahaba wasn't like that: There were no recorded deaths from gangrene, none from scurvy. It was pneumonia and dysentery, digestive failures, guards' bullets, and simply giving up on life that killed men at Cahaba.

Like every prisoner under his authority, Capt. Henderson was also a fervent believer in exchanges. He didn't want men starving inside his walls; he wanted to send them north, trade them, bring back the Confederacy's own. What point was there to just warehousing human flesh? When no one would have his prisoners, when it became as apparent to

Henderson as it already was to the Muncie men and others that his inmates were there for the duration, Henderson did the nearly impossible: He requisitioned and actually received supplies to ease their misery, to soften their burden, a Christmas gift that should have been the stuff of legend: two thousand coats and hats; two thousand pairs of pants, drawers, shoes; four thousand pairs of socks; fifteen hundred blankets all delivered on the last day of 1864 to the landing just beside the prison by a Union packet that steamed up the Alabama under a flag of truce.

It didn't do any good, of course — or the good that was intended. Capt. Henderson had been cold, but never so hungry as the Cahaba men. He didn't realize that between the two it was no contest at all. The townspeople were lined up outside to trade before the packet after left the landing. Jake sold his blanket for $50 Confederate and got to keep $30 after the wall-eyed guard had taken his commission. With his $30 Confederate, he bought a stale Christmas pie that cost $25. (The Wall-Eye kept that $5, too.) Jake's shoes, socks, pants, and drawers he bundled into a swap for an only partially molded half slab of bacon. (The shoes wouldn't have fit him on a bet.) The coat and hat he traded for an armload of kindling. All the Muncie men did the same: sold or swapped or traded the clothing as fast as they could, before the townspeople had had their fill, before one of their fellow prisoners stole it away. Ephraim got a half-filled bottle of Plantation Bitters, S. T. 1860 X — alcohol, water, and flavoring; famous throughout the land — for his woolens and sent his quarter share in the bottle promptly down the hatch. George bartered for a double armload of bread; Henry, for an iron cooking pot. When their clothing was gone, they traded the incidentals that had come in on the same packet: writing paper, envelopes. They wanted to eat, to drink. George would have given every last thing he'd received for a half-pail of warm cow's milk, but there wasn't one to be had for love or money or fresh new blankets. The cows had all gone off, or their udders had all dried up. How were they to know which? But if they weren't any warmer those bitter weeks of January, they were far better fed, and they would need all that strength and more.

H.A.M. Henderson didn't just shrink away after the war, either. He became state superintendent of education in Kentucky and then returned to the ministry in Jersey City, New Jersey, at a Methodist church favored by Hannah Simpson Grant, mother of Ulysses, whose army had defeated the nation to which Henderson had once pledged his sacred honor. When Henderson committed Hannah Grant to her final resting place in 1883 — ashes to ashes, dust to dust — the ex-president was standing by his side.

Trouble was, Henderson was too good, he cared almost too much. High councils summoned him for his wisdom on the prisoner issue. As the war wound down, he became one of the main planners for the final exchange, after all arms had been laid aside. In late January 1865, Capt. Henderson left Cahaba for the last time, never to return. As always when Henderson was away, the place descended to the care of Lt. Col. Sam Jones, and Sam Jones was another story altogether.

Unlike Henderson, he's a cipher at both ends of his tour at Cahaba. Jones hailed from New Orleans, had maybe worked there as a bookkeeper before the war, served with the 23rd Louisiana Volunteers, later the 22nd Louisiana, and had twice very briefly been a prisoner of war himself, captured after the falls of New Orleans and Vicksburg and paroled back to Confederate lines. No one seems to know how Jones got from Vicksburg to Cahaba, but by early 1864, he was a lieutenant colonel, commander of a prison guard force of 179 men, "totally inadequate for the duties required of them," in Col. Chandler's estimation.

What Sam Jones and his guards might have lacked in training and numbers, he made up for with intimidation. He liked to punish men by making them hang from the underside of a ladder that leaned against the stockade: hands on a high rung, feet on a low one, for as long as twenty minutes. Try that, too: Men were lame for whole days afterwards. Jones also had a fondness for kicking the bags of bones under his authority. Sit too close to the deadlines, be too slow to answer at the daily roll calls — 7:30 in the morning, five in the afternoon — and bodies that couldn't be abused much more would feel the thump of his boot.

Under Sam Jones, guards shot to kill, and they learned to be tougher themselves, but even for the guards, he took it too far. It wasn't just the prisoners who asked to be allowed to convene on higher ground during the Great Flood. Sixty guards, a third of the force, petitioned Jones on the prisoners' behalf as well, to no avail. The Yankees could drown for all he cared, and maybe the guards as well. For good reason, Jones simply disappeared after the war, vanished, went *poof* into the night, but he would live on in dreams, in nightmares, in dusty vows of revenge.

It seemed impossible that Lt. Col. Sam Jones could really be the cause of the bad times, but he was there whenever they happened: the mutiny, when it finally came on; the flood; the fever that came up when the waters finally went down. Christ in Heaven Almighty, the dry for a while seemed worse than the wet. The last pockets of water had just leached out of the earthen floor when a brace of men suddenly seemed at death's door. Soon, whatever was making them sick was racing through the prison, grabbing every third man. Jones, the Wall-Eye, everyone who owned a bandana or could borrow or fashion one was wearing it over his mouth, and camphor under that if they had it; if not, garlic, onion, sage leaves, anything to cut the vapors, to keep death in its place.

The warehouse gate was kept locked almost all the day long, opened only at meal time, and even then the men weren't allowed in the yard until the last of the guards had cleared from the walkway and taken to the high ground to the west of the stockade. Cooking wood was all but gone; rations, cut to almost nothing. Little point in feeding men who were going to die at any rate.

The stench, always bad, grew near unbearable, and not just the doomed. Men would have sold their fingers for soap, half a limb for a bushel of crisp red apples. Teeth came loose. Skin peeled off their feet in sheets, rotted from the damp and cold and filth. Lice grew so thick in the scalps of the sickest men that their crowns of hair seemed to be moving on their own, as if a gentle breeze were blowing over them.

There was an Irish boy among them, fiery red hair, fiery red face, begging with what he thought was his final breath for last rites, extreme unction, absolution for a lifetime of sin. But the Catholic priest who had been coming weekly ever since the Muncie men arrived declined to enter the compound until the nature of the fever was determined, and the Congregational minister, if he ever was that, announced he had lost his vocation.

Townspeople took to gathering with the guards around feeding time, on the upwind rises — not from cruelty, or so it seemed, nor for entertainment, but simply out of respect and awe. Whatever it was had yet to jump the stockade, sneak through the palings, travel backward through the artesian spring to infect Cahaba itself. To keep it that way, the Bell Tavern hospital would accept no new patients from inside the warehouse.

The fever came on Ephraim the fourth day: black spots on the tongue, the shakes and chills, somewhere inside him a furnace roaring full, the raving delirium. The Muncie men did everything they could for him. Jake and George wiped Ephraim down with their own damp shirts, wet their shirts again and held them to his brow. Henry begged some kindling and made a tea of a piece of sassafras root-bark that he had long ago squirreled away for such a moment.

Finally, George prayed: *Dear Lord, forgive me my many sins, this war, this whole mess we got ourselves in. Watch over my little brother. See him to health. Help me get him home again where he belongs. He and Henry never had any business coming along in the first place. Amen.*

Hell, they all prayed in their own way: every man in the prison, sick or well. And it must have worked because just as suddenly as the fever arrived, so it went away, lifted from the place as it had been a Biblical curse and the gods had finally been propitiated. Even the Irish boy survived though, by his own pronouncement, he was no longer a Roman Catholic.

Not that the sickness didn't take a toll, leave weary men even more worn, take bodies so long abused and abuse them just that much more. From where he sat with the writing kit spread across his knees, George could hear Ephraim wheezing in his sleep, could see him shivering beneath what thin cover he had. The captain's coat would help that, George thought, and his britches and what-else too. He would volunteer to drag him outside; dig the ditch himself, then strip him clean before he rolled him into it. The boots alone were worth the labor.

7

An eye popped up over Ephraim's rattly chest, a shock of blonde hair all cowlicked on top, a face open as daybreak. In some ways, the biggest mystery of them all.

We also seem to have picked up a boy. I don't know nothing about him. He won't talk, or maybe can't. Same difference. The boy walked into this place at night, so near as I can tell, and must have just stumbled on us in the dark cause he was squatting by Jake's feet come morning. He's like a stray dog, and like any stray, I reckon he'll take off just as soon as he figures out we don't have the food to spare him.

Just as had the fever, the boy seemed to rise out of the earth after the waters finally went down, or maybe he had been waiting there, underwater, all along. He didn't exist, and then he did, hunkered down, waiting for them to awaken on that first morning afterwards, quietly watching George and Ephraim un-mat their joined hair, pull the clods of mud out of it. (This before they knew that quiet was his only option.) Appropriate for someone who had arrived thus, the boy seemed capable of astounding feats of legerdemain, prestidigitation, vanishing acts and sudden reappearances. If he had placed himself in a wooden box with his feet sticking out one end and his head out the other, then reached around and sawed himself in half, Jake wouldn't have been the least surprised.

The boy followed them everywhere that first day, dogged their steps, was their shadow and after-breath. When Henry took their unit's small ration and headed for the cook yard, the boy went with him, cupped his hands to the tiny bit of tinder Henry had brought along as it sparked, added some dried grass from his own pocket and out of his hair, puffed gently on it all until it had burst into flame, then laid it beneath the stacked shreds of green wood, and bent and puffed some more. Then he watched Henry as closely as if he were removing a human brain from its skull, not just trying to coax some small amount of flavor and nourishment from cornmeal that was half stalk and chaff. The noxious clot of smoke didn't seem to bother him in the least, as if he had been living in a cave the winter long, conditioning his lungs for this moment. No one exactly approved when Jake fed the boy a heaping spoonful of mush afterward, but not one of them would have had the heart to do otherwise. Later, the boy followed Jake clear across the warehouse to the water closet and would have gone inside with him had Jake not put a firm hand on the boy's chest and told him loud enough for George to hear way back yonder: "Wait here, dammit, boy. I'm shitter bound!" The boy did, and he was waiting when Jake came back out. A dog trained for the fanciest shows on earth could have performed no better.

The boy plopped down beside them that evening, unasked, burrowing into the dirt between Jake and Ephraim. When George awoke sometime in the middle of the night — torn out of a dream he didn't want to remember by a screech owl that seemed to be perching on his ear — the boy was gone. Perhaps he, too, had needed the water closet. George waited on him awhile, then gave it up, figuring him for a one-day wonder. But when George opened his eyes in the morning, the boy was back in his burrow, his pocket stuffed with pecans, which he pushed on the Muncie men as soon as they were all up.

It became the boy's pattern, or maybe it always had been. He would be with the men when they closed their eyes and with them when the morning bell was sounded, with them every moment of the day, but almost never when one of them rose in the middle of the night to shake off a dream or answer nature's call. And the things he showed up with! A sheet of newspaper wrapped around a whole dinner's worth of tender, fresh pokeweed; a pack of playing cards barely broken in at all; a pillow slip that still smelled of laundry soap and sunshine; four carved chess pieces; two cribbage pegs; a cobbler's form.

"What in the hell?" Ephraim asked the morning he revealed his chess pieces, but Henry saw it immediately. Kindling! Anything dry that would burn!

Curiosity killed the Muncie men. They had to know where the boy was going, what he was doing. One evening they all pretended to sleep. When the boy finally rose and slipped away, they set off by pre-arrangement. George took the water closet. Maybe it really was possible to slip in and out of the prison through the latrine holes and the artesian spring below them. Jake headed to the front of the ware-house. Could the boy pick the lock? Had he found some crack in the thick plank doors that sealed them in every night? Even if he had, he would have to cross the dead-line zone. He couldn't make himself invisible, or could he? Jake had to practically crawl like a snake to his watching post. George had the plausible excuse of loose bowels if one of the sentries stopped him. What was Jake going to say? That he was sleep-slithering?

The youngest, Henry and Ephraim, had the hardest assignment: to try to tail the boy, pick up his route, keep him in sight. They might as well have tried to turn base metal to gold. The boy skittered on all fours that barely seemed to touch the dirt floor, and he must have had cat eyes, not human ones. Tracking him along his right flank, Henry tripped over a pair of feet and fell headlong into a sleeping pile of Buckeyes. Naturally, they assumed he was out for their few possessions.

"Hold him tight while I gouge his eyes out," one of them growled.

"Too good for a goddamn 'un like this," another groused.

"I implicate the resentment!" Henry said, struggling free and doing his best imitation of a prisoner many sheets to the wind on cornmeal beer. It worked, or the Buckeyes didn't have the strength or will to stay angry any longer. But by then, the boy was long gone.

Ephraim had more luck. He trailed the boy all the way to the west wall, had him clearly in his sights, then stopped to see where the nearest sentries were. When he looked back, the boy was gone as if he had simply walked through the brick. Ephraim crawled over to where he had last seen him, pushed on the wall to see if he could find a magic door, searched with his finger tips for toeholds, finger rungs in the wall, felt the dirt floor for a trap door of some sort, then gave it up and crawled slowly back to his own burrow.

The men took forever waking up the next morning. Their detective work, the whispered note comparing when they all got back together had taken it out of them. When they finally did open their eyes, the boy was sitting up brightly among them with two dead doves under his shirt, necks wrung and feathers plucked.

"Thieving?"

The boy looked up and up, his eyes growing so wide that it was wonder what kept them in their sockets at all. The man towering above him was nearly seven feet tall, face like the butt end of a railroad tie, fists the size of watermelons.

"I said, *thieving.*" Angrier this time. More a statement, than a question.

"Not from any of us, Big Tennessee," George answered.

To prove it, the Muncie men emptied their possessions on the ground between them: the plucked doves, two chess pieces that had not yet seen the fire, the pillow slip that Jake pulled from inside his shirt, a short length of rope that Henry and the boy were unwinding evening by evening for tinder, the playing cards far too crisp to have come from inside, a lady's shoe that no one had yet figured out a use for.

Big Tennessee — his real name was Richard Pierce, and he hailed from Barboursville, in Kentucky, but he had signed on with a Tennessee unit and was "Big Tennessee" to one and all — sifted through the evidence, crouched down and had a hard look at the boy, then gave his hair a good rub and rose painfully on creaky knees.

"Hell, George, Jake," he said, shaking his log of a head with disgust, "we must be losing this damn war if a boy this old has been in uniform long enough to wash down to us."

The other prisoners reached out and patted Big Tennessee as high on the back as they could reach as he set off to the other side of the warehouse, wished him a good day, or shared some joke or special intelligence. He was the reason the weak inside were not more preyed upon by the strong. Over in Andersonville, the thieving, the mugging, the predation got so bad that the prisoners finally had to run down the gang leaders and hang them high themselves. The worst of the worst, it was said, were New York boys, fresh from the city's teeming street mobs. Cahaba had men just as bad, just as raw — the government had recruited bodies to fill the front lines, not ethicists to sift good and evil — but there was nothing like the crime that plagued prisoners over in Georgia. Big Tennessee saw to it: He was the law: sheriff, judge, jury, his fists the instruments of punishment and deliverance. Like Capt. Henderson, he was loved — by the boy, too, and in that single instant of first meeting. The next morning he brought Big Tennessee his own plucked dove and a squirrel skinned and ready for the pot. No one could claim that the boy had deprived any man inside of those rightful possessions.

George watched him rubbing the sleep from his eyes, wondered where in God's name he had gone and what treasure he had brought back this time. The boy's eyes missed nothing, but they were the eyes of the hunted, not the hunter — the vole that scampers through the grass, not the owl that drops on it out of the night. He must be about thirteen, George thought, a tick away from manhood. His own oldest son, George Junior, would be eleven any day now. He had missed seeing him turn that corner out of boyhood, first start exploring the world with a man's eyes, might miss seeing him become a man altogether. Time went on and on. Hours became days; days, weeks; weeks, months; months, years. He sat still, and the world he had left behind turned, changed, grew: his parents, his wife, what they had created between them.

Three sharp whistles split the morning stillness. He could hear shouts, heavy hawsers hitting the landing not far beyond the stockade: some sort of steamboat or another. The boy was staring at the source of the noise as if he could see straight to it, through brick, mortar, and stockade. When, George wondered, when will it end?

8

O, Eliza. Hug the children for me. Don't ever let them go.

With deepest affection,
Your husband,
George Ethridge

George folded the letter he knew he would never send, slipped it into an envelope he was certain would never go anywhere, and wrote as carefully as he knew to do on the front: "Eliza Ethridge, Muncie in Indiana," a place the letter would never get to. Just writing her name in his careful schoolboy script made him feel connected, as if he were reaching across near six hundred miles of tortured land to touch her hand. George fingered at the bottom of the writing kit, found a small stick of sealing wax, pulled it out, bit a piece off, and began to chew. His mouth at least could soften the wax: There was nothing to heat it over. What else was in the kit? Coin? Some sort of stamp for the wax? He was about to dig in again, turn it over, shake it, get anything useful out of there he could — a prisoner's economy — when he heard the lock at the front of the warehouse turning, the gates creaking open.

"Form up!" It was Jones' voice, an early roll call, some new punishment for some fresh slighting of the rules. George had long ago stopped asking what or why.

"Form up, dammit. In the yard. All y'all. Now!"

Someone was standing beside Jones, taller than him by a good half foot, an officer's hat, some sort of plume sticking out of the band. A dandy, George thought. A peacock. Just what we need.

The early morning sun slanting in from the side back-lit the two officers and mixed with the usual pall of dust to make it impossible to see either of them clearly. As the men rose wearily from their burrows of dirt or spilled out from what remained of the bunks, George edged along the western wall, hoping for a clearer line of vision. The plume compelled him on: Pigs would fly, wolves lie down with lambs before Jones ever wore a feather like that. He had just about worked his way down to a spot where the sun would no longer blind him when one of the men up front, toward the dead line, saw the light.

"Ain't gray," he shouted. "The other one ain't gray. It's blue! Hell, he's one of ours!"

One of ours? George could see him clearly now, a full colonel, spit and polish Federal.

"Goddamn it to hell and all, form up in that yard afore I have every goddamn one of you shot!"

The Union colonel just stared at Jones as he ranted on, never moved a muscle, an eyelid, never said a word of his own, and then it came to George. The lambs really had laid down with the wolves. Stunned, as if someone had hit him over the head with a timber, George slumped against the wall behind him, slid down to the dirt, pulled the envelope from what was left of his pants pocket and the letter from the envelope, then dipped the pen quickly into the last drops of ink, and scribbled hastily at the bottom:

My darling, my darling. War's over. We're Muncie bound!

Who would have ever believed it? He bit off a piece of the wax, pressed it as hard as could down on the envelope flap, and hoped for the best. Pandemonium had seized the warehouse: shouts, hoorays, anything that could fly thrown up into air by anyone still strong enough to launch it. George had buttoned the writing kit together, was getting ready to add it to the general array of celebratory missiles when he saw a prisoner barely able to raise himself up on his elbows staring at him.

"Here," he said, "here," handing the kit to him. He had no further use of it, nothing more to write. The man cradled the kit as if it were a baby while prisoners hopped and hollered all around him, and then George thought: Captain Downey!

He pushed, raced, shoved his way as best he could back toward where he had left the captain lying only to see another prisoner he could never reach slinking away with the captain's flawless underthings. He'd been stripped clean, nothing left to him but his graying skin, the crown of hair on his unthinking head, a circle of it around his useless pecker. George turned and saw Jake, Ephraim, and Henry staring at him. They had gathered up the very few possessions they had and piled George's together for him as well. The boy seemed to be sitting up on something between them. George walked over, put a hand on his shoulder, and leaned him aside. Beneath him, dusted — it looked almost oiled — was Capt. Downey's hand-tooled saddlebags.

hey were already loading the hospitalized prisoners on
to the first paddle wheeler: men with broken limbs,
men doubled over with dysentery, a Pennsylvania boy
done in by frostbite. As Jones' guard corps carried him on
board, the Muncie men could see where half his foot had
been cut away. They remembered the night he had been
hobbled, could never have forgotten it: A miracle that their
own feet and toes and fingers had survived. A second paddle
wheeler waited just off the landing, ready to take the first
one's place when it was full.

Like the mercy ship that had steamed up the Alabama on
New Year's Eve day, both these flew Union and Confederate
flags side by side, a sight to see. Back then, though, the dual
flags had been a necessity: a guarantee of safe passage behind
enemy lines. Now, it was more a formality. Jones still barked
orders. He still had his guard corps under arms. He still
required the prisoners under his authority to swear no harm
against the Confederate States of America before he would
officially parole them and send them on their way. But the
Federal colonel looked to Jones for nothing, seemed not to
fear him or his men in the least, barely acknowledged his
existence. No doubt about it: This war was over for sure.

The colonel had brought along a quartermaster with
him, some corpsmen — a dispensation to offer succor behind
enemy lines that spoke volumes about who was in charge.

Across from the Muncie men, maybe two dozen naked prisoners stood in a tight circle, ass ends out, while the quartermaster rummaged through his stores for shirts, pants, flour sacks, sugar sacks, scraps of tent canvas, anything to cover them with. George and the rest could see their ribs and spines, vertebrates and tail bones, stretching the flesh. The sun climbing overhead seemed to rake them with shadows, each one a lash mark.

There was vinegar as well, a whole cask of it, but it was the food that gave the Federal colonel his final authority: crates of beef jerky. Everyone was chewing it — prisoners, guards, even Jones himself — whether he had teeth left for the purpose or not. The jerky seemed a miracle of its own: a meal that didn't need cooking, a fire that didn't have to be built out of wood that wouldn't light, with tinder that barely existed.

"Kind of got used to them boys in their birthday suits," Jake said, gnawing at a thumb-size chunk of the dried beef as he nodded toward the quartermaster's club. He was wondering if his teeth would ever settle right in their sockets again. It was disconcerting to have them rattle so. Still, his mouth was full. Nothing to complain of there. "Seemed like it wasn't no big thing. Looks a tad strange now though."

With the gates to the landing left open, dogs as bad looking as themselves had come wandering in, pulling bones George didn't want to think about out of holes he wished he'd never seen. Jones' guards were working their way through the crowd, trying to get the men to form up into companies, units, anything rational — a losing effort. The men had left any semblance of military discipline behind months upon months ago.

"Might as well herd ghosts," Jake opined. One of his molars had come unmoored altogether.

Not twenty feet away, Millbank was curled in the dirt, drawn up in a tight circle, bawling like a baby. One of the

Union corpsmen was trying to raise him back to his feet, stroking his head, whispering in his ear.

"First fat man I seen in forever," Ephraim noted. The corporal's gut sprawled out from under his tunic.

"You reckon they could shoot me before I got to Jones?" Henry asked, staring at the cadre that surrounded the acting camp commander.

"I reckon they could," Jake said, eyeing the distance, maybe fifty feet in all, plenty of time to level a rifle and squeeze.

"Well, you reckon they're good shots?" Henry persisted.

"Never known 'em to miss that much before when they set their minds on killing someone. They got numbers of their side, too. Why?"

"I would sure like to feel my hands on his throat as I died."

Jake was steadying yet another errant molar with his tongue. Henry wasn't going to strangle no one. He was just being Henry.

Steamboats were the troop carriers of the Civil War, but the Alabama wasn't the Mississippi, or even the Potomac, the James, the Arkansas, or the Missouri; and the war had taken a toll on shipping channels. To get upriver to Cahaba, a steamer had to be small enough to handle narrow turns and light enough to keep its rudder out of the mud below. That and the general paucity of river traffic that comes with any economic catastrophe slowed the evacuation of Cahaba Federal Prison to a crawl.

As should be, the sickest men went first: the hospitalized and those who should have been, the men who could barely walk, the sticks-and-bones. Day Two of the clearing had just begun when George saw Capt. Downey's writing kit chugging up the Alabama, held high by the man he had befriended as if the kit contained a sacred scroll. Millbank left later that afternoon, practically carried on board. He looked back at George, over the corpsman's shoulder, but George couldn't meet his eyes. Too much history there.

Nothing seemed standard, nothing regular. Some ships headed down the Alabama to the Tombigbee River, almost to Mobile Bay, then followed the Tombigbee to Gainesville, Mississippi. At Gainesville, the men would disembark and march overland until they had made the tracks of the Mobile and Ohio Railroad. There they would wait for a train to carry them to Meridian. At Meridian, they boarded the Alabama and Mississippi line to Jackson and west toward Vicksburg. Other ships steamed north the scant eight miles to Selma to meet the Alabama and Mississippi line — the easy route, the men said; everyone hoped for it. They were all headed to the same place, or so it seemed: some new camp that had been set up just east of Vicksburg, and from there up the river and then by rail again to Camp Chase in Ohio, to be mustered out, soldiers and prisoners no more.

Men traveled on northbound packets that held barely two dozen people or on southbound passenger steamers that had to back and fill at half the river bends. Sometimes a clot of guards went along to escort the prisoners through enemy lines; sometimes only one or two went along. It wasn't just prisoners Cahaba was emptying out of. It was guards, too, and residents. The Muncie men watched what had to be the Gardners — mother and daughter, Amanda and Belle — board a southbound steamer arm in arm, followed by a dozen or more heavy wooden boxes: their library, off to some new destination, some place less inclined to soaking all who lived there. The place was already well on the way to the ghost town it would soon become. What prisoners went which way when in what numbers was all a matter of what trains might be running, where the regular river traffic was going. Half the time, George expected, it was the Federal colonel's best guess.

The chaos of war had become the chaos of impending peace. For the moment, from the Muncie men's perspective, the two looked much the same, but there was this: They were going home. They would wait out anything for that, and they damn near had to. Better off than most despite their long imprisonment — Henry's cooking, their sharing, the boy's additions of late, always blind luck — they chewed their jerky, scuffed the dirt with their bare feet, and watched the prison empty out day by day.

"The war, how'd it end?" Ephraim asked. They'd been watching the colonel from afar as the place emptied. Now they could hardly avoid him. There couldn't have been more than 125 or so men — prisoners, guards, Jones, the few Federals — left in the whole place.

"We wore 'em out before they wore us out, I guess." His voice surprised them: It was soft for a tall man. Maybe that was why no one yet had heard him speak more than a word or two.

"You think it's really over?" It seemed impossible to George that something so momentous, something that had ground up so many months and years of their lives could just stop. It was like God's suddenly deciding there would be no more days or nights, no seasons, no nothing. How could that be?

"I know it's over for Lee, and I suspect it will be over soon enough for Johnston up in North Carolina and the others," the colonel answered. "No point in it any more except for the dying and destroying. We're an army of occupation now, not a fighting one, but that doesn't mean there aren't plenty of raiders out there, just waiting for too few of us to come by without enough men or arms to protect us,"

He took a deep breath, let it slowly out. His eyes seemed to be set on some spot far beyond the horizon. The Muncie men would swear days later that they could see the whole history of the war, maybe of warfare itself, in that look.

"Some say the fighting won't be over all the way until Jeff Davis is hanging from a tree," the colonel finally went on. "Some believe it'll go on 'til the last Reb's dead. Hell, Forrest is going to be waging this war long after the rest of us have forgotten what it was about or maybe invented some new reason for all this madness."

A purple crease ran across his forehead and down by his right ear almost to the jaw line, as if his face had been half peeled off, then sewed back to that corner. His right hand was a claw, not much more.

"What do you believe, colonel?"

"I stopped believing anything two years ago, soldier. Hasn't been anything to change my mind since."

The plume in his hat appeared to have come from a great blue heron, or maybe a sandhill crane. It was exotic, ridiculous.

"I'm Corporal George Ethridge," George said it only half intelligibly — anything to keep the conversation going. "This here is Jake, my uncle, and Ephraim, my little brother." He was patting Ephraim on the shoulder like he was getting ready to burp him. "Last one's Henry. He and Ephraim been joined at the hip practically since they was babies."

George capped his oration by snapping off a salute so fast that his thumb almost knocked his eyeball out. He was rusty. All of them were. The colonel laughed.

"Corporal Ethridge," he said, pulling his own hat off and bowing deeply to them all, "I deeply appreciate the genealogy, sir. It couldn't be more fascinating."

Now that he was bareheaded and bent over, they could follow the purple crease as it ran a zig-zag pattern far back into his graying hair. What had happened? Some Indian wars? Had he really been scalped? The thought made George want to grab his own hair, hold on tight. Maybe a half dozen of their guards had been Creeks, Choctaws, who knew what. They had long since melted into the night, but the thought of being scalped by one of them had kept more than a few prisoners awake, until worse fates intervened.

"We're Muncie men, sir." George couldn't leave it alone.

"Muncie?"

"Yes, sir, Muncie. Indiana 66th Volunteer Infantry. Had to go all the way to New Albany to join up. Muncie men stick together."

One of the remaining prisoners was circling a dog, dangling a length of twine done up into a slip-noose. For the first time since he didn't know when, George was willing to consider the possibility that the man was after companion-ship, not a meal.

"And the runt?"

The colonel was pointing to the boy, half hidden behind Jake. A good question. What was the boy? The runt? They knew less about him than they knew about the Man in the Moon, and weren't likely to learn much more. The boy had come from nowhere; he disappeared to nowhere half or more nights still, even now that they didn't need his filching. During the day, none of them, Jake especially, could turn around without practically tripping over the boy. He was underfoot every moment: watching, learning, taking everything in. George wasn't sure he'd ever seen a better mimic, a quicker study. The boy had never danced in his life — that was clear as moonshine — yet at the dead-line romp not long after he'd tied himself cheek to jowl to the Muncie men, the boy had jumped right in, picked up steps in an instant, caught the music, added some steps of his own. When Jake took hold of him at the end of one number and threw him up in the air, George thought for a moment that the boy might just sprout wings, keep on flying over the stockade, over the rivers, over God knows where. That he didn't, that he bounced right back down to earth just like any mortal had almost surprised all of them.

What was he? George could see in the boy's eyes that he was awaiting the answer along with the colonel. The boy's mouth was stuffed with jerky — his jaws looked half ready to snap apart from the work of it all. He was dressed in rags, filthy like all the rest of them.

"That ain't no runt, sir," George finally answered. "That's a short-limbed Muncie man through and through." The flicker of a smile passed over the boy's face; then it broke open into sunshine: a full-toothed grin that not one of them had ever seen before. That much settled, at least. They were five now.

The major was fitting his hat back on his head with his good left hand, the plume fluttering slightly in what little breeze there was.

"Why so he is, corporal. So he is. Don't know how I missed it." He picked the saddlebags off the boy's shoulder, turned it over in his good hand, held it up to his eyes to check the stitching. "That's a fine-looking piece of leather you got there, son."

"Spoils of war, sir," George answered for him. Ever since he had saved it from Capt. Downey's corpse, the boy had insisted on carrying the bag everywhere with him.

"Spoils, you say? Even here?"

The colonel turned, started toward the gate on the far side of the stockade, then turned back to see if the Muncie men were following him.

"Well, c'mon," he called. They all but ran to join him.

At the gate, the colonel lifted the crossbar out of the way. A pair of guards watched him from the walkway above, rifles leaning against the wall behind them. It was all show, now, yet the Muncie men found themselves crossing the deadline to the gate as if they were walking on hot coals, ground-up glass. The colonel signaled to the boy to pull back and secure the one gate. He took the other half himself and swung it open. Just beyond, half a dozen yards back from the outer wall of the prison, stood maybe two, three hundred Negroes: men, women, children; white-haired ancients, babies still at their mother's breast. In their hands were hoes, mattocks, sickles; hammers, mallets, and mauls; cross saws and rip saws; crowbars; every kind of hand tool the Muncie men had ever imagined. Among the Negroes, there wasn't a sound, not even a little child's whimpering, nor hardly a movement. It was like staring at a painting that kept looking as if it would walk off the canvas.

"Ever seen anything like it?" the colonel asked.

The men didn't even bother to answer. They didn't know whether to be scared or awed. The quiet was monumental.

"What do you think they're doing here?"

It was Ephraim who first got the courage to speak up.

"Waiting, sir."

"Waiting? For what?"

"For us to leave."

"Well, then," the colonel said, swinging his half of the gate back in place, "It's about time we did."

10

They departed at precisely 7:07 the next morning — the packet captain checking his pocket watch with a great flourish, giving three sharp toots on his whistle, and pulling gently away from the landing. The Muncie men, five now, were among two dozen or so headed north to Selma and from there to the Mississippi by rail: the easy route, good luck at last. For escorts, they had the Wall-Eye and two other guards they barely knew, a pair of drawn-looking soldiers, maybe even brothers, who had come on duty only a few weeks earlier. The Federal colonel, his quartermaster and corpsmen, all the rest of the prisoners, even Jones had all left only minutes earlier on a passenger boat heading south.

Just as the larger boat was throwing off its mooring ropes, George had snatched his letter out of the saddlebags on the boy's shoulder, jumped their own railing, and raced down the boards.

"Colonel!" he shouted, waving the letter, "Colonel! Could you post this for me somehow? I'd sure like it to get home before I do."

"Anything for a Muncie man," the colonel called back. The boat was already pulling away from shore. "Give it a toss!"

George held the letter flat, gave it a spin in the colonel's direction, and prayed. The envelope seemed to waver over the water, stand still in the air. Then it dipped down toward the deck, just far enough out for Big Tennessee, who was standing next to the colonel, to snatch it from oblivion. More luck. Everything was turning. George waved once — it was the last time he would ever see either man — then turned full-throttle for his own transportation. He had to leap to make it and managed to do so only because leaping was his special talent and Jake was the one who snatched something from oblivion this time.

"Goddamn foolest thing I ever saw in my life," Jake groused. "I've got half a mind to toss you back," but he didn't. The milk of human kindness was flowing in him.

They leaned against the railing, watching the water churn against the landing, as the space grew wider between them and their confinement. Feet became yards; yards, fractions of a mile. One of the dogs that had been foraging the prison for bones jumped from the landing and took off after them. The men cheered it on for a while until the dog gave up, turned tail, and swam for home. They rounded a sharp bend, and the warehouse disappeared from view, behind a point of land still covered with pines. When it reappeared across an unplowed field, the prison seemed huge, dark, menacing. This was a vantage not one of them had ever seen it from before, and they were all glad of it, glad to be seeing it this way for the one time when they were leaving for good.

"Looks sort of like a castle, don't it," Ephraim said.

"Castle Morgan," Henry added. "I never knew for the life of me what that was all about."

That's what the guards had called the place: Castle Morgan, in honor of the Confederate cavalry raider John Hunt Morgan. The prisoners didn't call it anything — it was what it was, beyond words, nearly beyond description — but John Hunt Morgan made an oddly appropriate patron saint for the Muncie men who'd been held there. Morgan had been born in Huntsville, a day's ride north of their misery, and raised in Kentucky, scene of that awful first taste of battle.

In the early summer of '63, when George, Jake, Ephraim, and Henry were still settling into Cahaba, Morgan led his men straight into Union territory. Cincinnati quaked while the raiders skirted her, panic spreading like smallpox through those flat alluvial plains. A militia was raised, cavalry called in. At last, at New Lisbon, Indiana — not thirty miles from Muncie, deeper behind enemy lines than any other Reb force would ever push — Morgan and most of his command staff were captured, hauled across the state line into Ohio, tossed into prison, and the key thrown away. Five months later, Morgan sprang himself free — Houdini before anyone had ever heard (or made up) the name. The party ended September 4, 1864, at Greeneville, Tennessee. Flushed in the early morning, Morgan was shot in the back by a Yankee private named Andrew Campbell, a local boy who'd declared himself for the Union. Famous for his daring exploits on horseback, John Hunt Morgan bled to death bootless and face down on a dirt street. R.I.P.

"Not going to be a castle for long," Jake said, looking one last time. He had the boy hard by his side, couldn't have shook him with a stick.

The Negroes had already torn most of the palings off the stockade on the north side of the prison. Others were swarming across the roof, pulling loose the planks, passing them down, starting in on the timbers. As the men watched, a section of brick along the northwest corner swayed, then came tumbling away, dust and mortar rising into the still morning air. George had visions of a brand-new shantytown; narrow, rutty streets; tom-toms instead of their snoring and moans. On the whole, an improvement. The vermin, he thought, must be licking their chops. Negro or white, it couldn't matter much to rats.

The little packet turned again, went around another bend, beat north, left Cahaba and its prison behind for good, just as history soon would do, the dreams of all those hard-working Negroes up in smoke once more, along with their labors. Water won. It always does. Always.

Beneath their feet, the Muncie five could feel the boiler thrumming, the steam driving. Over on the starboard side, one of the men started up a song that seemed to fit the beat of the engine. There wasn't a person among who was well by anything other than their own dismal standards of health, but the jerky had put some backbone into them, the vinegar had chased away the worst of their stomachs' ills and furies. The sun was out. They were heading north, then west, to home. Why not a song?

Our Jimmy has gone for to live in a tent,
They have grafted him into the Army,
He finally puckered up courage and went,
When they grafted him into the Army.
I told them the child was too young, alas!
At the captain's forequarters, they said he would pass,
They'd train him up well in the Infantry class,
So they grafted him into the Army.

"Oh, Jimmy, farewell!" Ephraim joined in at the chorus, his lovely soft tenor. There didn't seem to be a song in Christendom he didn't know. "Your brothers fell / Way down in Alabammy, / I thought they would spare / A lone widder's heir, / But they grafted him into the Army."

"If your brother was as good at mules as he is at singing, we might have had ourselves a more fruitful tour of duty," Jake said. "That's your mama in him."

George nodded. He could see Jake's bad ankle bowing out to the right, an odd half moon of sinew and bone. "Might have caught us a bullet, too, or one of them cannonballs." For every road not taken these last three and a half years, an equal chance for worse disaster. That was his consolation.

Now in my provisions I see him revealed,
They have grafted him into the Army;
A picket beside the contented field,
They have grafted him into the Army.
He looks kinder sickish -- begins to cry,
A big volunteer standing right in his eye!
Oh, what if the ducky should up and die,
Now they've grafted him into the Army.

"You're feeling mighty chipper," George told Ephraim as soon as the last chorus died down.

"Can't help myself."

"Still, I'm wondering if you couldn't put a little more feeling into that part about your brother falling way down in Alabammy. You were a touch too lilty when it came to that."

"It's that jerky, for sure. Feel I've had me half a steer."

"You smell like the half that ain't been eaten yet," Henry chipped in, and the two of them were off and running.

"Say, Henry, you remember that Lucinda Hopkins woman?"

"Cockeyed face? Lives out by the Barley road in that three-cornered shack with the green paint splotched all over the door?"

"That's the one. I believe this is what she smelled like last time you visited her."

"Wouldn't know. I borrowed your nose that night."

"You two might as well be married," George said. "You couldn't talk any more nonsense than you do now."

Jake's neck was scarlet, the red seeping upward to his cheeks and brow. He'd all but clapped his hands over the boy's ears. The primly named Lucinda Hopkins was a notorious bawd. Her father had carried her out with him to Muncie sometime in the late 1840s, only to die the next winter of exposure complicated by being too drunk to know it. She had been maybe fourteen then, forced to make do ever since with what she had to offer, a diminishing asset. Some said that, in spite of her name, Lucinda was half Indian or more, but that's what they always said in Muncie when they couldn't figure out any other reason.

Overhead, the sun had begun sliding between clouds, climbing toward mid-day. The scent of new growth was in the air. Grasses, reeds, daylilies filled the river banks. Birds were darting everywhere. A second song was just starting up when the captain gave another sharp toot on his whistle and the men looked up to see Selma Landing all but staring them in the face. Beyond it lay a scene of utter destruction, and right in the middle of it waited their train, windows open, a fine plume rising from its stack.

11

On June 1, 1865, Maj. Gen. George H. Thomas, U.S. Army, reported to Headquarters, Department of the Cumberland, in Nashville, on the raid deep into the heart of Alabama led by Maj. Gen. James H. Wilson in March and early April of that final year of war. Wilson had at his disposal 13,500 Union cavalry and mounted infantry. His immediate goal was to capture and destroy the critical Confederate arsenal at Selma, sweeping through the narrow valley and mountains of what was to become Birmingham along the way and destroying the ironworks there. By occupying Confederate forces at the center of the state, Wilson also hoped to ease the pressure on the Union soldiers who had laid siege to Mobile.

> *On the 30th of March General Wilson's cavalry reached Elyton, after an extremely difficult, toilsome, and exhausting march, on account of bad roads, swollen streams, and the rough nature of the country, which had also been almost entirely stripped of all subsistence for man or beast. At Elyton, Croxton's brigade, of McCook's division, was detached and sent to capture and destroy Tuscaloosa, and then march to rejoin the main body near Selma. With the remainder of his command, General Wilson pushed rapidly forward to Montevallo, where he destroyed five extensive ironworks, and other valuable property. On the outskirts of the town*

the enemy's cavalry was found in force, attacked, routed, and pursued through Plantersville, leaving in our possession three pieces of artillery and several hundred prisoners.

At 3 p.m. on the 2d of April, General Wilson reached the immediate vicinity of Selma, and rapidly formed Upton's and Long's divisions to attack the defenses of the town — Long attacking on the Summerfield Road, and Upton across a swamp deemed impassable by the enemy. Dismounting two regiments from each of the brigades of Colonels Miller and Minty, General Long and those two officers gallantly leading their men in person charged across an open field, 500 yards wide, over a stockade, which they tore up as they passed, through the ditch and over the enemy's parapets, sweeping everything before them. Our loss was 46 killed and 200 wounded; Colonel Dobb, Fourth Ohio, among the former, and General Long and Colonels Miller and McCormick among the latter. General Upton met with less resistance than Long — entered the enemy's works and the town, capturing many prisoners.

In the darkness and confusion following the assault Generals Forrest, Buford, Adams, Armstrong, and others made their escape. Lieut. Gen. Dick Taylor had left earlier in the afternoon. As the fruits of the victory, however, there remained 26 guns and 2,700 prisoners, besides large amounts of ordnance and other property of great value. Twenty-five thousand bales of cotton had already been destroyed by the enemy. General Wilson remained at Selma from the 2d to the 10th of April, resting his command and completing the destruction of the immense workshops, arsenals, and foundries...

Selma, in short, got it both coming and going: from its own defenders, who would rather have destroyed the last wealth left to the place than have it fall into devil hands, and from its conquerors, who took it upon themselves to tear down just about everything else left standing. The place looked like a bomb the size of a city church had exploded right in the middle of it.

In front of them, the old landing might as well have been attacked by a herd of crazed elephants. All the planks were splintered, ground up, crushed, axed, askew every which way. Someone had lashed the few half sections that remained to a pair of logs — hardly any landing at all, but it had to do. The packet captain kept up a steady stream of cursing as he backed and filled to come up even with it.

Beyond the landing, what must have been some old shack of a custom's house lay burned to the ground. Further back, in what had been warehouses, the remains of those 25,000 bales of cotton — more than 6,000 tons of it, for God's sake — made up their own smoldering ruin, a little Pompei still puffing out smoke weeks after the great conflagration. The brick walls of the arsenal leaned precariously — or had collapsed altogether. The few buildings that stood on their own were charred and wounded, as if some giant had taken a notion to bludgeon them with the jawbone of an ass.

Still, in the middle of this devastation, their train was waiting for them. It was like something out of a bedtime story you might tell children. The packet captain tooted his whistle twice, the train engineer tooted back, and the men got off at the ruined landing, negotiated the rough first feet of that slippery, make-shift pier, then walked the few dozen yards to the track and climbed aboard. And with another toot and a *chug-chug-chug*, they were off to Vicksburg and home.

The Wall-Eye was the only one who refused to go any further.

"Can't get on," he kept telling the two guards he had been joined with. "Just can't."

It was obvious to everyone that the two of them could have cared less. Finally, Henry couldn't stand it any longer.

"Wall-Eye," he asked, "did you really bayonet that guy the way you said you did?"

The Wall-Eye's face went white with shock, then red with anger.

"I do it," he said, stabbing some mythical bayonet in Henry's direction. "I do. I do. I do. I do." Tears were streaming down his face.

The boy was pounding George's arm, pulling on his shirt, his own face twisted into a giant question mark. It seemed as if the boy had been with them forever, but he hadn't been there back then, thank God.

"It's a long story," George told him.

The boy turned to Jake, bursting with curiosity.

"And nobody wants to tell it," Jake added.

The Wall-Eye was still standing by the tracks when they pulled out, bayoneting everything in sight.

12

The locomotive was one of those half-armored ones that became popular as the war wore on: enough iron to keep a rifled musket ball from piercing to the interior, enough of a slit for the engineer to see the tracks, enough danger from a sharpshooter with the slit in his site to keep the ride interesting, and all of it vulnerable to torpedoes (what would later be called mines) buried under a tie, just waiting for the heft of the train to compress its fuse. The war had raged on for four years; nothing would be safe for months and months to come.

Behind the locomotive, the tender, unarmored, the fireman a sitting duck. Behind that, two enclosed cars with benches and a flat car at the back that had been rigged with a tent like a traveling circus show. The Muncie men settled in the second of the enclosed cars, five abreast on the last bench to be had. There might have been fifty people with them in both cars, physical wrecks every one, but almost all of them with liberation smiles on their sunken faces. The jerky had gotten to them, too, and hardtack as well — one more thing impossible to chew. They could see men gumming those rocky biscuits row by row by row as they made their way back to the empty pew.

It wasn't long before the flat car behind them got their attention. Two Union guards were posted at the back of the car, but why seemed as uncertain to the guards as to the Muncie men.

"Where's everyone coming from?" Jake asked, still talking his head off.

"Camp Sumter. Most got sent to Jacksonville, down in Florida, to be shipped north up the coast, but this batch is heading up the Mississippi with you."

"Camp Sumter?" Jake was looking at him with a blank stare.

"Andersonville, over in Georgia," the guard explained.

Even then, the name had a muting quality, one of those words that compels silence in its aftermath.

"And them?" Henry asked, looking through the glass of the door into the last car.

"Same," one of the guards said. "Only worse. There's a hospital up in Cincinnati that might be able to help."

He left the rest unsaid — that the state of rail transportation after four years of blowing up each other's tracks left water as the best alternative, if only they could get them to Vicksburg.

"Can we have a look?"

"You don't want to."

But they did, or thought they did. They'd known plenty who had been shipped off to Andersonville in the clearing of the October before. Unlike the Muncie men, though, the Andersonville ones had never returned.

"Here, take the boy," Jake said, pushing him back to George. "Stay with him." But, no, the boy was one of them now. He went where they went, however bad, and this was awful.

Words are inadequate, even the tongue of a poet. Only photographs can really convey what the Muncie men saw. Get them out some time. Have a good look. The dead break your heart, but the undead sometimes are more instructive.

Sure, they hung Henry Wirz for what happened at Andersonville. They had to. It doesn't matter what the facts were, what duress he was working under, what a miasmic swamp he'd been handed to run his prison on top of. Wirz was commander most of the time the place existed. Someone had to take a fall. But what they saw that late morning in that rolling field hospital of a railroad flatcar wasn't the work of just one person. This was mankind failing itself.

The best of those they walked among were the merely starved, the living skeletons lying upon their straw pallets: men whose heads seemed impossibly large for their shrunken bodies, whose ball joints (shoulders, knees, hips) bulged out of their bodies like monstrous tumors. Bones, craniums — you couldn't starve those down to scale, just the muscle and flesh that hung from them and around them. From there, it descended downhill through various rots, unset fractures, still-open wounds until the Muncie five came to the footless men, and there they were literally floored: a half dozen or so men — of the more than 45 in all so afflicted who were recovered from that hellhole in Georgia — whose feet had simply rotted away from the damp, the cold, the infestations and diseases. One of those things in life you see that you would give a fortune to forget.

Open eyes stared blankly back at the Muncie men. It was as if they were there and not there, as if they walked among humans and ghosts at the same time. The four who had been in the prison when the inmates were first dispersed looked for familiar faces, peculiarities of brows or cheekbones, moles or birthmarks that might led them to someone they had known. Finally, Ephraim dropped to his knees beside a shriveled man whose blond hair and beard had been freshly barbered by some kind soul.

"Hundt?" he asked.

George recalled the name — a Pennsylvania German, an alto. He and Ephraim had spent hours harmonizing among themselves and with a few others.

"Hundt?" Ephraim asked again, but there was no expression, no hint of recognition, no acknowledgement that another person existed beside him or even that he existed much himself.

Very gently, so as not to scare anyone, Ephraim began to sing:

When Johnny comes marching home again,
Hurrah! Hurrah!
We'll give him a hearty welcome then,
Hurrah! Hurrah!
The men will cheer and the boys will shout
The ladies they will all turn out
And we'll all feel gay,
When Johnny comes marching home.

And slowly, ever so slowly as Ephraim sang, they could see something like life coming back into Hundt's eyes, but not just Hundt. The man lying next to him stirred, and the skeleton on the other side seemed almost to smile.

"That's enough," Jake said, putting his hands on his nephew's shoulders and lifting him back to his feet. "Let's leave the poor souls to their rest." It was the boy: Everyone knew that. He'd seen more than he ever should have.

Back on their bench in the last car, the five of them wriggled this way and that, found spaces along each other's sides to lean into, and were soon asleep. A dusty breeze blew in through the window. The sun had gone hot overhead. Soon it would bake the car. A New York hotel room couldn't have been more comfortable.

Ephraim had no idea what time it was when he awoke. Had he dozed off for a few minutes? An hour? More? He slipped off his spot at the end of the bench; took Henry's head, which had been on his own shoulder, and leaned it into George, who was set up in the middle. The guards, or whatever they were, had found themselves a sheet of newspaper to pore over. They didn't even look up this time when he slipped through the door.

"One. Two. Three. Four."

Four what, George wondered? He heard a small clatter at the end of their bench, the sound of muffled metal. One head was leaning against his right shoulder. What felt like another head was cradled into the bend of his left elbow. He popped an eyeball open and saw the two federal guards standing in the aisle, stacking four canteens on the empty seat.

"Five," George said.

"Five what?"

"They're five of us."

"Ain't four but I see."

George bent his head left and saw Jake snoring against the window frame. The boy was packed between the two of them. He'd slobbered all over the sleeve of George's shirt. Henry flanked him to the other side. Ephraim was missing. He could see now that the canvas sheaths the canteens came in were stamped "C.S.A."

"What in the hell?"

"Found a warehouse full of the damn things when they took Demopolis," one of the guards explained. "Put 'em on when we stopped there. Figured you boys might be getting thirsty."

Demopolis? They must have been sleeping half the day.

Still half asleep, Henry reached out and raised one of the canteens.

"Forgot to fill 'em."

"Train's going to stop when we get closer to Meridian," the guard said. "They say there's a creek up there with sugar water in it, so sweet you can put it on a birthday cake. You can fill the canteens there."

Fair enough. They sat waking up each at his own pace, feeling the hot breeze on their cheeks, smelling the new season on the air as Alabama disappeared behind them, waiting for Ephraim to wander back from wherever he had wandered off to. When he didn't, George rose to have a look. He was about to turn toward the front of the train when he glanced through the door behind him and saw his brother sitting cross-legged in the middle of all those poor and desperate men.

> *Get ready for the Jubilee,*
> *Hurrah! Hurrah!*
> *We'll give the hero three times three,*
> *Hurrah! Hurrah!*
> *The laurel wreath is ready now*
> *To place upon his loyal brow*
> *And we'll all feel gay*
> *When Johnny comes marching home.*

Ephraim had sung himself hoarse. His voice wasn't much more than a croak now. "Shhh," he signaled George. "Shhh," his finger to his lips. George could hear the snores of the men around him, could see how the pain had been lifted off their faces. How long had Ephraim been at it? And then he noticed something else. His brother was red in the face, trembling; sweat was pouring off him. My God, he thought. The fever is back.

George put his arm around Ephraim and walked him into the forward car. They had just sat him down in Jake's spot by the window and stretched his legs out along the bench when the train let out a sharp whistle and screeched to a grinding halt.

13

It didn't take a minute to see what the problem was once they had stepped down from the car: The train had no rail to ride on. Four sections of track had been yanked up, along with the sleepers. The ties fed the fire; the fire cooked the rails. Once the tracks were red-hot, the Reb raiders had twisted them, then bent the skewed metal into arcs. The men could see a live oak maybe fifteen feet away covered with charred marks just at the height of a man's chest.

"Sherman's Bowties," the ruined tracks were called, named for the scourge of Dixie, Gen. William Tecumseh Sherman; and it was the twist that made the difference. Track that had been heated and bent could be reheated, unbent, and laid back down again, even by as pathetic a posse as this foray had netted. But getting the kink out of the track took know-how. No fool, Sherman had marched with 10,000 men specially trained to do just that. Until he reached Atlanta, the rails were Sherman's supply line. He needed them as a baby needs a mother's breast. After Atlanta, Sherman destroyed everything in his path, railroad tracks included. Thousands of his bowties littered the Georgia landscape, all the way to Savannah and the sea. The South was never going to rise again if William Tecumseh Sherman had any say.

The raiders who'd done this didn't have anything so grand in mind. They'd torn up just enough track to slow down rail traffic, not cut if off: a nuisance, more than an act of war; a last tweaking of the nose of the conquering hordes from the infidel Yankeeland. As far as the prisoners were concerned, though, the raiders might as well have torn up every piece of rail in sight and chewed it into metal shavings. Sherman and his crack rail-repair crews were hundreds of miles to the east. Wilson had left Selma for Georgia a week earlier. No one was rushing out to unkink this rail and put it back in place. Instead, a puffy faced captain and a company of raggedy looking infantry waited on the men. Half the company was going to stay with the rolling field hospital until ambulance carts could be dispatched, the captain announced. The rest of the train load, its mixed assemblage of guards included, could start marching.

"Water's not but an hour or two down the road," the captain shouted, standing up in his stirrups so he could be heard by one and all. "You can fill your canteens there. Get some beauty sleep tonight, and we'll march into Meridian by mid-day tomorrow. Plenty of trains waiting just west of there to carry you on to Vicksburg. Hell, they'll probably have a banquet table set up for you when you arrive — roasts and potatoes and all the pie you can eat."

Just to be on the safe side, the men stuffed their pockets with hardtack before they set off. It was strange to be on foot again; strange to have somewhere to march to after all that round and round in the prison yard; strangest of all to think they might really have the strength to get where they were supposed to be going. Even Ephraim had rallied — the sweats gone, his color back almost to normal. George felt his forehead, still warm to the touch but nothing like what it had been back on the train. Maybe he had been wrong; maybe the singing had just plain worn him out.

Ephraim and Henry walked in front; George and Jake followed, with the boy attached to Jake's side like some third leg. The empty canteens slapped against their sides like a promise of plenty to come, but when they got to the creek where they were to fill them, the water put up a terrible stench. A party was sent to explore upstream. At length, just where the creek flowed out of a thick field of brambles, they peered into the near darkness — the odor by now almost unbearable — and saw the water washing over the rotting corpses of what seemed to be dozens of skunks, muskrats, possums, and raccoons, strung out along a line.

"Unstring 'em!" the captain bellowed when the party reported back, but who would do it? Who would wade into those brambles? And who knew what the brambles held? Someone, after all, had turned the track into bowties, and someone had tied all that carrion up there. What if they were one and the same? The prisoners hadn't been liberated that very week so they could walk into a Rebel trap. Nor had the soldiers who were escorting them dodged death this long only to make its acquaintance now that the war was at an end, or nearly so. As for the captain himself, George counted two canteens hanging heavily from his saddle, and two more strapped across the chest of his sergeant. The pistol in the captain's holster had the polished look of a weapon never fired.

"Don't want to spoil you boys!" he barked out as the sergeant sent the line marching onward. "This is the Army, not the Palace Hotel. You get your water when you get it."

Ho. Ho. Ho. But anything to get away from that smell.

14

" Fall out!"

Truth told, they'd fallen out miles earlier: minds numbed; bodies wracked; feet moving forward from habit alone, no more from will, no more because they were going somewhere they wanted to get to. Not only had they gone without water; the sun had turned punishing by mid-afternoon and the breeze dropped to nothing. Ephraim had his arm over Henry's shoulder so Henry was half walking for them both. Behind them, Jake was wondering what might happen if his ankle just gave out altogether, ceased to be an ankle, became something else instead. Could he build boilers with but one ankle – with one working foot, with one working leg? (He refused to think of the men they had left behind with no feet, with nothing but rounded purplish stubs to stand on. He'd figured death for part of the bargain when he signed up to watch over his sister's boys, the only two she would ever be able to have, but not that.)

Jake ran through his workday — what he would do while Old Quincy sat back on his keister and barked orders, the things he had to hold, the places he had to be. He could do it, he decided, one-damn-legged if it came to that; he could do it. He had a vision of a helper, the boy, still by him, and at that very moment, the boy suddenly looked up at him in complete agreement, as if he could read every word that passed through Jake's mind. The mute, the blind, the deaf

— Jake had always figured that those who lacked got gifts in return. More and more, the boy seemed proof of it. Don't, Jake told himself. Don't.

"Henry," he said, talking to his back, "you think maybe they've gone and started speaking in some new tongue in this Army since we been gone? 'Fall out' now means 'keep going on'? Is that what's happened?"

Men were peeling off in front of them, plopping down on whatever inviting space they could find beside the road, sprawling in the fresh grass and new weeds poking through the crust of a dead season. It had been, so one of the Cahaba guards had told the men, the coldest winter in his memory. The day they had just walked through had seemed inclined to make up for the heat deficit all at once, but the sun was almost to setting now, a glint of orange to the horizon, blessed relief. Three Vermont boys — like them, tight as ticks around one another — fell face down together down into a clump of weeds that looked like a goose-down mattress. If it was good enough for them, Henry thought, it's good enough for us.

"Uh, George?" he tried.

Finally, George pointed with his nose towards a little clump of cottonwood. "Those trees might kick up a breeze, and if the rain comes on, we can rig up some way to keep us dry."

"No rain in that sky," Ephraim volunteered, a fact crushingly obvious to everyone but his older brother.

"Don't go wandering," the captain bellowed as they were settling themselves in. "You saw what it's like back at that creek. If those Graybacks lure you into their lair, they'll eat you up for sure."

Food — the underlying theme of everything these last years. No sooner had the captain mentioned eating than the Muncie men pulled out their hardtack and began in on it. Here and there, a few campfires were firing up, men hauling in dry fall wood for the sheer joy of being able to find it. As the sun sank into the horizon in front of them, gold went to orange to red to purple. Almost exactly at dusk — just as the last colors faded out of the sky — the silent road they had been walking along seemed to come alive with spirits.

"Cigars!" someone cried out. "Four to the two-bit piece."

"Whiskey! Who wants some whiskey? Got it right here. Moonshine to make the moon shine!"

George ached for the coins that must have been in Capt. Downey's pockets, the coins he had let get away the morning of their first deliverance. How could he have done that? He could taste the tar of a cigar lingering on his lips, the burn of whiskey on his gullet. A rising campfire not far from them lit the spacious curve of a woman's bosom. No need to ask what she was selling. You did what you did to survive.

"Silver?"

George turned to see a woman his own dead grand-mother's age standing over him, dressed in black lace as if she had just come from a funeral, a parcel wrapped in a soft gray cloth in her hands.

"Ma'am?"

"Silver, young man. Would you care to buy some silver?"

"Ma'am, I've been a prisoner these — "

She lifted a corner of the cloth, showed George what might have been some kind of tea caddy, a jam jar covered with filigree, something else he couldn't identify.

"Oh, don't you worry," she said. "I've got more, plenty more where that came from. My people are Bevingtons, you hear? *Bevingtons!* That means something around here. You'll never find the silver. Don't even try. I've got it buried, buried deep, my own secret place. You could kill me and I still wouldn't tell. Would you care to buy some?"

"I'd be pleased to, Ma'am, but I don't — "

"You've got to pay me in Federal money, U.S. dollars. I don't take any Confederate bills although I would consider a ham if it's of a good size and has been cured just right. I'll need a sampling."

"It's like I've been trying to tell you, ma'am. I don't have any money."

"Should I just put you down for a gravy ladle then? Why don't I just do that."

She seemed to be writing on some kind of pad although George could see neither pen nor paper. The woman moved on to Jake.

"Would you care to buy some silver?"

"Sorry?" He was holding his right leg out straight in front of him, practicing for the day when he wouldn't have its use, but the woman had already marked him down for a ladle and turned to the boy.

"I'll just put you down for one, too," she said. "Every boy needs a ladle of his own."

The boy stared back at her, mesmerized.

"Cat got your tongue?"

He nodded.

"They don't teach social conversation the way they should anymore. Your friend here" — she was looking at Ephraim — "looks piqued. You need to get him out in the fresh air more."

Then she was gone, disappeared as instantly as she had arrived. Glad as the men were for food, the hardtack was like sawdust in their mouths without any water to wash it down. Or beer or whiskey, George thought, again ruing the hard specie he had let get away.

"Everateashoe?" Henry asked, the sound all a garble.

"Ain't I doing that now?" The words were barely out of Ephraim's mouth before he seemed to suck in one time, go still, then let out a burst of gasping that rattled every bone in his body. Jake picked him up like a baby thrown over his shoulder, while George gave him three, four sharp raps on the back until whatever piece of volcanic dough was trapped inside him came flying out. Henry uncorked his canteen and handed it over to Ephraim, forgetting it held nothing but air. Equally forgetful, Ephraim tilted his head back and went to take a soothing swallow that wasn't there.

"Goddamn it all to hell," he said. "Either you got too much water or you got too little. It's no good either way."

George didn't even think about improving his brother's language this time. He was too busy looking. Now that the sun was down completely, the cloudless sky was coming alive with stars. A nearly full moon had begun to rise behind them. In the distance, over an idle field, George could see a tiny wisp of something rising into the night. Mist? Some kind of haze? More than that? He couldn't say, but if you were to head into the field precisely where those two withered stalks of field corn split into a vee and set a course toward that lone oak or whatever it was outlined on the horizon, the path should bring you to the source of whatever it was.

An argument had started up by one of the campfires: shouting, threats, whiskey-talk. Someone had been hoarding hard currency — or managed to steal it. George thought about getting up and having a look — anything for enter-tainment, even fisticuffs — but the grass felt deep and soft beneath him.

"Somewhere out there is a well with water sweet as honey," George said. Ephraim looked over at his brother as he talked, a weak smile on his lips, or maybe the beginning of pain. Both were all but asleep. "It just stands to reason."

15

The revelry was over, the boasts and angry words drained away with the whiskey. The makeshift camp beside the road had gone still as a tomb. George guessed it might be midnight — the full moon directly overhead, something about the feel of a night halfway through — but he had no way of knowing. Somewhere out there surely one of their guards was doing sentry duty, or pretending to, but it was the first night they had slept outside prison walls in two long years. Strange that none of them had thought about that earlier when they were nodding off to sleep. One day of freedom, and they had begun to think like free men, or as free as any man can be in another man's army.

Everything hurt: arms, shoulders, legs, feet. Even George's tongue felt swollen and chafed. He rose on one knee, pulled his suspenders up over his shoulders, and tip-toed across to Jake, who was sleeping on his canteen — George could see it tucked half under his shoulder. He swung wide around the boy, still stuck to Jake, and tugged gently on the canteen strap. Impossible: Jake slept like a mountain on top of it. He tried tickling Jake under the nose with a piece of the grass bedding. Maybe that would move him, give George a moment's chance to free the canteen without waking him. He might as well have tried tickling a lump of coal, a mound of dirt. Jake didn't budge. Finally, George hunkered down, put his shoulder into Jake's side, and slowly, slowly pried him up as best he could. He had just freed the canteen when a hand shot out and grabbed his wrist in an iron grip. George could feel his tissue bruising, all the small wrist bones starting to compress dangerously.

"Jake," he whispered. "Jake! It's me. Let go."

To his surprise, Jake did. He patted George once on the wrist and raised a single weather eye that seemed to be trying to gauge whether his oldest nephew was just being dumb or this time had gone truly over the edge. Then he was back asleep as deeply as he had been moments before.

Henry's canteen was on the ground beside him, as sprawled out as Henry was. It always astounded George how people in their sleep become themselves years and years younger. Tangled up in his clothes, that hard pinch of tension around his mouth, Henry looked maybe all of ten years old lying there. George felt like his own mother or father, sneaking a peek at Henry as he slept next to Ephraim after some disaster or another in his own household.

Next: Ephraim. His lips were moving. George could see that in the moonlight. He picked his canteen up, as well; threw it over his shoulder with the others; and bent to hear what words there were.

> *The men will cheer and the boys will shout,*
> *The ladies they will all turn out,*
> *And we'll all feel gay,*
> *When Johnny comes marching home.*

No louder than a tiny puff of breeze.

"George?" His eyes not open. "George?" The smell — something animal telling him his brother was nearby. All instinct. Christ in heaven!

George walked back over to where he had been sleeping, added his own canteen to the mix, then squatted low and turned in a slow circle until he spotted the two old stalks of field corn splayed like a vee with the lone oak on the rise caught in the center like a giant rifle sight. Maybe the thin wisp was still there. Maybe not. It was that hour of the night when things imagined are more real than things heard and seen.

Raised up on his own elbow, his eye just visible above the rise and fall of Jake's barrel chest, the boy watched George walk into the rough field. He waited until he was nothing more than a rustle moving through the stalks, then rose slowly, inch by inch.

16

He imagined himself leaving huge red footprints as he forged deeper and deeper into the fields, like some martyred Martian giant. Thistles had torn at his ankles back when he was moving through the corn. Now that he was into some other untended remnant of a planting — sorghum, maybe? — the near petrified remains of old stalks sent jolts of pain shooting from the soles of his bare feet to his eyes, ears, everywhere. The rest of him had grown hard and gristly, but his feet had become soft pacing around that worn dirt yard at Cahaba. My God, he used to walk this way through his Papa's field to town and not feel a thing. He didn't want to look at his feet even if he could. Blood must be everywhere.

George stopped, thought he heard something rustling somewhere in the field behind him, but it was only the echo of his own footstep — too regular, too much like his own breath for anything else. He sited again on the oak on the rise, closer now, then peered into the field in front of him and could see it beginning to break apart not far ahead, some kind of blank wall of red that might be a barn; beyond that, a block of dirty white. Birds were darting overhead — split-tailed, picking mosquitoes and other insects out of the night air. Swallows, he thought; a barn for sure as he stepped out of the coarse vegetation into a broad farmyard. So it was here after all, he said, only half to himself.

To his left, the red barn. In the moonlight, he could see the hayloft open and empty. The mud yard in front of the barn was bare, only the least hint of manure in the air. Whatever animals had once been penned there were long gone: eaten, sold, hidden, stolen; maybe disease, maybe just inattention. The house in front of him argued for inattention. It was the kind of place George always guessed governors lived in: double storied, gabled on top, with a wide porch wrapped around it, elegance at every turn — beyond, the outline of a tree-lined drive leading to the front of the porch — except it was all in a state of decay. Walking toward it through the farmyard, George could see the white paint blistering off in huge sheets. Windows were missing, sometimes the whole thing, more often in part, dagger edges jutting this way and that. Here and there, the clapboard siding hung straight down toward the ground, suspended by a single remaining nail. A scattering of porch chairs flanked the front door, but Lord, to even think about sitting in them! The railing that surrounded the porch looked as if bears had been gnawing on it. Up top, the roof bloomed with vegetation. George couldn't imagine its keeping out a thing: rain, snow, even sun if it came to that, much less possums, raccoons, squirrels, mice, rats, snakes, bats, whatever other exotic creatures scaled the upper heights in this forlorn outpost of Johnny Reb land. Four chimneys in all, two at either end: no wisp of smoke now coming from any of them. No mind, they'd led him here.

Straight ahead was what he had come for: a well. His feet seemed to heal themselves as he neared it, as if the crabby grass underfoot was the Balm of Gilead itself.

The bucket was down the hole, far from his seeing. At least, he hoped there was a bucket, hoped there was water down there, hoped it was sweet and clear. Lots of pitfalls in so much wishing, not to mention three years of disappointment behind him. He laid his canteens on the ground beside him; put his hand gently to the crank, careful lest it make a racket; and found it wouldn't budge. The teeth were broken, the gearing rusted tight. The rope looked almost new, a blessing among so much dilapidation. He began to pull it up hand over hand, felt the comforting heft of a full bucket on the other end, and started pulling harder. He figured three feet to the handful, ten pulls before he could begin to hear the bucket scraping against the sides, and another five pulls after that. Maybe forty-five feet down: plenty deep for soil like this, it seemed, a good omen. He set the bucket on the stone lip of the well, dipped his hands in (no algae, nothing dead floating there), and put the water to his mouth. It tasted like no water that had crossed his lips since before he had been carted out of Muncie: a nectar almost. The moonlight danced across the surface of the bucket as if it wore tiny slippers of diamonds. Miracles all around.

George set himself and the bucket on the ground beside the well, pulled the plug from the first canteen, wedged it had between his knees, and filled the canteen as carefully as if he were pouring blood back into a vein. The second canteen, too, nearly to the top, before the bucket ran dry. Back down he sent it. Up he pulled. Canteen four was half full this time when the water ran out. One last time, George told himself. The memory of that sweet taste gilded his tongue as he heard a gentle splash echoing back from all those feet underground. He'd hauled the bucket almost back within sight when he heard the unmistakable sound of a hammer being pulled back, the hard click of a rifle cocking.

"Let it go." A woman's voice. Hard. The teeth clenched tight together.

George hauled the bucket up the last ten feet and set it on the ground by his feet.

"I said let it go." She was standing behind him, not far off.

George sat back down on the ground, took the last canteen between his knees, and began pouring.

"You're going to kill me or you're not going to kill me, but I come here to fill these canteens up, and that's what I aim to do."

"There had to be one last thing left to steal, didn't there, Yankee?" George could hear schooling in the voice, culture, what his mother always called "society."

"The furniture, the silver, the china and crystal, smoked hams, corn, the wine and whiskey — none of it was enough for you. You had to come back and steal our water, too, the last thing we got to live on."

"Your name Bevington?" George asked.

"What are you going to do when the water is gone? Cook us up and stew our bones? Maybe flay us and make purses for your pretty northern ladies out of our skin?"

"Is Bevington your name?" A guess, pure and simple. Too much of a coincidence to credit. For all he knew, this flatland was full of fine houses, silver and crystal spilling out the windows and doors. He grabbed the straps of the four canteens in his right hand, down to the side where he judged she couldn't see.

"Bevington is my mother's family." Mystery in her voice now: a riddle to untangle. "What's my name to you?"

"We're camped out on the road over yonder." He was in a crouch now, slowly rising, his back still to her, wondering whether to swing the canteens fast at her ankles or try to catch the rifle barrel with them. "Been there just since sunset."

"You think I don't know that? You think everyone around here for 50 miles doesn't know Satan is camped on that road? Federals are like cow patties, my Daddy used to say. Flies are just naturally attracted to them. Except now, instead of flies, we got hucksters and harlots."

"I seen her."

"Seen who?"

"You're grandmother, I reckon. She tried to sell me some silver. Said she was a Bevington."

George rose to full height now, turned to his left to look at her, the canteens hanging from their straps down behind his legs. She was younger than Eliza, maybe no older than Ephraim and Henry; raven hair piled on top of her head; dressed for housework or so it seemed; almost sinewy although that might just have been the times, hunger reducing everyone to what God deemed essential. The rifle was a twin-barrel, side-by-side. George could see the brass tracery on the stock: fifty dollars if it was a dime. The right barrel was cocked and ready; the left, still harmless. He judged himself about a foot shy of reaching the barrel end with his double brace of canteens and took a step toward her.

"Close enough, Yankee man," moving back a step herself, on to his game. Catastrophe was in her eyes.

"War's over."

"Not in this farmyard. Not while I have a loaded rifle. Not as long as you're trying to steal my water."

"My brother needs it. We all do. Creek we were supposed to fill up in had gone rotten."

"Brother?"

"Ephraim. He's — "

"Mine are dead — one at Shiloh, one at Petersburg, the oldest at Chattanooga. You want the details?"

George just shook his head. As little as he had seen of real war, he knew that every story of a man shot to death came down to the same ending. What was going on in her eyes? He couldn't read it, couldn't read anything.

"'Water, water, everywhere, but not a drop to drink.'" He almost shouted it, nearly scared her into shooting him dead, or so he imagined. Keep talking: That's all he could think of. "You ever heard that?" He didn't look up, didn't wait for a response. "My Mama likes poetry. She used to read it to us when we were little."

"Empty them," she said, nodding toward the canteens he was still trying to hide behind himself.

"Empty what?"

"You know."

"It's not but water."

"It's my water, Yankee. And my Daddy's water and my brothers' water — they dug that hole. All three of them. Got down there with the coloreds and sweated water out of that ground. Not you. Empty those canteens back into the well, or so help me God, I'll shoot you where you stand."

Now that she had the canteens in full sight, he was never going to get close enough to take a good swing at her. A long shot, at any rate.

"Go ahead then."

"Go ahead?"

"You're going to shoot, then shoot. Get it over with."

The blast astounded him. The flash of light almost blinded him. This is death, he thought, his side exploded into wetness. And then the dawning light: It was water, not blood, that had drenched his right side. She had shot the front canteen, not him.

"That was my mother, you goddamn Yankee son of a bitch!" The thumb pulling the cock back on the other barrel. "My mother!"

"Ma'am?" Thirty-one years of living, and he had never heard a woman say anything like that. Maybe "society" was just different down South than in Indiana.

"It was my mother who tried to sell you that silver, not my grandmother. My grandmother's been dead since before I was born. My mother was fifty-one years old — you hear that, fifty-one. That's what the war did to her. That's what you Federals did."

"Was?" Fifty-one? My God, she looked eighty.

"She got back here about two hours ago, laid down in what's left of a drawing room, and said she couldn't do that anymore. The Bevington silver's been in this family since England!"

"Was?"

"She's dead." She had drawn the rifle barrel up; set it on his chest, his heart, his vitals. "Dead! Her heart just burst."

She is going to do it, he thought, and this time it's not going to be any canteen gets a hole blown through it. It's going to be me. The woman's face went wide with surprise. She gave out a kind of *oof*, like air being popped out a bellows. What in the heck? Carefully, as if she were about to settle back on a bed of nails, the woman uncocked the hammer with her thumb and let it gently down. Then she laid the rifle stock-end first on the grass, and let it fall. Her upper body seemed to be in a state of paralysis. Soaked all down his pant leg from the seeping canteen, George stepped to the side and had a look behind the woman. The boy was holding a hayfork sideways, pressed hard down the length of her spine, his feet dug into the ground beneath him as he leaned into his work.

"You can put that down now," George said, picking up the rifle. In the moonlight, he couldn't tell if the boy looked relieved or disappointed.

"Your Daddy dead, too?" he asked.

She shook her head no. With tears streaming down her cheeks, she looked more girl than woman. The boy had put the fear of God in her: She hadn't yet dared to move anything but her arms.

"He's off near Vicksburg. A camp surgeon. They said he was too old for anything else."

"Be home soon then."

"That's not his way. I know him: He won't come back until the last man has been seen to."

"We ain't no thieves. It's just water. Water ought not belong to any person. This land's been burned in hell, salted for its sins. There's no decency left anywhere."

"Your salt, not ours. Your sins, too."

George left the two of them standing there and studied the terrain as best he could in moonlight. There was a clearing near the porch steps, a low swale at the middle of it. He bent over, dug his hands into the soil, and felt it give way almost like sand.

"You think you can pick me up a shovel where you found that hayfork?"

The boy nodded his head and took off running.

At the clearing, George thought about handing the rifle to the boy, decided it was too risky — he had no idea what the boy knew about guns or anything else for that matter — and told him instead to go fill the canteen that had been shot up as best he was able. No sense in not bringing back all the water they could. Then, when he was gone, George handed the rifle back to the woman and picked up the shovel the boy had found.

"You through shooting me?"

She cradled the rifle across her arms and nodded yes. Half an hour later, covered in sweat, George pulled himself out of the hole he had been digging, stepped back, and had a look. It would do. The two of them, boy and woman, were standing side by side, in front of a row of boxwoods, watching him. Behind them, the house and its gables put him in mind of another journey west toward Meridian, a house glanced from the railroad car across ruined fields, his brother's beautiful voice.

"Lorena?" he asked.

"Like the song?"

Who knew for sure? Dixie might be filled with such places. He stood the shovel upright in the ground, next to the hole he had just dug.

"You think you could find a horse if you put your mind to it?"

"I could."

Society or not, she had done work. There were calluses on her hands, little knots of muscle on her forearms now that she had pushed her dress sleeves up. Her mother had been tiny, frail. She wouldn't be much burden at all.

"Wrap your mama up in whatever you can find — curtain, blanket, it doesn't matter — put her in this hole and bury her until you can do a better job of it, then go find that horse you got hid and ride on to Vicksburg to find your daddy."

In his mind, George had visions of raiders, rogue Yankees, that band of Negroes they'd seen outside the prison, waiting to tear it to the ground. It was war, hard times; every form of predation was on display. He tried to imagine Eliza living out here, all alone, and went cold in the stomach.

"Don't stop nowhere neither, unless you know who or what you're stopping with."

She gave no nod, no answer, no hint. Her face was a blank slate of intentions.

"Take that rifle with you, too, and keep it loaded."

That much as least he was sure she could handle. George hoisted the three canteens he had filled, threw their straps over his shoulder, and started out across the farmyard toward the field he had come through. The boy followed, holding the fourth canteen like a baby in his arms, water gurgling where the rifle ball had ripped a piece of metal away.

"No."

What did it mean? He turned slow, half expecting to see the rifle leveled at him again. No fool, the boy slid over directly behind him.

"You don't need to go back through the fields," she said. "Follow the alleé," gesturing with her free arm toward the tree-lined drive. "Just past the fence, you'll come to a path on your left. Go along that, and it will take you practically straight back to where you're camped."

Alleé? Another word he had never heard anyone use, man or woman, society or not. The path must have been how her mother had come and gone. The thought of that woman pushing through those fields had been tugging at him the whole time he hollowed out her grave.

George was starting to feel the terrain in his feet, understand the place in his bones: an alleé that led who knows how far — a mile? two? more? — to some offshoot of the road they had marched along; this path to the smaller houses of overseers, plantation managers, farm stewards, whatever they were called; off still more side paths, the smaller houses of still lesser workers; somewhere out of view the hovels and shacks of the slaves who had done the real labor on this land, hardly humans at all in the scheme of things. How much of this was Bevington property? A thousand acres or more? Unimaginable tracts.

They had already passed two houses, frame, falling down like the main house, and were just working their away around a third when both of them felt a shadow pass overhead and looked up just in time to see a horned owl crash into the brush not twenty feet from them and rise up again with a mouse or vole squealing murder in its talons.

Mother of Mercy, George thought. Were they alone? Was anyone left in these houses? Had the whole plantation been deserted except for the girl-woman and whatever, whoever was living in the forests along its edges? He watched the boy carefully set his canteen on the ground and dart into the brush just where the owl had struck. Lugging his own canteens, George went in after him, following the crushed grass ten, fifteen feet until he saw the boy in a tiny clearing, staring at what might once have been a kind of drying shed. The vents were all wired up now, or stuffed with mud and grasses and other makeshift caulk. Limbs, branches, half trees almost had been laid against the far side of the shed to hide it from the path. Now that they were standing in this little hemmed-in circle, the shit smell was overwhelming.

Is that what had led him here? The boy searched around at his feet, found a stick thick as his wrist and half as long as his arm, reared back, and hurled it as hard as he could at the shed door. A horrible squawking came from inside. George counted maybe four birds joining in before the racket died out as quickly as it had begun and the night was silent again.

"Someone's hiding their hens in there."

The boy just stared back at him.

"You ain't going to tell anyone, are you?"

At last, a second grin. No, he shook his head. No. No. No.

17

George's job, his sacred trust and beholden duty, was to make sure everyone got home safe and sound, but how to do it? He would lead them down broad meadows that ended suddenly at sheer rock faces so that their only exit — no way to turn back up the meadow — was a slim defile that became an ever-narrowing mountain ledge that hung over a vast abyss. Sun-lit roads led into caves that dipped into caverns that seemed to run forever through limestone fissures deep into the earth's core. (Horses stabled there, too, and all the lost mules and jennies of northern Alabama, if only they could reach them to ride.) Once he led the four of them boldly into a building he knew as well as the back of his hand — a Muncie general store, oddly displaced from its own geography — only to have its single flight of stairs branch into a second set of stairs which branched into a third and fourth and fifth, each choice worse than the one before. Another time, pursued by marauding Rebs, he sought to hide his band in a gabled, clapboard mansion, but the siding melted away as if it were butter on a stove while the raiding party circled the house playing trumpets and waving banners. (Where did he know that house from? It seemed so familiar.)

Water was impossible. Gentle springs doubled their width each time they tried to step across them. Creeks became torrents, eating the soil from beneath their feet as they stood powerless along the banks. Rivers boiled with snakes, larger serpents; catfish with hippopotamus jaws lingered in their depths. One such river split around them, gobbling a channel through the field they had just crossed over, so that they soon found themselves inexplicably on an island, which became a raft, borne by the river toward a crashing falls just around a bend. (Rescued that time at the very last minute by an overhanging limb that was the trunk of an elephant that lifted them high in the air and was about to dash them into the ground and trample them underfoot except something else happened then that George could no longer remember.)

As for drinking water, there was none. Half the time, the water almost glowed with disease. The other half, it became strangely solid at the most inopportune moments, refusing to pour through wide open canteen mouths though the sun beat down and dust caked in their mouths.

Poor as it was, the water out shone the food. Steaks walked off plates. A bowl of beans dodged one way, then another, the beans shouting awful curses as he tried to dig his spoon into them. An unplucked hen came out of the oven beautifully baked, singing a Union marching song. A suckling pig jumped out of the roiling waters into a frying pan that became a coffin that silent, angry Negroes bore to its grave. He had, he decided, rather starve to death than sit down to any table again.

In truth, the Muncie men themselves might have been the most impossible task of all. What a contingent to have pledged himself to lead home! Jake walked straight ahead wherever he went, like a blind man, like a zombie: into walls, trees, nothing seemed to stop him, nothing to hurt him. And yet there were sudden cracks in the earth's crust that George would have to constantly lead him away from. He looked back one time to find skin grown over Jake's eyes so that there were only fleshy bulges beneath his brows. Henry would be carefree one moment, covered with sores the next, and beaten and pierced an instant later, as if he had borne the cross to Calvary himself.

Ephraim was more remarkable still. Suddenly, without announcement, he would begin to float skyward. George would have to complete his greatest leaps ever just to grab some part of him — a lace, a suspender, a scrap of trousers or shirt — so that he could keep him tethered to the ground, and even that sometimes wasn't enough. Where were they? Crossing some stubble-strewn field when a gust of wind caught Ephraim and sent him scudding along. George snagged him by his belt in the nick of time, but his weight wasn't enough to hold his brother down, so that Henry had to leap up and save the two of them and finally Jake to leap up (and he was no jumper, ever) and do the final anchoring. Thus they proceeded beneath a purple noon-day sun: blissful Ephraim a-high, George dangling from him, bloody Henry next down, and Jake walking blindly below while George called out to him to avoid this fresh chasm or that one. Meanwhile, the boy, dressed head to toe in a clown suit, darted this way and that, between Jake's legs, straight up his side across his head, and down the other. He was juggling corn cobs, dead doves, anything he could lay his hands on, barking like a trained seal. Not the biggest circus show in the world could match it for novelty.

"Jake, how come you ain't never got married?"

My God, where had that come from? It sounded like Ephraim, grounded, terrestrial again.

"Told you before. Didn't want to be tied down." And that was Jake, who held them all to ground.

Where now? George risked one eye, found it pressed into the bedding grass, and dared the other instead. Ephraim was propped up against the tree he had slept beneath. Beside him, Henry was bent over, cooling Ephraim's head with a damp rag.

"Tied down to what?"

"Well, to some woman's apron strings. To a bunch of little ones running around under foot. I figured a man's got to keep his possibilities open."

"Possibilities?" Henry had a canteen to Ephraim's lips. What was going on? Ah, the fever! Still and all, he didn't look so bad, just spent, the way they all were after yesterday's march but more so.

"Well, sure. I might want to light out for the West some day. How am I gone to do that if I'm weighted down with a wagon load of obligations?"

Obligations? Jake who lived practically in a shed? Who could pack everything he owned in a single crate? It was enough to drive George into speech: "Like me?"

"Well, George, I'm mighty glad you got your beauty sleep, although I suspect you still could use a little more. I also suppose we have you to thank for this delicious water, and I imagine there's a story there, too. But you know I wasn't talking about those young ones of yours. Why I — "

His poetry, his protestations of fealty and love interrupted by Ephraim: "But you never been more than five miles from Muncie until we put on these uniforms and went off to war."

Now that he was fully awake, George was heartened by the color in his brother's face, the strength in his voice. Yes, for sure: He'd worn himself to a nub.

"Didn't see any need to," Jake said. He was cleaning his nails with a twig.

"You been out there with old Quincy, building boilers, since before Ephraim and I was born," Henry added in, the two of them doubling up on Jake now.

"Nothing wrong with sticking to something, I hope; nothing wrong with being a little *steadfast*."

"Jake — " George tried to join in, but his uncle cut him off before he could go on.

"You know them boilers Quincy and me build out there produce the steam power that makes the world go around these days. Wasn't for us, you wouldn't have no steamboats or trains or anything else. Hell, *everybody'd* have to stay home."

"Jake — " Trying again.

"Confound it, can't a man want a little privacy in life without a bunch of yapping dogs nipping at him all morning long? I done what I done, and I ain't sorry about a moment of it!"

"Jake's getting a little steamed himself."

Henry was right, George thought. Jake had a definite burr in his pants, not at all like him.

"You'd know about that, wouldn't you, Henry. You would know about folks getting steamed up." Regretting the words as soon as they were out of his mouth. "Goddammit all and hell, I'm sorry."

"It's nothing."

It was, though. They could all see the wince, the flush of rage, gone as quickly as it rose. George remembering his dreams now in random bits and pieces. That was the boils, the stigmata. Of course!

Henry picked up the canteen lying on its side at the far end of Ephraim, tipped it this way and that, listening to the water slide around inside. "Jake's right. That's about the best water I've tasted in forever, but this drinking can could use a little weld itself." Wanting nothing but peace.

"And you," Jake said, turning to George, unable to leave anything alone this second morning of his liberation. "What business do you have sneaking off in the dark, and getting a man's canteen all shot up, especially when he just got the damn thing? I should have broke your wrist when I had the chance last night. I damn well should have. I probably ought to do it now just to go and teach you a lesson."

Well, he might, George thought, as Jake started to rise. Stranger things had happened, and Jake had about worked himself into a fit.

"Form up!" came the cry. "We're moving out in ten minutes time."

Groans and grumbles in every direction. Aching legs, memories of tortured feet, the debacle of yesterday's water. (That much, at least, seen to for the Muncie gang.) The sun was already burning off the gentle chill of this spring morning. Ahead of them, though, lay Meridian and just beyond that another train, the river, home. George reached in his pocket, found a last bit of hardtack, and jammed that into his mouth, thinking of flapjacks, sizzling bacon, potatoes chopped with onions and golden browned in a pan. Coffee: pots and pots of it, and Eliza in her nightdress still.

"Where in the hell?" Jake was at full roar now, bellowing, eyes darting every which way. "Where in the hell is that boy? If he's off peeing, he's been doing it since before I woke up!"

So that was it! They'd all gotten so used to the boy living in Jake's shadow that they hadn't noticed he was gone.

"If you took that boy with you last night." Again, turning menacingly toward George. "If you — "

And at that moment, as if expressly to rescue George from sure mayhem and worse, the boy walked out of the field behind them, shirt pulled up in front of him like some kind of cradle. He walked over to Ephraim first, still leaning against the tree; reached into whatever he was holding; and pulled out a perfect, beautiful brown egg. Henry got the next one — looking at it in awe, as if the boy had handed him some emerald ripped out of a maharajah's forehead.

"You didn't tell no one," George whispered to the boy when he presented him with his egg. Again, the head shake: no. That sly little grin.

Jake got the biggest — that much was obvious: a giant of an egg that must have come from a hen the size of a turkey.

No surprise there, but unless George was mistaken, the boy had saved the second biggest one for himself.

"Form up!" The cry again, louder, more insistent. "Form up! We're moving out right now."

Each cracked the egg in his own way: Henry on Ephraim's head, Ephraim on a tree root beside him, Jake against his own knuckle, George on a sharp edge of the shot-up canteen. The boy just bit off the narrow tip of his egg and spit it on out. Then they all leaned their heads back and let the yolk and white slide down their throats. My God, the taste of it. The sensation.

18

"What are you most looking forward to when we get back Muncie way?"

George had a vision of that bend in the creek where he had first kissed Eliza. The banks would be wild with flowers now. He could see the two of them — man and wife — cradled in the soft grass, the daylilies arching over them, painting their skin a bright orange wherever they brushed against them. God alone knows where the children might be. Not with them.

Henry had his own kissing spot and a blind he'd built by himself for when the last leaves left the trees and he could pick off the geese one, two, three, four, just like that. He thought, too, of the rhubarb pies his mother, Alma, always made this time of year.

"Anything at all?"

"Anything."

"Josephus being buried six feet down where he can't do anyone no more harm."

He had his shirt off already, tied around his neck. George could see the stripes crisscrossing Henry's back and wrapping around his chest and stomach. "He's gone to grow out of those scars one of these days," George's Mama used to say. Instead, he seemed to be growing into them.

"She had to marry again, Henry. You know that. Wasn't any way the two of you could keep going on your own."

"Didn't have to marry no man with a bullwhip."

Henry had just turned ten when his father climbed up on the roof one bright March morning to lay a patch by the chimney and fell back down more quickly than he had ever ascended. They'd seen his body hurtling past the front window, heard it thud into the still-frozen ground. His neck was broken – that much plain — but what no one knew was if he was dead before that happened. His heart had been fluttering for weeks. "Just getting sick of winter," he kept saying, but no man on that side of the family ever seemed to make forty.

Henry and Alma had tried to make a go of it on their own: harnessed themselves up like draught animals, plowed and sowed, fought back the weeds, shot the varmints (even then, Henry a born marksman), harvested when it was ready (what got ripe and escaped other destruction), milked the cows, churned the butter, even slopped a pig or two for hams and bacon. But Lord, it was hard going. Alma had lost a son, Henry's younger brother, only three months before she lost her husband: The grief for what had gone weighed her down more than the plow straps. Henry, the last thing left (another child dead at birth), was only a boy. When they were through — when the first hoarfrost lay on the ground — there wasn't enough remaining for the winter long. George and Ephraim's parents could help. Others would too. It was a community; communities pulled together. But living on handouts is just existence. It's no way to raise up a boy.

Josephus Estes showed up on horseback the second day of the New Year, wrapped in a blanket. Near a foot of snow was on the ground, the wind howling. Alma had brought up the last of their apples the day before. The firewood Henry had been able to chop and saw — himself not much taller than the ax — couldn't last the month, and they'd still be seven weeks shy of even the beginning of spring. Josephus had come to buy the farm, he said. He'd heard of their troubles. Everyone had. And he already owned the farms on either side. It just made sense.

"I've had an idea, Mrs. Wellington. You might call it a dream, even a vision," he said, warming himself by the stove. Josephus's eyes had gone wistful, far away as he talked. A dream, was it? Alma saw a palace, terraces spilling down a hillside, fountains like geysers, peacocks parading through the park in full plumage.

"Hogs!" Josephus slammed his fist into his open palm so forcefully that Alma jumped back and pulled Henry to her side. "Thousands of hogs! Hogs and wallows as far as the eye can see! Can't you just imagine it!"

"Why, of course," Alma answered, nodding her head, the palace crumbling inside, her peacocks now pink and fleshy. "Of course, Mr. Estes. Hogs." Henry's mouth was agape.

"Might even have my own railway siding. Load them hogs up right up here to ship back to the feedlots in the East. Hell — begging your pardon — I might even own them feedlots, too. With your farm and mine and what I already got, I'd have land enough to do it right. You got to think big, Mrs. Wellington! Man who thinks small ends up small. You understand that?"

He was pointing now at Henry, all fifty-plus inches of him.

"Yes, sir," Henry nodded, forcing out the words, frozen like a deer at a campfire.

The math was clear, yet to Alma's surprise, Josephus didn't make an offer that first day. Instead, he showed up nine days later, hauling along a bushel of his own apples and a fat slab of salt pork. Two days after that, he caused a towering wagonload of dry split oak to be delivered and stacked just to the side of Alma's front door. The following Monday he appeared dressed as if he was still coming from Sunday meeting, as antsy as a preacher in a saloon.

"I hear your full name's William Henry," he said when he'd settled down enough to take a cup of tea. As he spoke, Josephus reached out and grabbed the boy under the chin in his lean, bony hand. "You must be named for the president. Old Tippecanoe."

"Not that," Henry said. "I'm named for my daddy and granddaddy: William Henry Wellington."

"So you say." He dropped the boy's chin then, looked at his hand as if maybe he'd run it through a grease bucket and rubbed it on his black suit pants.

"Alma," he said, turning toward her, the first time he'd ever assayed her Christian name, "I'm fixing to make you my wife."

He was twenty years her senior; a long, wiry man all hard knots of muscle with a face like a muzzle-loading cannon. So far as anyone knew, Alma and Henry were his only acts of charity in three decades of living in and around Muncie. Even his own Methodist minister barely got a dime out of him. More children, even a shared bed, were out of the question. Nor did Alma have any desire to be the Swine Baroness of Muncie, Indiana. She couldn't stand the stink of the things, their grunts and groans, watering them down in heat, enduring them in the cold. But what choice did she have?

"I'm honored, Mr. Estes."

"Josephus."

"Well, then, I, too, am honored, Josephus," putting what lilt she could into her voice, her son's eyes on her in abject consternation.

The temper didn't come up 'til later, after he'd moved in and set about making their house his and filling the land with hogs, as he loved to say, "straight to the horizon." (The railroad siding was yet to arrive.) Nor did Henry's stubbornness. Granted, he was at an age where boys start to struggle their way into manhood, but Alma had no idea, had never seen that side of him. Two trains running at each other in opposite directions at high speed on the same track could not have been more certain of disaster. Alma had been Mrs. Josephus Estes exactly one month when her husband drove a sixteen-penny nail into the front wall, just by the door, and hung his coiled bullwhip from it — "my only recreation," he explained, recreation being, like so much else, in the eye of the beholder.

Three turkey vultures were circling to the south, just over the top of a small knoll covered with scraggly pines.

"You still held on to it?" George asked.

"Sure I have." Henry fished in his pants pocket, pulled out a large wad of a rag, folded the cloth back with his thumb, and produced a silver watch out of its filthy depths.

"Shame you didn't know him longer. Your daddy was a good man," George said. He took the watch and popped the cover with a thumbnail. "W.H.W.," the inscription read. "1841."

"I know that, too, and his daddy before him. I didn't know him at all. Just this watch. That's all I got of him."

Behind them, Jake was humming a song known only to himself — his ear for music as flat as his forehead. To his side, the boy whistled his own tuneless tune and chewed what looked like six blades of grass at once, a calf at its cud. The road had stretched out flat in front of them. They could look to the front of their small column and see the dusty heart of Mississippi awaiting them.

"Listen, Henry," George said, "I been thinking. When we get home, you, me, and Ephraim, we can open us up a general store right in the middle of Muncie. Not like old Jervis's place. We'll sell everything a man or woman could want: meal, clothing, tools, you name it. Way I figure it, Ephraim here can sit behind the counter — "

"Why me?" Ephraim was bringing up the rear. The vultures had disappeared into the pines, to their reward at last.

"Cause we need someone pretty to draw all the girls and widow women inside."

"I see your point. But ain't I going to be doing all the work?"

"Hardly. Henry and me will be going out in our own carts, taking orders all around the countryside and delivering stuff right to their door. No reason why we got to do business with all those farmers on Saturday only."

"I'll bet that place down on Division Street that used to be the saloon is still empty," Henry chimed in, warming to the idea, letting it draw him out of his gloom.

"Why, I'm sure it is. I wish I'd thought to write Eliza to go on down there and have a look. But come to think of it, why do we even need a store? We'll just keep the inventory in some barn, and do all the business out of carts! No overhead at all in that."

"Now I ain't got a job at all," Ephraim groused, but George could see it all: an armada of wagons, "Ethridge, Ethridge & Wellington" painted on their sides in a flowing gold script, the business growing by leaps and bounds, bigger houses (a porch wrapped around it), fancy clothes, Eliza in diamonds, little George taking over (and maybe some little Henry and Ephraim, too) when the three of them turned old and gray...

"Well, why stop at a store that ain't a store?" Jake piped up. "Why not buy you some horses that ain't horses and some wagons that ain't wagons. Then you take a load of flour that ain't flour out to some farmer's widow who ain't a widow and charge her hard money that ain't money at all. You'll have a fortune that ain't a fortune in no time!"

"Dammit all, Jake — "

"I'm not done as long as we're having grand ideas round here. Not done by a longshot." He elbowed the boy hard on the arm. "How bout wings on trains so they can soar right over the rivers! No need for bridges that way."

The boy's eyes were full of wonder, as if he'd never heard of anything so practical.

"Or chickens that lay fried eggs so you wouldn't need to bother with no shell or pan?"

Yes! Yes!

"George," Jake shouted, "you getting these down? We must have ourselves about five thousand dollars gold in ideas back here, and I'm just getting started, just getting the hang of it all. By the time we make Vicksburg, I'm likely to be the next John Jacob Astor!"

Ahead of them, the column was slowing down, backing up on itself. What now, George wondered: Raiders? Snakes? Another river they couldn't drink out of? Some general done up in furs and feathers? I wouldn't bet against anything, he was telling himself, when he saw the empty ambulance carts heading up the road toward them — nothing more than hay wagons with some railings pounded onto the side and two horses just short of the slaughterhouse hauling each one. He thought again of that sea of broken humanity they had left behind at the ruined rails. Could they even survive the ride, he was wondering when the call came echoing down the line: "Food!"

"What did I tell you!?" Jake called out.

"What did you tell us *what?*"

"Hell, I'm already John Jacob Astor. They're bringing the restaurant right to me!"

The food turned out to be a half dozen loaves of bread rimed in mold and a barrel of some river water that had been sent along on one of the ambulance carts. No banquet to be sure, but after the hardtack, the bread tasted like French eclairs, and the river water could have had cow turds floating in it for all the Muncie men cared. The water in their canteens tasted as if it had been drawn from the Garden of Eden itself, some liquid version of the world as it was before sin came along.

"Damned but I could get used to this," Ephraim declared, peeling away the bluish-green crust from the chunk George had handed him. "And don't go worrying." He'd seen the look cross his brother's face. "By the time we get back to Muncie, I'll have forgotten every cussword I ever learned." Food brought him around, there was no denying that.

The five of them were sitting on a pile of boulders that had been levered off the roadbed. No telling how the stones might have gotten to such a place. There wasn't so much as a rise, much less a mountain, within seeing distance of where they sat. They seemed to have ascended out of the molten core.

"Tastes like cake on one side and pie on the other," Jake said, shifting the bread back and forth as he measured the play of his teeth in their sockets. The boy was still popping his eyes up and down in a yes, yes, yes at every fool thing Jake had to say.

"Meridian in an hour!" the sergeant roared. He had just helped the captain up into his saddle. Back the road they had just come along, they could see the ambulance carts retreating into the distance like some thunderhead only narrowly avoided: dark, full of silent fury.

"Makes you realize," George said.

"Realize?"

"There's always someone worse off than you are."

Ephraim had broken into song again, just loud enough for the Muncie men to follow.

In the prison cell I sit,
Thinking mother, dear, of you,
And our bright and happy home so far away,
And the tears, they fill my eyes
'Spite of all that I can do,
Tho' I try to cheer my comrades and be gay.

Henry started off again beside George, strange for a man who had spent half his life walking practically arm in arm with George's younger brother. Odder still, he dragged his feet until the two of them had dropped back out of earshot of Jake, Ephraim, and the boy. Henry wanted to say something, that much was clear. Finally, he got it out.

"You seen me that day back at Cahaba, didn't you?" His jaw was clenched, his words just loud enough to be heard. George could see how hard his mouth worked just to get words out.

"What day?"

"You know."

George knew. Wish against wish, he hadn't forgotten. Nor Henry.

"I said, did you see me?" Half hostile. Half pleading. Time to air things out.

"I seen you."

"Must be hard to miss a man blubbering like a baby."

George just nodded this time. No need for words.

In the nearly twenty months they had then been captives, nothing equaled it for drama. (This was the middle of January, before the flood, before the burst of fever.) And yet none of the Muncie men had been awake when it began.

The idea had been simple: Just before the last guard shift of the night at 3 a.m., the prisoners — or at least the plotters among them — would overwhelm the nine sentries on duty inside the warehouse. Then, armed with their weapons and emboldened by superior numbers, the entire population would burst out of the prison when the gates were thrown open, mow down anyone who opposed them, and break through the stockade before the cannons could be swung into action. In practice, nothing so efficient happened. The prisoners rose up too soon. The sentries inside were nowhere near as compliant as they were supposed to be. Rather than seize the guards, they simply angered them, like swatting a wasp's nest with a stick with no clear idea of how to escape the consequences. The guards had orders to shoot to kill, of course; they'd proved their willingness to do so from every angle of the walkway, hunted earlier escapees as they would rabid foxes, blown holes in men whose only crime was that they were too sick to scurry across some dead line before the hammer came crashing down. This time, though, the guards seemed to lack the heart for it, or maybe they just calculated the numbers and saw no benefit for themselves in blood rage. For every one or two they might kill, ten or twenty would survive to rip them to shreds before the doors could be thrown open and the cannons trained to mow the prisoners down as if they were sheaves of wheat in an open field.

Instead, the guards worked their bayonets: thrust, parried, all the time working toward the door, crying out to open it, telling the men to "Stay back! Goddamn it and all! Stay back! I mean it now!"

The strategy worked — more or less. The prisoners crowded around the guards, stayed just out of range, spit, threw dirt, jeered, called them names they never would have used had they been alone. But the bayonets were sharp; the men, defenseless. Time, tide, momentum — they were all on the Graybacks' side.

"Seems in a hurry," Ephraim opined as one of the guards, a bent-back piece of gristle, burst out of the crowd, jabbing and slicing in every direction. Ephraim yawned as he said it, not entirely certain this wasn't one more dream from the sleep this insurrection had wakened him from.

"Them, too." Henry added. Not more than a dozen feet from them, a cluster of guards, three in all, with bayonets out and ready inched back-to-back towards the door and rescue.

"Shouldn't there be another sentry back that way?" Jake, curious.

"The Wall-Eye," George said. "The Wall-Eye ain't been accounted for." Nor would he be. Just as Col. Chandler had predicted, Cahaba was in mutiny.

The talk buzzed the rest of the night long: They had trussed the Wall-Eye up in the back with suspenders, had him tied tight as a roasting goose, his mouth stuffed with his own boot. Phase One might have come up short, but not Phase Two. Come daylight, the Wall-Eye would be their ticket out of here. The prisoners were bound for Union lines.

"All of us?" George wondered.

"All or none," came the answer — some born-again reactionary, his eyes bright as burning coals. None of the Muncie men knew his name.

"What are we gone to do when we get to the river?" Jake asked.

"River?"

"The Tennessee. We come across it this way on a raft and just barely got to the other side."

"Why, we'll take rafts back the other way then."

"All how many thousand of us?" Jake persisted, but the man was already gone, a whirlwind before the storm. "What we going to eat along the way? Dirt?"

The rain came on just as dawn finally struggled into existence. A hard, bitter wind out of the north drove it. The only ones asleep were those too close to dead to be awake. By seven, when Col. Jones came walking alone across the yard, the sky behind him was lead gray.

"Anyone in charge here?" he shouted out, the rain running off his broad-brimmed hat and cape in small rivers.

"I am."

The mass of men opened in front of Col. Jones as if Moses had just parted the Red Sea, and out of its middle walked a short, dark-haired man George recognized from the yard. He'd been brought in six weeks earlier, captured near Nashville by Forrest's men: a civilian, or so George thought, though how he had managed to put himself in harm's way no one knew. The man had a lawyer's habit of always debating, of always being at some discussion or another, jabbing his finger with each new arguing point. The Muncie men had figured him for one more rooster: someone who had bought his way out of serving only to be swept up at any rate. Maybe not. Stranger things had happened.

"What's this about?"

"We got your guard."

"Hell, I know that."

"We got demands then."

"Give 'em to me."

"Safe passage for all of us to Union lines, jerky and hardtack to see us along the way, river transportation where needed."

(That much solved at any rate, Jake thought. The rest just plain crazy.)

"Who in the hell are you?" Jones asked.

"Captain Hiram S. Hanchett, Company M, Sixteenth Illinois Cavalry," the rooster answered, drawing himself to full height.

"That right?" But Hanchett had already turned to face his ragtag forces, a smile of pure triumph upon his face. When he turned back, Jones smashed the butt end of his Winchester revolver square into the middle of his face.

"Goddamn it all, but there ain't nothing dumber than a Yankee who thinks he knows it all."

"Hold it, mister. We negotiating!" The words mushier now, less distinct.

"No more," Jones amended, smashing the face again. "Where in the hell is that guard?"

Hanchett was sprawled on the ground, blood and teeth all over creation, when the wall-eyed guard came flying out of the crowd as if he had been fired from a slingshot. Someone had covered his face with ashes. The Wall-Eye was black as the ace of spades.

"Who in the living hell are you?" Jones asked.

"Me! The Wall-Eye!"

"Shee-it!" came the answer, and that was it. Or so for a few anxious hours it seemed.

The rain had just gone to sleet by the time the men were called out at noon, each drop hard and mean. No need for more proof that the temperature was in free-fall.

"Strip down, goddammit!" Jones shouted out. "I wanna see every man's pecker, and if you don't got one, I wanna see you when we're through. Har!" Rebellion had put him in a good mood, apparently. Wasn't a man in Dixie, George thought, who didn't have something dirty on his mind every minute of the day.

"This here soldier" — Jones's arm was draped over the wall-eyed guard's shoulder — "says he fought valiantly against superior forces. Stuck a man in the butt with his bayonet, he claims, before you all overpowered him. I'm walking out to that gate. By the time I get back, I want the man got stuck in the butt by this here *he-ro* to present himself."

He did as he promised, to no avail.

"All righty," the colonel yelled, "we gone to have ourselves an inspection. Guards!"

And so they stood, preparation for that later, epic standing, while the sleet beat down and the guards circled around them, slapping their bare flanks for the sheer malice of it, or maybe just to warm their own hands.

"Check all 'round them," the colonel bellowed. "This here guard might have been so courageous that he didn't know an ass end from the other."

Even in the extreme conditions, a low murmur of humor greeted Col. Jones — anything to see the Wall-Eye squirm.

"Next man makes a sound gets to meet his Maker a day or two earlier than I intended. And, boys, I got rounds enough for every sorry one of you."

That much, George doubted, nor manpower enough to put them all underground either, and that much had to be done too. Otherwise, there'd be pestilence. The sight of us, he thought, stealing a sidelong glance at Ephraim, Henry, Jake, the rest of them: the goddamn sight.

A few men saved the colonel his ammunition, staggered to the ground or just dropped over dead where they stood, more precursors to what was to come. Finally, even Jones seemed to tire of the pageant.

"Aw, hellfire!" he bellowed, "I don't got time for no pack of prisoners with miracle healing powers. Didn't know Jesus Christ was no Unionist."

He started down the line, peered hard at Ephraim, harder still at Henry, then picked out some boy a half dozen or so spaces down from them, pulled him out front, took a knife from under his tunic, and shoved it an inch into the withered flesh of his buttocks. He was from New York State — that much George knew — a private with a pleasant manner, not really much more than a boy himself. George might have even played checkers with him one time, back before someone had burned the board to warm his mush by. Strangely, the New York private didn't seem to be in all that much pain. Maybe it was the shock of having God desert him.

"That the one, Corporal?" Jones asked, wheeling on the Wall-Eye as he wiped the knife blade on his sleeve. "That the one? Sure seems like it to me." The guard's good eye was looking on in near horror. "Have a study there, Corporal. Have a good one. It's a fresh wound. Any man brave enough to inflict this wouldn't just turn his rifle over to a bunch of half-starved, near-dead prisoners, would he? Oh, hell no!"

The Wall-Eye was shaking his head, trying to work himself up to speech: Yes. No. Yes. No.

"That's him," he finally got out, sounding like his tongue was stuck halfway down his throat. "Damn sure yes. That's him!" Convincing himself as he went on.

"Figured so." Jones turned toward a sergeant who had been standing by him, waiting for orders. "String the sumbitch up." Then he turned to the Wall-Eye. "You, *he-ro*, find me a whip."

The word caught Henry like a hatchet between his shoulder blades. George watched him pitch forward, almost lose his balance all together. His skin had started to go blue.

"That what passes for a whip round here? Sumbitch, no wonder you got to rely on the bravery of this one, lone man to keep peace around all these goddamn desperados."

The Wall-Eye had come racing back with some sort of a long thong dangling from the end of a pole, more buggy-whip than anything else but barely that either.

"Here, teach this damn prisoner a lesson," Jones said as he shoved the buggy whip into the Wall-Eye's hand and stepped back to have a look.

The guard pushed his chicken chest out as far as it would go, took a few steps forward, measured the distance, and all but missed the New York private completely. Blood was flowing down his leg from the knife wound.

"You got the distance down now, corporal? You got the measure?" Jones was bellowing.

"Yassir. I got it now."

"Well?"

He connected this time, somewhere on the side of the private's head. Even in the sleet, they could see his ear begin to swell up.

"God in heaven help us," Jones muttered as he grabbed the whip out of the Wall-Eye's hand. "We got us an army of girls."

"Do you admit that you sought to impede this soldier in the performance of his duties?" he shouted now at the private.

"But I wasn't anywhere near the Wall-Eye," the New Yorker shouted back. "Ask them!" He was looking over his shoulder, straining round from the post they'd lashed him to, his eyes on the Muncie men.

"And do you repent of your sins?"

"I — "

The whip came crashing down on him — half thong, half pole.

"Do you admit and do you repent?"

"Ask 'em!"

But Jones wouldn't turn around. This time he hit mostly with the thong — a long slash from scapula to tailbone. The next hit paralleled that one. Then the colonel reached back again, flicked the whip between the previous two lashes and flayed the skin right off the private.

"Do you admit?"

"Oh, hell, yes. I done it! I done it!"

"And do you repent?"

Blood streaming over his ass now, joining the river from before.

"God! God! God! Yes!"

"Show's over boys," Jones cried, even him sounding almost relieved as he dropped the whip in the slush. "Button up tight. This sleet might go to snow." He walked out the gate then without ever looking at the Wall-Eye or any of them, went wherever he went in town when he wasn't among them, said nothing else to anyone that they could hear.

Henry was quaking like a palsied man as they bent to pick up their rags of clothes, but it was more than that.

George could see tears still streaming down his face and a yellow puddle steaming by his feet. In the morning, the New York private was gone — cut off the post sometime during the night, led away to who knows where or what, everyone's shame upon him.

Four days later, while being transported south to Mobile for reasons never explained, Capt. Hiram S. Hanchett, who launched the entire insurrection that ended in such specific misery, was murdered presumably in cold blood by the guards sent to accompany him, almost certainly upon the orders of Col. Samuel Jones, CSA. Four months after that, Jones upped and disappeared. A written parole exists for him — issued May 17, 1865, the last of three that for some insane reason were granted — and with that, he walked out of history, changed his name, went to Mexico, stuck that goddamn Winchester that he'd used to bash in Hanchett's face into his own mouth and dissolved his horrible weight of guilt and sin into a mush of brains and shattered bone. No one knows, but it is a safe bet that had he hung around, Henry Wirz would have had to share the distinction of being the only Reb prison commander found guilty of capital offenses upon the Union soldiers under his tutelage. Sam Jones was Old Nick, the Devil himself, the Worst Man in the World.

19

Tramp, tramp, tramp the boys are marching,
Cheer up comrades they will come,
And beneath the starry flag
We shall breathe the air again
Of the free land in our own beloved home.

Ephraim was still singing; the road, still long. The dust kicked up by their feet hung in the air like something alive and avian. Where in the living hell was Meridian?

"What all did you see?" Henry persisted, the mid-day sun making everyone irritable.

"I seen you shaking," George said. "We all were — buck naked in the middle of winter."

"You seen more than that."

"You already said it. You were blubbering."

"And?"

"Aw, hell, Henry, and you pissed yourself. You been letting that bother you all this time?"

"Heck of a man to go off to war with, ain't I? Just what you want marching by your side." He was speaking in almost a fierce whisper now, cutting each word off hard. "I'd have turned my own mother over to him to keep that colonel from whipping me."

"You been through one war, Henry. I think you ought just be glad to have survived another."

"Not yet."

"What?"

"We ain't survived nothing yet."

A cold sweat had started crawling up George's back when Jake stumbled behind them and nearly pitched off the road himself.

"You okay back there, old man?" George called. The boy was holding on to Jake, trying to prop him up.

"I'd be a lot better if those damn Graybacks hadn't stolen my Garber No. 12s. Best boots I ever put on. This ankle's about to pop loose on its own without them. Hated to see them in that fat Reb's pack."

"You'd still have 'em if you hadn't gone jenny herding," Henry joined in. "Mules and such is a young man's calling. You just left them boots sitting up on the rise, begging for a new owner."

"Looky there!" Jake was pointing with his chin. Through the dust raised by the column in front of them, they could just see the faint beginnings of a town in the distance — a grove of trees, the outline of a few low buildings.

"Must be Meridian."

George had no sooner spoken than the boy handed him the saddlebags he'd been hauling for miles now, broke from Jake's side, and took off running toward the front of the column.

"Don't look like he's going to stop anytime soon," Henry said as they watched him disappear into the distance.

Jake was shaking his head in wonder. "That boy spooks worse than a wet cat in a tornado."

20

Meridian! When they had arrived here six months earlier, the name had conjured magnificence: the Prime Circle that divides East and West, the place where time begins and ends. They'd escaped Cahaba then, or so it seemed — been freed from the crush of so much humanity. Surely, their lot was bettering. But they had come by night, left by night, lived inside yet another stockade the whole time they were there, as starved in one place as the other. Now, arriving a second time by foot, they could see what a dispiriting spot it was. The buildings they'd seen in the distance were a pair of mills, burned clean through to the rafters. Before they got to them, their thin line marched through a camp, a big one, maybe division size, long deserted. The packed earth where tents had stood was struggling back to weeds. Beyond that, trees were already sprouting out of the fecund night soil of a long row of slit latrines.

It was more than a year since Sherman had come through Meridian, intent on destroying its supply depots, a rare failure. He was just entering town from the west when the last of the supplies left by train east to Demopolis. Warehouses stood empty; the opposing army — that abandoned camp — gone. Disappointed, Sherman's men did what they did best: bent the rails into those famous bowties, torched half the town, pillaged the surrounding farms, ravaged the countryside, made the enemy feel in its bones and bellies the cost of rebellion.

"If the people raise a howl against my barbarity and cruelty, I will answer that war is war and not popular seeking," Sherman once said. "If they want peace, then they and their relatives must stop war."

Atlanta, of course, would be the final testament to his words, but Meridian and a dozen other places like it were the precursor: the foreboding cloud upon the horizon that announces the hell-storm to come.

When George, Ephraim, Henry, and Jake had ridden out of Muncie back in the summer of 1862, it was a town of near three thousand souls. There were brickyards, a general store, old Quinn's boiler works out beyond the edge of town, two watchmakers. A man could buy a steak in six places, have a whiskey in just as many or more, overnight in five hotels, and board his horse at a dozen different stables (if, that is, he hadn't steamed into town on the Indianapolis and Bellefontaine Railroad). Muncie was a place with gumption, spirit, enough churches to keep a man honest and enough other temptations so honesty wouldn't get too much in the way, Masonry and frame and log houses sat along its streets, some of them surrounded by picket fences with roses twining along them. The town was ringed by farmland, black and fertile. Four different Muncie docs could bring you into the world if you needed their services, and any one of the four could declare you dead and begin your journey to a half dozen burying grounds. And this all from someplace that been named for a damn wolf clan of the Delawares!

By contrast, the grandly named Meridian was limp at its edges, rising from what seemed a pall of gloom. It had come into existence only seven years before the war broke out, sired by the railroads as surely as Cahaba had been born of water, of rivers. The Mobile & Ohio had reached north; the

Alabama & Vicksburg, west. Where they finally intersected in 1854, a place first known as Sowashee Station had sprung up. The town had been christened Meridian in 1860, and it had boomed through the first part of the war: a rail hub, an army camp; the grifters and slatterns and ostlers that come with both; shopkeepers to feed them, innkeepers to bed them, parsons and ministers and priests to pray for them all; a schoolteacher; and then like an avenging angel, Sherman to make them pay for their hubris, their temerity, their insane hope that the war might simply prosper their town and then pass by. It didn't.

A pack of bird dogs barked the prisoners along the road, the only sign of life other than themselves. Whatever body of water the place sat along had been over its banks more than once these last weeks: A film of silt sat over everything, untouched by plow or hoe in this new planting season. George could see some sort of huge plantation mansion off to the south, but even from a distance, it made that other one with its chewed railings and jagged windows seem tailored and trim. Maybe this one, too, had felt the torch — too far to tell from here.

The town itself was nothing more than a village that had bulged out of its corset: some battered churches, a school miraculously spared, a charred hotel, maybe two or more of them, ringed by homes half of which looked as if they had been hammered together by great apes, then by even more ramshackle wartime construction and, farthest out, lean-tos and huts and falling-down this's and that's where the village and the army camp had agreed to meet.

It was the streets themselves that surprised the Muncie men, and the others, and left them near slack-jawed in wonder. They were barely into Meridian before they came upon an old white lady in a kind of ankle-length gunny sack tied at the waist with a raveled scrap of twine. She was standing in her front yard (or so they surmised) separated from the street by a hedge of forsythia that had already bloomed and gone green with leaf. At first George thought it might be the Bevington woman, miraculously risen from the dead (or from her daughter's lies, come to think of it), but this woman really was old. You could see it in the pink scalp showing through her thin strands of white hair, in the sunken cheeks that couldn't have covered more than a half dozen teeth, in the gnarl of her hands. She was hacking at the grass and weeds with a rusted hoe, each assault barely enough to part the blades much less dent the soil. A piece of fine white lace a few feet square lay on the ground beside her, covered with onion sets and a green potato or two, chopped into quarters. My God, George thought, did she really believe she could plant them, and live to eat the produce?

A muscular Negro — legs like oaks — was leaning against the front gate post, watching her.

"Mrs. Deering?" he kept imploring, "Mrs. Deering?" as if that alone might stop her.

"No, Joseph, no. These is new times, new times is come." She never looked up from her labor as she talked.

A few houses further on a colored girl and a Federal soldier sprawled side by side, flat out on their stomachs, on someone else's lawn. From what the Muncie men could see of them, she might have been sixteen, barefoot, her hair all done up in ribbons. He couldn't have been older by more than a few years. It was hard to imagine she'd ever worn shoes in her life. A book was spread out on the grass between them: a grade-school reader. The boy was pointing with his finger to the words, working his mouth around each sound the way the deaf sometimes do, as if the words were taffy: "Papa, will you let me ride with you on Prince?"

"Pa-pa," the girl echoed beside him. "Wi-eel yall .... "

A cottage stood just beyond them. Lilacs framed its doorway. Empty, rotting planter boxes were tacked below each of its lopsided windows. The drawn curtains gave the house a vacant, musty look, but as the men drew even with the front door, they saw a corner of one of the curtains part, a white face pressed against the glass and just as quickly pulled back. That was followed by another face at the same spot, and another, and another, and on and on.

"How many people you think might live in that place?" Henry finally asked. "I've seen rabbit warrens less crowded than that."

If the girl and boy on the lawn, tutee and tutor, were even aware of being watched, they showed no sign of it. "Get up, Prince," the boy was saying. "You are not too fat to trot as far as the barn." Each word stretched, chewed, worked over. As he spoke, a half dozen quail burst out of the roof of the cottage, all but burned away.

Meridian, it turned out, was full of bluecoats. One detachment of scrub-faced recruits marched by without ever once looking at them. Bad luck to cast an eye on those so far removed from Divine Providence.

"I wish to heck I'd never seen them feetless men," Jake said out of the blue. The thought was on everyone's mind, already afraid of what the night's dreaming might hold.

Another passel of bluecoats was gathered around the front door of what had to have been the town's grand house: a two-story brick affair with four pillars supporting a curved portico and set-back wings on either side — the only structure within eyesight that had a hint of permanence. The soldiers had used a log twice as long as any of them to stove in the door. A tiny arsenal of rifles sat stacked on the front walk, with more coming out in the arms of each new soldier to emerge from the depths.

"Goddamn Yankee thieves! Goddamn bastard thieves!" The sound rang out from inside the house — an old man's voice, cracked but strong as thunder. It didn't matter your station in Dixie, George said to himself again: You were either cussing like a soldier or thinking a soldier's dark, lewd thoughts.

They had come to the main crossroads. North and south didn't look much different from east and west: tired buildings; wooden sidewalks shaded by their overhang; rutted, muddy roads. And yet nothing was what they expected. The crates and chairs and stumps of logs along the shaded walkway were filled with coloreds taking their leisure out of the midday sun. Meanwhile, the whites who were out trudged through the dust in the middle of the road, as broken as the roofs and siding that flanked them.

A dozen yards to their north, a little gnome of a black man held a bayonet point to the chin of a Reb officer. The officer's tunic already hung down nearly to the gnome's knees — the Muncie men could see a brigadier's star glinting on his shoulder. Now the gnome was obliging the officer to step out of his trousers. A pair of Federal soldiers sat on the edge of the wooden sidewalk, cheering the gnome on and passing a bottle back and forth between themselves. The Reb brigadier had just shed his trousers completely when the gnome gave a wild whoop, twirled around in the air, nearly fell down drunk in the dust, then popped back up, the knife this time pointed straight at the brigadier's vitals. What was he going to oblige him to remove next?

"Don't seem real, does it?" Jake said. He was right: It didn't. Some conjurer had touched the world with his wand and turned everything upside down.

"This how it's going to be now that the war's over?" Henry asked. No one knew. No one had anything to say. They'd been locked up for going on two years, blinded by the brick walls of their prison, the wooden ones of its enclosure, while the world spun and spun and spun around them. Now that they were out, it was all too topsy-turvy to contemplate. What had happened?

The far end of the village was in sight — and beyond it, more played-out fields, more miles upon miles of dusty road — when a commotion broke out to their left, up on the raised walk. The men could see the back of a Union corporal, rifle slung over his shoulder; the front of what looked to be a shopkeeper, gut pushing out the middle of his grimy apron. Between them, whatever it was they had caught was half wrapped in a gunny sack. The soldier reached in to grab a hold, let out a yelp, and pulled out his hand again.

"Bit me! Goddamn, bit me," pounding against the gunny sack with his good hand.

The shopkeeper took advantage of the distraction, reached in himself, yelled "got him!" and let the sack fall away. It was the boy, face torn with pain. The shopkeeper had his right ear twisted practically into a pretzel.

"What in tarnation?" Jake shouted out. "What in goddamn tarnation?" He'd stepped out of line, ready to jump on to the sidewalk, when the soldier unslung his rifle and leveled it on Jake's chest.

"Stay where you are. You don't damn move!"

"You know this boy?" It was the shopkeeper, a clipped New England accent, not the lazy drawl any of them had been listening for. The man had pig eyes, what appeared to be flared nostrils from their vantage below him, bristly tufts of black hair growing from his ears. Behind him they could see a crudely painted sign slapped beside the door: "Meridian General Store." And below, "If we ain't got it, it ain't." And below that, "J. Tutworth Esq., Proprietor."

"I said, 'You know this boy?' Because if you do, you know a thief. A common goddamn thief trying to cheat a Christian man out of his livelihood." The shopkeeper was holding a pair of black boots in his hand, wrestled from the boy's grip. The corporal hadn't moved. Jake was still dead in his site.

"What do you got to say for yourself, boy? What do you gotta say?" J. Tutworth, Esq., if that's who it was, had the boy's ear turned so far around most of it was upside down. When does an ear fall off, they were all wondering? How much holds it to the head after all? It can't be more than skin and some cartilage.

"The boy don't speak," George said, stepping forward, "and he's no thief."

"No thief?" The shopkeeper was yelling now. "No thief? It's not thieving anymore when some little sneak comes creeping into your store, grabs a pair of" — he stopped, turned the boots over, had a read — "grabs a pair of Garber Number 12s, best damn boots made in the patriotic Yewnited States of Union America, and goes bolting for the door? That ain't thieving?!"

"I sent the boy on ahead to pick out a pair of Number 12s for me," George said. Ephraim and Henry both had their arms around Jake, for all the good that might have done. "I figured we wouldn't have no time to stop, so I'd have to buy 'em on the fly, so to speak. He must have heard us coming by and just startled a little."

"You don't look like no Number 12s to me." A crowd had gathered around them. The shopkeeper was playing to them like some grossly overweight thespian, smirking and smiting his brow.

"All this walking expands my feet."

"Oh, I'm sure. I'm sure!" Smirk. Smite. Smirk. Smite.

"Listen here," serious again. "I don't have time for this. I got customers, honest men and women, people with *needs* just waiting to get into this store." Another smirk, this time for the corporal only. "You're blocking their way."

"Why don't they just go somewhere else?" Ephraim asked. He was leaning on Jake — George could see that now, not so much holding him back as holding on for dear life. That's probably all that kept their uncle from taking a bullet into his lungs.

"Isn't anywhere else," the shopkeeper crowed. "Can't have these people buying their necessities from any damn traitor reb storeowner. I got the franchise, you hear? I got the franchise. Bought it fair and square." He looked over at the corporal, who was licking the bite mark on his hand. "Fair and square! And I have the soldier here to prove it. How are you going to pay?"

"What if we don't?" Henry this time, enough murder in his voice that the corporal moved his rifle site an inch or two to split the distance between Henry and Jake.

"Then the boy belongs to me until he works off his debt to society." There was something horrible in the way he said it, half greed, half something unspeakable. He lifted the boots up for the Muncie men to see, then set them carefully by his feet. "Those boots cost a fortune. He'll be here a long time." The hand that wasn't twisting the boy's ear was on his shoulder now, lightly, almost a caress. The boy was trying to squirm out from under it, but the ear gave him only so much play.

"I was figuring I would trade for them," George said, pulling the saddlebag off his shoulder. "This is hand-tooled, soft as a baby. Must be worth four times what those boots cost. I'll swap you even up."

"I've already got saddlebags," the shopkeeper spit out, "and I don't care if they been hand-tooled by Jeff Davis himself and autographed by Ralph Waldo Emerson." Who, they all wondered? Ralph Waldo Who?

"Don't even look like leather at all," the corporal added. "Looks like some kind of mule skin. That 'hand tooled' just where it got itself run into some wire."

"You an expert?" Ephraim's face had gone red; sweat was beginning to drip off his nose.

"What?"

"I said, you an expert in leather goods, are you?" George couldn't stop thinking of his dream. His brother seemed on the edge of floating away.

"I sure as hell know more about leather goods than you do about fighting. Didn't hide out from battle in some fancy-dan prison."

"Battle tested, are you?" Jake threw out his arms in amazement. Somehow, in the process, he managed to shift Ephraim so that he was hanging on to Jake's back now. "Been in the rough and ready, have you?"

"We got the rule of law here." The corporal was nearly shouting himself now. "I'm protecting this man's property from looters and thieves, just like I been told to do, and by God, I'll shoot anybody that — "

"There you go, George. There you go!" Jake's arms were practically flapping over his head now, like he wanted to take off, too. "There's one more thing happened in the world while we was lollygagging away in prison. They learned to make shit that could talk!"

A dead man was all George could think. He's going to be dead before we ever move off this spot, but J. Tutworth Esq. had grown tired of the banter and bi-play.

"No one's answered my question yet!" He was kneading the boy's shoulder now with his free hand, still twisting his ear with the other. "Somebody pays up for these boots, or I own this boy. Who's it going to be?"

"Me."

It was Henry, reaching into his pocket.

"No," George told him. "No."

"There's things worse than a whipping."

Henry was unfolding the cloth as he stepped forward. "You might have saddlebags, mister, but you don't have nothing like this." He wrapped the chain around his index finger, held the watch out to the shopkeeper, stood there still as a post while J. Tutworth Esq. turned the casing over and over in his palm, ran his teeth along it, flipped the cover open and held the inscription up to the light.

"It might cover the debt."

"Might? This watch is worth half of everything you got in that store."

"What am I going to do with these initials — 'W.H.W.'? Where am I going to find someone like that who wants a watch? I got inventory to worry about. I've got to move goods! What do you think, corporal? You the law around here. You think we can relax the standards of justice long enough to give this here thieving boy a second chance at the straight and narrow even if I got to take a beating on this damn tin chronometer?"

He yanked the watch from Henry's hand as he talked, lifted the boy into the air by his ear, dropped him in the road at Henry's feet, and turned toward the store at the same time the corporal was depositing the boots down on the boy's throbbing head. The Muncie men could hear the two of them laughing as they walked into the general store. Some joke.

A Negro in a Union uniform had been standing just down the way from them, arms folded across his chest, watching the show. He was shaking his head back and forth as the Muncie men fumed past him.

"Mr. Lincoln know about this?" George barked at him. "He seen his army in action now that the war's about over?"

"Mr. Lincoln?" His voice complete bafflement.

Surely, George thought, he'd heard of Lincoln: Father Abraham, the Railsplitter. The man had a sergeant's stripes on his sleeves. Colored or white, he had to know *something*.

"Ain't he the president?" George was sick of Meridian; sick of stupidity and greed and cupidity and all the other sins of the species; sick of everything.

"Mr. Lincoln's dead. Mr. Seward, too, or about so."

"Dead?"

"The Rebs murdered 'em both, about a week back. Mr. Johnson president now."

Andrew Johnson? The Tennessee Unionist? The one who wanted to hang everyone?

"With malice toward none, with charity for all, with firmness in the right as God gives us to see the right ...." The sergeant was talking quietly to himself, George or anything else long gone from his mind, tears pouring down his rutted cheeks.

Where in God's name, George wondered, had a colored man learned words like that?

21

Spit traveled faster than the men were walking now, promises didn't mean a tinker's damn, and they didn't have a Chinaman's chance between them.

Rails waited when they got to where they were supposed to be picked up west of Meridian, but no trains to travel them. A day's march west in Jackson, trains waited without the tracks to ride on. Some damn group of Reb raiders had struck again. In between, so promised the dough-soft captain who had led their column this far from the comfort of his dappled mare, sat a wide stretch of river so serene and luxuriant that it's a wonder the three Magi hadn't traveled here instead of to that stable in Bethlehem.

"Hell," he shouted out, up in his stirrups for once, "I'm just sorry I can't go with you."

It was, Henry noted, only the second time they had seen him on his feet since their mercy train screeched to a halt almost twenty-four hours earlier, but at least they were rid of him. The sergeant would take them on to Jackson, along with the guards they had been dragging with them since Alabama, and there were crackers and hardtack to go around for everyone.

Ephraim started stumbling not a mile or so later. George didn't have to feel his forehead: He could see the fever on him. Another half hour, and his brother was dead on his feet. Henry, George, and Jake began taking turns carrying him, an arm over each of their shoulders, but no two were the same height, and only Ephraim and Henry stood eye to eye. George had to stoop. Even in his new Garber No. 12s, Jake still had to stretch up as tall as he could. The load shifted this way, then that. Whichever combination was doing the hauling, Ephraim's feet dragged behind him in the dirt, an anchor against their progress.

"Need to make us a litter," Jake announced as the road wound its way up a rise, through stands of hardwood — rare shade from the pitiless Mississippi sun. No more than a dozen feet into the woods he came upon a pair of felled limbs that looked right for the occasion. Back along the road, Jake and Henry tied their shirt-rags to the timber as crosspieces, something to lay Ephraim on. George rigged the saddlebags so they would cradle his brother's head. The boy tried to add his shirt to the mix, but Jake stopped him before he had half unbuttoned and wouldn't let him be until he had done it up all the way again.

"Tow-headed thing" — he almost said "thief" — "like you be burned up by this sun." He was right: From what George could see beneath the dirt, the boy's skin was white as mother's milk.

Ephraim's eyes were closed when they laid him on the litter. Jake took the back end so his nephew's feet would be lower than his head. Henry and George hoisted the two front handles. Threadbare though they were, the shirts held through the ascension.

"Ole' Ephraim's going home in style," Henry said as cheerfully as he could muster, but Ephraim was out. He didn't know he was going home at all. And the style was short-lived.

They had just reached a lowland stretch, the road mounded up over the swampy forest on either side, when the right-hand strut of Ephraim's litter groaned and cracked with a sharp snap like an old dry bone, followed moments later by the left strut. Limp as a rag, the patient slid between the collapsed cross-cloths and settled himself rear-end first on the dirt.

"My turn this time," Henry cried, bounding off into the trees to their right. "Jake never did know nothing about building a litter." This was wetland, though, not dry ground. What fall wood Henry found was too thin to bear Ephraim's weight; the few pieces that seemed thick enough, already damp and rotted. There were snakes, too, to watch out for, and God knows what else in the murk and ooze. Barefoot, Henry leaped from hummock to hummock, drawn deeper into the swamp. Whether it was his imagination or not, the still black water seemed alive with possibilities, none of them pleasant. He'd heard stories of crocodiles, alligators, whatever they were called, with jaws big enough to clamp down on a whole pig; of swamp panther black as coal and quicker than any horse could run. Henry was bending over, trying to judge a length of straight wood sticking out from below a toppled tree — the light now too weak to tell by anything but feel — when a spider the size of his fist dropped down on a strand directly in front of his eyes.

"Ai!" he shouted, leaping up, ready to race back where he'd come from. He was longing suddenly for the comforts of a prisoner's life when he heard a kind of sucking noise in the sodden earth just behind him. He turned. Something huge, dark, eyes on fire — Christ! The Devil himself! In his hand, an axe. Henry watched him raise it up in a giant arc, saw the glint on the cutting edge, one last piece of light seeped into this inky morass, even wondered as the blade started down what it might feel like to have his head cleaved in two. A *swish*! A kind of *chank*! Was that it? Am I dead? But then the blade raised up again, the glint, another great sweeping arc. *Swish! Chank!.* And that *was* the last, absolutely the last thing Henry remembered. He came to supine on a large hummock, only a few leaps from the road.

Beside him lay a pair of thick, sturdy green poles, cut to the length of the litter and trimmed clean. He thought he could see moving deeper into the swamp a man's back, shoulders as wide as an ox cart or so it seemed, maybe an axe hanging from his arm, the man dark as midnight though that could have been the light, too. Jake and George were talking up by the road. He could hear that. Also the boy standing a few feet into the swamp-woods, peeing against a tree. *Splash. Splash.*

When Henry got back to the road with the litter struts, their short line had nearly passed the Muncie men completely by. They fitted the shirts to new poles, the saddlebags too, laid Ephraim down again on the cross-cloths, picked him up gently, and began on as they had been going: Jake in back by himself, George and Henry on either pole at the front, the boy tagging just off to Jake's side.

Four days and nights would pass before Henry tried to tell them what had happened, or might have. He wanted to sit on it first, think it through for himself. Had he been saved for some purpose? Was that it? (And a miserable proven sinner like himself?) Was it just a chance encounter, or the Devil trading life for soul? Or had it happened at all? Always a possibility: Thirst, fatigue, the long captivity — they do things to a man's mind. Yet he had the evidence of the litter poles, shaved by some blade, practically fitted with grips, and green as any fresh wood could be. Surely, if that had been his own work, he would remember. The side of the road now seemed to Henry to have eyes of its own, ears, a life just barely invisible. When he finally got around to saying his piece, to explaining those beautiful, limber poles with which they were to bear Ephraim nearly across the breadth of Mississippi, there wasn't a man (or boy) among his listeners who believed the first word he said. He couldn't fault them a lick.

At least the captain, lying son of a bitch that he was (the non-train, the non-banquet waiting for them), hadn't lied about the wide spot in the river.

The water was clean and the current just strong enough to keep it that way. Cottonwoods lined the shore, but where the river was widest, the trees opened up to a broad beach of fine silt and worn, rounded gravel. Better still, the bottom was firm enough so a man didn't sink down to his knees with each new step and the incline so gentle that someone suspect of swimming or without the strength to attempt it could baby his way out until he was up to his waist or more. Best of all, this was April, spring. The water was cool, refreshing, not the hot, murky soup full of mean-tempered moccasins that it would become in another month or two.

The whole short column took all of two minutes to rid itself of its remnants of clothing and start wading in. Even Ephraim, fevered as he was, rose from his sick litter, stripped clean, and started thrashing out to the deeper water with Henry close behind. No better medicine for a boiling constitution than this.

Jake was flat on his back, arms stretched to his side, floating gently downstream and nearly asleep, when he happened to cast an eye back to the shore from which he had come and see the boy standing there, naked as a jaybird and frozen as any statue. What now?

He rolled to his side, took a dozen long pulls in the boy's direction until he could feel the river bed below him, and hauled himself to his feet.

"Ain't you coming in?"

The head shaking back and forth: No.

"How come?"

Nothing. The boy's big toe was just touching the river's edge.

"You're not scared of the water, are you?"

Head shaking harder now. No! No!

"Oh, yeah?" But Jake had already grabbed the boy, thrown him over his shoulder, and started heading out into the river proper.

He'd gotten all of knee-deep — the boy pounding on his back hard with both fists — when Jake stopped, drew the boy back over his shoulder, and cradled him on his back between his arms.

"Now, we're getting wet," he said, but the boy was already way ahead of him, stiff as a board, teeth clenched, eyes shut so tight that it might as well have been midnight, not noon.

"I ain't gonna let you go."

The boy seemed almost to levitate when Jake finally touched his backside to the river, practically jumped out of his own skin, but Jake wouldn't let him be. Lower, he went, and lower, and lower still, until the boy was almost resting in the water.

"Now take a deep breath," Jake said. "Hold it inside. Don't let it out."

And then Jake took his arms away ... and the boy floated, laid there like the river was a bed just made for him. First his eyes opened tiny inch by tiny inch, amazed to see the world from this perspective. Then his teeth unclenched, his lips relaxed and turned upward in a smile. Slowly, delicately, as if they were French crystal, he moved his arms away from his body, moved them back again, kicked one leg up and down, then the other. Then, in an instant, the boy was on his feet and racing through the water back to shore.

"Hell," Jake called after him, "I thought you liked it!" But at least one question had been answered: The boy hadn't been sneaking out through the crapper holes and out to the river back in Cahaba. He wanted nothing to do with water.

Jake could see the boy back on land, digging into his pants pocket, and pulling something out. And then as quickly as he had run out of the river, the boy ran back into it, pulling some kind of paper wrapper off whatever he had retrieved as he came, and finally handing it to Jake.

"Mother of Christ!" Jake yelled, holding it in his hand, dipping it in the water, rubbing it, smelling it: What wouldn't that boy grab hold of?

"Soap!"

He might as well have yelled "Gold!"

The soap was rough, red, and oily. If the men had stopped to read the thin paper wrapper floating down the river, they would have seen the name — "Oleine" — and the distinctive logo of the Proctor & Gamble Company of Cincinnati, Ohio. But the men weren't stopping for anything. Though it was only a simple square of lye and additives, that soap led to an orgy of washing such as few rivers have ever witnessed. Men who had never exchanged names, men who had never seen a manufactured piece of soap in their lives were scrubbing each other's backs, passing the square back and forth as it grew smaller and smaller, scrubbing their own dismal hair, their own crusted and caked bodies, reveling in the faint violet scent as an epicure might revel in the aroma of a simmering truffle sauce.

A New Jersey infantryman that George had been sure was some olive-skinned, dark-haired Italian turned out to be a freckle-faced, blond-haired German. What had seemed to be moles, warts, disfiguring birthmarks washed off in the soap and river as if Christ himself had walked upon the waters and healed them. The soap piece was worn down to a translucent sliver thinner than a grass blade when splashing broke out, followed by chicken fights out where the water was deeper and song although Ephraim for once kept out of it. Even the sergeant and guards, such as they were, got into the spirit of things, stripped, left their rifles on shore (with one forlorn man-boy covered with sores to guard them), and wallowed happily among their charges, all of them dunking each other as if in another situation they wouldn't have squared off and tried to blow each other's living brains out.

An hour later, they were all lolling in the sun, drying themselves, half-clothed if that, every blessed one of them asleep or nearly so, when with a cascade of hoots and hollers a Rebel party came riding in on them, sabers drawn and pistols at the ready.

"Aw, hell," Jake said, feeling the boy practically burrowing into the silt beneath him, dirty all over again. "Aw, hell and tarnation."

22

For all their shouting, the raiders were as sorry looking a group of humanity as the Muncie men had ever seen: snaggle-toothed, scraggly haired. Half of them didn't even seem to have eyeballs the same size, or ones that matched with one another. The only one who looked as if he could add past four was their leader, done up in a gray major's uniform, riding the sole horse among them that wasn't ready for the glue factory.

"Sorry to intrude upon your bathing party, gentlemen," he said, suddenly a professor. "No one appreciates the solace of a good soak more than I, but if you would be kind enough to direct me to your ranking officer, we can conclude our little business here and be on our way. Y'all being all but buck naked, it's a trifle hard to tell who's in charge."

His own men looked at him as if he had spoken in Aramaic. What in the hell was he saying now? As for the prisoners, they were all on their feet, pulling on pants, shaking out shirts and throwing them on, too. Jake was only half dressed when he stumbled into his Garbers before some new Reb could claim them. They were going to have to cut his feet off this time if they wanted his boots. Behind Jake, the boy had his back turned to the raiders as if he couldn't even bear to look at them, or maybe it was just modesty.

"Reckon I'm in charge," said the Federal sergeant, stepping forward, "or them," pointing to the two Grayback guards, "depending."

"Depending on what?"

"I guess on who's asking."

"An honest answer. Rare in Mississippi. We'll need all your gold coin."

"Ain't got none."

"Your horseflesh."

"That neither."

"Provisions."

"Hardtack, maybe."

"Suppose you won't object if we help ourselves to those four rifles you got stacked over there."

No, of course not. His men had already hoisted them and added them to their own arsenal.

"Prisoners?" the major asked, sweeping his eyes over the bone-bags he had roused from their rests.

The guard just nodded.

"Hell of a way to spend a war. Hope you men make it to the Mississippi. I'm not in the habit of adding injury to insult."

He'd turned his horse and was about to give the signal to move out when one of his own raiders down the line shouted out: "Hey you!"

What?

"Hey you!" he yelled again, pointing at Jake. "What behind you?"

"Me?"

"You! What's that little thing back there?"

The boy was holding on to Jake's back, arms wrapped tight around him now, eyes just peering round his side, shaking like he was sitting at the North Pole.

The raider was edging his horse forward now, trying to get around Jake, Jake and the boy turning with him.

"Ain't you got the stickiest finger boy in all Dixie hiding back there? Ain't you got a boy crawl through walls? Ain't you got a boy disappear right in front of your eyes?"

"I got none of that," Jake said, turning, turning as horse and rider circled around him.

"Why course you do. Hell, I know. I taught him everything. I his goddamn pappy! C'mon, boy!"

With that, the raider lunged from his saddle, got hold of the boy by the shoulder and started drawing him forward until Jake grabbed the raider's shoulder, seemed to lift him straight out of his stirrups, and tossed him like he was some kind of match-stick on to the ground. The raider rolled once, twice, then scrambled to his feet holding a Bowie knife in his hand.

"Oh, I get him this time. I ain't going to let that boy go. He too good a thief." All the time circling, advancing on Jake, swishing the knife blade back and forth. "I feed him your heart. That boy eat anything!"

He'd closed the distance to a body length when he let go with his free hand and threw a fistful of silt right in Jake's eyes, and then, quick as anything, with Jake blind and defenseless, the major who was leading the raiding party shot the boy's father (if that's what he really was) dead as dead could be.

"Jesus," he said, as the rest of the Muncie crowd splashed water in Jake's face and tried to clean his eyes out, "the trash you gotta ride with these days."

This time he did turn and did give the signal to move out, and his raiders and the dead man's horse moved out with him as if they were a drill team that had been training for this very moment for years and years.

When Jake's eyes were finally clean enough to look out of, he saw the boy spitting on the corpse of what Jake assumed was his father.

"No need to do that," he said, "no need at all." It seemed worse somehow than tearing a Bible in two. He had his hand on the boy's back, pushing him forward. No one was hanging around. The guards had called "Form up!" The line was already moving. George and Henry on the front end of the litter again; Jake had taken the back. They'd just about caught up to the others when the boy broke free once more and ran back where they had just come from to stand over the corpse one more time.

Poor thing, Jake thought. Poor damn thing. And then the boy spit on that dead body again and was about to pee all over it when Jake shouted out, loud enough to hear back in Meridian, back in Selma, back in that new Negro village where they had first come together: "HERE! NOW!"

23

"Jake?"

"What is it, Ephraim?"

"You think it's possible you could go the rest of the day without nearly getting yourself killed again? I believe a third time might test the limits of good fortune."

Amen, they all chorused. Jake felt it, too. Good thing he hadn't spent any more time fighting that war — he would have got blown up by a cannonball for sure. Jake seemed to be discovering something new about himself every blessed day of late.

They were hauling Ephraim again, against his will this time.

"I feel better than a preacher in a house of sin!" he declared when George first insisted he lie back down on his litter.

"No doubt," his brother told him, "but you're not walking all the same."

"Oh, heck, I feel even better than that. I feel better than a man who — "

"That's enough." George could tell where it was leading, where it always led with Ephraim. He was girl crazy, and three years away from them hadn't done anything to help that. George broke off a piece of hardtack and shoved it into his brother's mouth. "Why don't you see if you can go a day without near to choking to death. We might not bother to get it out next time."

Ephraim had cooled off in the river, but George didn't like his high color or the gimp in his legs. It wouldn't hurt him to ride, and it wouldn't kill the three of them to carry him.

"When he stops chewing, throw some water into him," he called back to the boy, who had Ephraim's canteen thrown over his shoulder.

Head up and down: Yes. Yes.

A half hour later, just when the sun had reached its mid-afternoon hottest and the dirt beneath their feet seemed to have risen lava-like out of some deep fissure in the earth, Jake felt the boy put his hand on his own hand and leave it there. What a strange and distant sensation! It must have been fifteen years since he had known anything like it — Ephraim, probably, when he was just knee high, walking hand in hand with his uncle to town or maybe just across one of the fields. It all brought up the sweetest of memories, but why, Jake wondered, why was he in such pain? And then he realized: The boy was pulling back his thumb, was near to snapping it off, for God's sake.

He bumped the boy with his hip, practically sent him flying off the road; shook his arm at him as best he could without dropping the litter; all but growled, and still he wouldn't let go. The boy was working on his other fingers now, trying to rip them off the handle, was bent over close enough to his work to begin tearing at Jake's fingers with his teeth. Maybe he had gone mad, been bitten by some rabid dog when the Muncie men weren't looking, eaten loco weed. Or his father — who wouldn't be made crazy by having to live with that rot of human flesh?

Then Jake had a final realization: The boy wasn't out to hurt him, wasn't crazy, wasn't any of those things. He wanted to take his own turn on the handle, share an equal load. He could see it in the boiling frustration behind the boy's eyes, the way he wouldn't let go, how he was trying to push Jake off to the right so he could take the left to himself.

Well, why not, Jake thought? The worst that could happen is that the boy couldn't hold his part up and Ephraim would go crashing to the ground again. That, at least, wouldn't kill him.

"Here," he said almost in a whisper, "I'm letting go."

And then the boy fell in beside him, smiling, tendons already strained on his neck, a partner through and through.

No one could have begun to tell you what time it was when the sun finally began to settle into the horizon in front of them. For two years, they'd had three fixed points on their clocks, no more: the roll calls at 7:30 and 5, lights out at 9. All time in between mushed into pretty much the same dismal moment.

What mattered was that they had been walking ever since the river and hadn't even reached Jackson. One of the Grayback guards had told them Jackson was halfway across Mississippi, but surely they had walked half the state by now. What if no train was waiting for them when they finally got to wherever the hell Jackson really was? What if they had to walk across the rest of the state, too? They would have to start rolling Ephraim in front of them whenever they came to a little downhill grade, just to get a break from the load of him. Either that or make him walk on his own, and then they'd just end up carrying him some other way.

Sometime soon, they'd have to break, fall out, lie down and sleep away as best they could their aches and pains, their worn muscles and bones, but for the last mile, the road had been winding through broad patches of poison ivy, and all they could see was more of the same ahead.

Jake had both handles in the back. He'd tied the boy's wrists together with a piece of his own shirt so that his arms crisscrossed Jake's chest. The rest of the boy was hanging down Jake's back, gone to the world. A little bit further, Jake thought, and I'll be gone with him. Up front, George and Henry hadn't said a word to one another in an hour or more. They didn't have the strength in them. Ephraim, neither. Traveling like some Abyssinian emperor just seemed to have tired him out all the more.

They heard a rustling up in front of them, saw two armed men step out into the road, unable in the twilight to tell what colors they might be wearing if any. More raiders, everyone thought, and us with nothing left to take but our lives. Nothing in this war, it seemed, was more perilous than being set free.

"Where in the hell you boys been?"

Us? Had word so gotten around that raiders were actually waiting on them now? But, no, the armed men had hacked a trail through the poison ivy ten feet or so to the rails on the other side. Waiting there was an engine, a tender, and a single passenger car.

"Camp Fisk Special!" one of the soldiers called out. And they all climbed aboard. Salvation at last, and just like the Bible says, when you least expect it.

24

That night, lulled by the *clickity-clack-clack* of their little iron horse, they all slept in a world of magical connections, a place where the walls of time and geography gave way.

George dreamed of Eliza, as he so often did, but this time she seemed to somehow enter his body, be living there — her knee, his knee; her arm, his arm; her lips, his lips. He would whisper to her, and she would whisper back at the same moment, using the same tongue, the same mouth and throat and larynx. Their minds were open to each other; their thoughts, interchangeable. The children seemed to somehow be orbiting them as they lie in their bed, both beings and celestial bodies, unseeing and all-knowing at the very same time. George could not for the life of him figure out how they did it.

As if some thread had been stretched between them, Eliza dreamed of George at the exact moment he was dreaming of her. Madeleine had been up for hours, coughing. Unable to sleep, Eben had trailed around after his mother, watching her put the water to boil, spoon camphor in it, put a cloth over his sister's head and hold her over the fumes. "Breathe in, sweetheart," she whispered. "Breathe in." A stone could not have been more patient. Exhausted from chores, worn down by school, little George had slept right through it all.

Now, with Madeleine snoring on the bed beside her and Eben asleep in the one the brothers shared, Eliza closed her eyes and found herself falling into George's arms. Was the red on his chest blood? Was the black of his foot gangrene? Where were they? And was that *thud, thud, thud* someone at the door or cannonballs, shrapnel, musket shot falling all around them? George felt so strong and weak at the same time, so there and not there, and then as if by grace, he entered her too, became one with her, one with her world again, and then she really did sleep, fell into that blackness from which there is no recall.

Ephraim, hard by George's right elbow, dreamed of Lucinda Hopkins, the notorious Muncie bawd. But what a transformation since he had been gone! She rode now grandly around the countryside in a wagon with "Ethridge, Ethridge, & Wellington" stenciled on the side in the gaudiest of gilded scripts. Furs covered her, even in summer. A tiara sat plunked on top of her head, its diamonds blinding in the light. And this was no Muncie he had ever known. Spanish moss hung from everywhere. Mimosa trees in full blossom sprang out of the most improbable places. The tiniest crack in the largest boulder was all that was needed. How had Lucinda managed to grow that extra six inches? Where had that circle of flab under her chin disappeared to? Hair that was never more than mousy, full of string, had somehow transformed itself into a glistening, raven-colored main. Ephraim could see her beckoning to him, picking him out of the crowd as she passed by. "Sing to me, honey," she called silently. "Sing me a song." And so he opened his mouth and out flew the most astounding assortment of hummingbirds and butterflies, and moths he never knew existed.

What do prostitutes dream of? Not sex, but its absence? There'd been two customers that night in the little three-cornered shack out on the Barley Road, the one with green paint splotched all over the door: a brakeman and a fireman, both from the Indianapolis & Bellefontaine line. The brakeman, a Mr. Dodd, was rough trade, always had been. Lucinda charged him double, not for what he wanted done but for the way he wanted to do it. The fireman was all sweetness and light, or as sweet and light as can be a man who runs to whores when he's got a wife and kids back home. He preferred to wait outside while his cohort growled and tore. But it was money, a bundle of it, and maybe it was all that cash under her pillow that had Lucinda Hopkins dreaming now that she was queen of the May Day parade, riding down Division Street in a throne set up on a haycart with all of Muncie at her feet, waiting at her beck and call. My lord, she thought, who is that beautiful boy over there by the Maypole? Is that the one went off to war with his older brother and that wild-boy best friend of his? And why, why, why are whatever them things are just flying right out of his mouth?

Henry was standing atop a towering mountain, looking into wide open spaces. His senses, always acute, were a hundred times more so. He could see rabbits darting twenty miles into the distance; hear mice rustling deep in a box canyon, around the corner from anything he could see; smell quail roosting in a clump of brush that must have been a two-day trek away. Beside him — he only realized it now, didn't know how he could have missed — stood an African giant, dripping with swamp weed. Dreaming through the soft grunts of a thousand hogs, Henry's mother saw her son as if through the opposite end of a telescope: infinitely small, infinitely far away, disappearing as she watched. "Go," she said to him in a whisper. "Go." Across the hall, Henry's stepfather dreamed of nothing whatsoever. The railroad siding would come one day, the feedlots back East, too. No man, he would tell you, asleep or awake, had ever more completely fulfilled his ambitions than Josephus Estes.

Jake usually dreamed of boilers: of seams, of sheet metal, of rivets. Tonight, though, he was visiting with his father. He'd been a steady man — like Jake, strong as an ox and almost silent, and so he was tonight. They sat, side by side, hand in hand, on the bank of a wide creek that had cut through the back part of the land Jake's father had farmed along with his brother and sister's husband. Between them, they made so little noise that Jake could hear the grasses pushing up through the soil, not just the beating of his own heart but the pulsing of his father's blood. And then Jake realized that, in this utter silence, his father was telling him everything he knew. My God, he thought, my God, how can I remember it all? And who can I tell it to?

The boy, too, dreamed of fathers, was still sore that Jake had stopped him before he'd had a chance to give the old man a good pissing over. Standing on top of him, giving him a hawker in that dead, startled eye, he could smell every shit-hole they had ever lived in, every half-empty pot of shit the old man had ever put on a stove, every drunk piece of shit he'd ever dragged through the door, or into the tent, and off into some barn if they happened to have taken up residence there or, once, in a cave where even the boy couldn't stand up straight. What kind of man wouldn't find his own son a cup of milk? What kind of father makes his boy steal the clothes he wears. "Hell," he could still hear the old sack of shit yelling, "I don't care if you go nekked. Ain't got a pecker a man can hardly see any rate!" And somewhere off in the dark other voices, laughter. But he could feel it coming now, feel himself filling up with piss again. He got it out, got it *way* out, and aimed right between the old man's half drawn lips. Drink this, shitface! And then there was a screech, a series of jolts, and the dead body on the ground shifted, smiled, filled out to a pleasing roundness of form, opened its eyes, and began to speak.

"Tarnation!"

Startled, the boy looked at Jake, felt the train come to a stop beneath them, and heard someone — conductor? guard? — call out "Camp Fisk!" And with that, the boy bolted as he was wont to do for the nearest door. In all the history of Creation, no one had ever had to pee so bad as this.

25

As if to put the seal of approval on their new fortune, the first person the Muncie men saw after they stepped down from the train was Howard Andrew Millett Henderson, their old prison commander. Henderson now wore the insignia of a lieutenant colonel. He'd come up in the world, leapfrogged right past major, but at heart he was still a Methodist minister, still tending to his flock whatever pasture he found himself shepherding.

Ever since he had left Cahaba for Vicksburg just on the eve of Capt. Hanchett's infamous January mutiny, Henderson had been tirelessly promoting prisoner exchanges. The South was done for, *kaput*, unable to feed or care for its own people, much less the incarcerated Yankees among them. His previous duty had afforded Henderson all the proof of that he ever wanted to see. Was it really necessary, he argued, to wait for an official war's end to begin shipping the prisoners home? The North had food. It had hospitals and money to support them and rails to move men on. Let the Federal prisoners go back there to heal, to recover what health they could and begin new lives, and send Dixie her imprisoned sons, too. The hellholes they were being kept in were killing them as surely as the hellholes of Georgia and Alabama, South Carolina and Mississippi. At least, they could starve among their families, their kin, their own kind.

Neither Washington nor Richmond entirely agreed. There was too much red tape to cut through, too many forms to sign off on, too many agencies to satisfy and self-important bureaucrats to placate. Politics intervened as well, and hidden agendas. Even with the South destroyed, its cities burned or burning, cries for revenge — for a parity of suffering — had not yet died down. Andersonville, especially, was on the public's mind. The summer before, the Chicago Board of Trade had written Lincoln, demanding that the Union subject an equal number of Confederates to conditions similar to those Federal prisoners were enduring at that worst place in the world. Even into 1865, Ben Wade, the firebrand Ohio senator, was pressing a joint resolution of Congress mandating retaliatory treatment, as if that in any way would have punished those responsible. As if, too, there weren't Union prisons that already came perilously close to matching Andersonville for squalor. Of nearly 8,500 Graybacks held at Elmira, New York, fully a quarter were suffering from scurvy when an Army surgeon inspected the camp. Andersonville was run through by a stream so vile that even to stick a toe in it was to risk blood poisoning and sure death. Not to be outdone, Elmira featured its own small stream that the surgeon described as "a festering mass of corruption, impregnating the entire atmosphere of the camp with the pestilential odors." At current death rates, he estimated, the entire prison population would likely have to be admitted to hospital within the year and more than one in three would die. Already, he wrote, "the hospitals are crowded with victims for the grave."

Still, if mercy wasn't yet in the air — and might never be — a kind of terminal fatigue had set in where prisoners and prison camps were concerned. On both sides, the horror had worn down intransigence. Negotiations on a final exchange opened. Meanwhile, Grant sent word back to Secretary of War Edwin Stanton that he had begun sending Union supplies through enemy lines to the prisons at Andersonville, Macon, and elsewhere. No sooner had Henderson heard the news than he began planning for a second shipment of clothing to travel up the Alabama to the pitiable men he had left behind. (Did he even know what had happened to the earlier load, that virtually every thread had been converted to the least scrap of food available?) Inevitably, the planning was tedious; supplies, tardy. Meanwhile, the need was obvious and overwhelming. Henderson was in Vicksburg, discussing the prisoner situation with a Federal colonel, A. S. Fisk, when Fisk made a suggestion that would change everything.

Years after the war, Henderson recorded the moment:

> *Fisk casually remarked, "Why not bring the men here, under parole, and detain them in a camp on neutral ground until exchanged?" I caught up the suggestion, and added that I was ready to enter into such an arrangement if it were made to apply to the grays and well as to the blues.*
>
> *He agreed and before we parted drew up a cartel and the minor particulars in duplicate to be furnished the confirming authorities. The two governments ratified, and we set up the camp at Four-Mile Bridge, back of Vicksburg.*

The place was at first called Four-Mile Camp, after the bridge, but Henderson insisted it be named for Col. Fisk, and as he so often did in his quiet way, Henderson prevailed. Camp Fisk, it was, and it proved to be one of the more peculiar institutions of that peculiar and horrible war. By the terms of the agreement finally settled on March 16, the camp covered an area one and half miles wide, flanking on either side the shattered railroad that ran between Four-Mile Bridge and Big Black Bridge along the Big Black River. (One and a half miles! Compare that to the 196-foot by 116-foot enclosure the Muncie men and thousands of others had lived in for two years!) Yank and Reb prisoners alike stayed there while awaiting exchange, guarded over jointly by blue and gray soldiers, each group with authority over its own men.

"No hostile person or persons belonging to the Federal or to the Confederate armies shall in anywise molest or interfere with the prisoners, officers or men, or transportation of either Government," the agreement declared.

Although Camp Fisk fell formally within enemy territory — the Confederate Department of Alabama, Mississippi, and East Louisiana would not surrender until May 4 — Union forces agreed to rebuild the railroad through the region and to construct a pontoon bridge over the river. The west side of the bridge was designated the Federal side. That's the way Union prisoners would be leaving the camp for the Mississippi and home, so in the spirit of the agreement, it was guarded by Reb soldiers. The east side of the bridge, gateway to Dixie for the secesh prisoners sent down-river from places like Rock Island on the Illinois-Iowa border, was tended by Union guards.

If fairness were redeemable in diamonds and gold, the agreement worked out at the urging and with the help of Colonels Henderson and Fisk would have exceeded in value the crown jewels of England and the art treasures of the Vatican, but it was the United States Sanitary Commission that made the real difference. The Sanitary Commission provided the food for prisoners on both sides. (Or half-prisoners, or transitory ones, or whatever they should by then have been called.) Of course, it was cornmeal, beef jerky, bread, nothing more, but they hadn't been serving lobster thermidors at Rock Island or braising ox-tails at Elmira either. The food was nourishment; it was regular; it was there every time mess was called, and there was dry wood to cook over. The Sanitary Commission made certain water was drinkable. It paid to have latrines cut and provided lime enough so they wouldn't stink to high heaven.

With the help of Union officers and whoever and whatever else it could requisition, the Commission also set up a field hospital where the wounded and sick and exhausted could be treated and solaced no matter their pedigree, no matter which side of the picket line they had fired from. Ephraim had exited the train on his own steam, walked to the camp gate on his two feet. "No more litter for me," he boldly predicted, but his face even as he spoke was red as a beet. His shirt looked as if he had just gone swimming again, this time fully clothed. The Union guard who admitted the Muncie men took one glance at Ephraim and sent him straight to the hospital. No one among them, not even the new patient, objected.

Being mostly inspired by women and Christian groups, the Sanitary Commission also devoted inordinate attention to hygiene and to clothes. So many derelict men were walking around in clean, untattered shirts when they first arrived that Jake declared they had wandered into a revival meeting. Wash basins and crude ewers for rinsing were plentiful, too. At that wide spot in the river where they had first bathed less than 24 hours earlier, soap had seemed a miracle equal to the Resurrection of Our Savior — bones, blood, organs, and all. Now, the damn stuff was almost commonplace. The boy, in particular, took inordinate pleasure in such general attention to lavation. There was no mistaking what it meant: He'd climbed off life's dung-heap for good.

26

"How'd he get 'em?"

"Get what?"

"Them stripes. The lash marks."

George and Jake, nephew and uncle, were sitting on a log drawn up between the two tents the five of them had been assigned. At their feet smoked the last embers of a fire they had used to brew a chunk of chicory root the boy had dug out of the earth like some truffle pig. Whatever it was — not coffee, but closer to it than anything they had smelled or tasted in all this time — was steaming out of the tin mugs they held in their hands. Across from them, a dozen yards away, Henry had fallen into conversation with a knot of Irishmen who must have come straight off the boat into war and some Reb prison. George could barely understand a word they said. Henry had his shirt off: was dipping water from a barrel and washing himself down. More luxury. Even from this distance, they could see the rolling welts along his back.

"No one ever told you?"

Jake shook his head. "Nope. Guess I never asked either. Just figured it was Josephus's work."

"It was. Henry sassed him one time. I can't remember what it was about, something to do with those damn hogs. Any rate, he told Henry to do something, and Henry said he wasn't gonna to do it and started walking away. His first mistake, I guess, although there was no doing things right with Josephus."

George paused, took a long sip from his mug, and poured the dregs on top of the embers.

"Henry had gotten maybe 50 yards when he heard that bullwhip whistling overhead. The next thing he knew, it had just picked his shirt right off him and left him bleeding front and back. He showed Ephraim and me the spot where it happened, right where the farm road begins to bend up toward town. He started running then, he said, fast as he could, but Josephus came over the fence and through the pasture after him, and that first lash had slowed Henry considerably. He'd stumbled maybe another hundred yards before Josephus snapped that bullwhip around his legs and brought him down, and after that, he didn't have much choice but to lie there and take it.

"Way he told it to us, Josephus finally wrapped the whip around his ankles, dragged him back to the house with it, and left him out front in the farm yard half dead. It was early morning by the time he got up the strength to get himself loose. Then he walked to our house, just where he had been heading in the first place. I'd guess he was about twelve, thirteen back then, skin just hanging off his body. Papa got his rifle and was setting off to kill Josephus until he realized Mama had hidden all his ammunition away while Henry was talking. He stayed with us a week that time until his mother finally came and got him."

"What did she say?"

"Nothing. She was too ashamed. It was the most silent moment I believe I've ever known. Later she told Mama that Josephus had said if she went out that door to help Henry, he'd throw the two of them out of the house, drive them clear out of the countryside, feed them to the damn hogs for all I know. The way she figured it, the son of a bitch had her pretty much over a barrel."

"Could have killed him herself."

"I'm sure she thought about it, but then Henry might have had no one."

"Orphaned," Jake said, "just like the boy, at just about the same age."

"You reckon his mother's gone, too?"

"She sure ain't around looking for him. Nor him for her that I can see."

Jake finished off his own coffee, rose and stood up on the log. On tip-toe, he could just spy the crown of the boy's tow-head down in the mud along the river. He was trying to gig frogs with a stick he'd chewed to a point. If the boy had begun gnawing his way through whole trunks and building a beaver lodge right in the middle of the water, Jake would have barely blinked an eye. He'd moved beyond surprise a long time ago, except that the boy could hardly abide getting wet. Time enough to work on that.

"Don't seem natural, does it?"

Jake didn't have to explain what he meant this time. Not only had they walked through a Rebel encampment to get to their own side of the railroad tracks; the Rebs had barely looked up as they'd moved among them. Grays were eating blue food. Blue and gray guards patrolled side by side. Prisoners (or ex- or half- or whatever) lined up at the latrines together; they shit in the same holes, drew water from the same barrels.

"Don't seem as though there's been any war at all, and yet —"

Jake didn't have to finish that thought either: the dead, the maimed, the footless, the starved, the years lost, the lives put on hold. Why do men do it? The boy was waving his stick back and forth, jiggling it up and down. A fat bull frog wriggled on the end of it. Jake waved back with both arms, like he was trying to drive a bull into its enclosure, then sat back down. They'd been delivered: to their personal angel of mercy, Lt. Col. Henderson; to the Sanitary Commission; to the combined might and power of the Union Army, the greatest force from ocean to ocean and pole to pole. All of them had come through the hostility, through the inhumanity, to something approaching peace. It was a morning for revelations, for disclosures, for filling in the gaps and shining light on the empty places. Else for, what were these three years about? They'd come out the other end — a band of brothers.

"Your Mama ever tell you that I'd been in love once?" Jake had taken a stick, was stirring the sodden embers, looking straight down to the ground.

"I guess she hinted at it once or twice."

"No hinting to it. It was the real thing. I was. Her name was Eleanor Anne — Annie to everyone."

"Do I know her people?"

Jake shook his head.

"She just appeared one day in eighteen-hundred and forty-three. Muncie wasn't much more than a crossroads then. Some farmer near town who'd come from back east in Massachusetts had sent for her to teach manners to his children — a governess, I'd guess, you'd call her. We were both twenty then. She didn't know a living soul."

"Jake — "

"I'm talking, dammit. Just sit and listen. Anyway, we met the way everyone did back in those days: church, some barn dance. I don't even remember anymore, but whatever it is that sparks between a man and woman sparked between us. Wasn't long before she was sending back to her family in Pennsylvania for some sort of wedding dress, something her own mother had worn. Hell, I'd bought a suit for the wedding. My first one. My only one when it comes right to it."

Jake stirred the dying ashes, looked up to see if the boy was on his way back, over at Henry, who was still deep in conversation with his new Irish friends, then back at the ashes once more. Anywhere but to George.

"I've kissed a woman, you understand. I know what it's like." He fell silent once more. "I know what it's like to" — the word eluded him — "to crave companionship."

"And?"

"And she broke her neck. Or I broke it for her. I don't know to this day. We were out riding, my Daddy's buckboard. The road had washed out. We hit some rock. We both went flying. By the time I picked myself up and got to her, she was gone from this world. I buried her two days later and went to work for Quincy two days after that, moved into that shack I call home and I've been there ever since."

"Jake — "

"The point, dammit; the point, goddammit and all" — there was a tremble to his voice, some pitch of emotion George had never heard from his uncle before — "the point is that I never planned to be no hermit. I never planned to live my life alone. It just ... sort of happened."

The boy was walking toward them now, a second frog on his gig, his smile ear to ear. As he got closer, they could see that he'd skinned his catch as well. With his teeth again, George wondered. If not, with what?

"I thought I should tell someone that," Jake was saying as he rose to meet the boy, proud as any papa could possibly be. "I thought it needed saying."

But George was already walking away. A premonition had passed over him as Jake was talking about his Eleanor Anne, one of those clammy moments when the future seems horribly revealed. Half a day had passed since Ephraim had been hauled off to the field hospital: time for them to cross the camp, be issued tents and mess supplies and the clean shirts they were all wearing now, time for the boy to root out his chicory and for them to brew it up and now for all this revelation and the skinned frogs. George didn't know if his brother was living or dead.

27

L iving, as things turned out, and loudly.

"Lorena! Lorena!"

At this rate, Ephraim would cause the earth to open up and shake spirits from their graves. What George took to be a doctor was standing by his cot. Men seemed to be groaning from every direction. The air was still, the day hot. Even without sides, the hospital tent reeked of rotting flesh, cauterized legs and arms, piss, shit.

"Ephraim." George laid a hand on Ephraim's arm. He was burning up.

"She's here, George. She's here! My Lorena, she's — "

A fit of coughing seized him. Ephraim's eyes rolled wildly in their sockets, as if they were trying to escape. The doctor turned him on his side, gave him a rap at the center of his spine sharp enough to unplug whatever it was, then rolled him back over again. In that instant, Ephraim had miraculously passed from raving lunatic to sleep. How did it happen? Or was he dead?

The doctor held up a narrow roll of paper twisted at either end, undid one of the twists, and gave George a look inside: a thin trail of some sort of yellow powder.

"I'm about out," the doc said. "He'll sleep for three, four hours. Best thing for him. Who's Lorena?"

George closed his eyes and pinched the bridge of his nose. A new gesture for him — his and Ephraim's father to the tee. Where to begin?

"A train ride," he told the doctor, still not looking his way. "Seems like forever ago. They were transferring us to Meridian, or said they were. Some place we saw off to the south of the tracks — I guess a plantation, a mansion after where we'd been living, maybe just a mansion to anyone. It was across a field, beyond a line of trees. We could barely make it out. Ephraim took a notion that the love of his life was waiting there for him. Lorena, like the song."

"Really?" There was something odd to the doctor's voice, as if he might have seen the same house, too.

"I'm his brother," George explained, nodding toward Ephraim. He could see it now. Deep creases etched the doc's face on either side of his mouth, a riot of crow's feet by his eyes. He was sixty if he was a day — amazing he wasn't worn more. The air inside the tent was made of lead. George had to pull it into his lungs.

"I figured as much," the doc answered, not surprised. "He mentioned you. Truth told, he's mentioned just about everything there is to say. You his brother, too?"

George had no idea who the doc was talking to. Then he felt the boy standing beside him, staring down at Ephraim. He moved like an Indian, like night.

"He don't speak," George said for him, but the doc just nodded. Maybe Ephraim had mentioned the boy as well. What hadn't he raved on about?

He watched the doctor move the boy's head this way and that, bend over and peer into both ears, pry open his mouth and stick an eyeball halfway down his throat.

"You sure?" the doc said when he was through. He was patting the boy on the head, mussing his hay hair.

"Sure about what?"

"That he don't speak?" They were both smiling now, the doc and boy, in on some private joke that George was never going to decode. He wished Jake had come along, or kept a better eye on things. The boy was a goddamn mystery. No point in letting him run wild all over the place.

"Lorena."

More like a sigh from Ephraim this time. A nurse, some sort of orderly was kneeling by his cot, a bucket of water beside her, wiping his head, his arms, his neck and shoulders down with a wet rag.

"Lorena."

She worked slowly, as if she had all the time in the world, as if lines of beds didn't stretch right and left, up and down. A tangle of black hair fell down her back.

"That's her," the doc said.

"Lorena?"

"Sarah actually." His face was lit up like sunshine.

The boy noticed it first, started tugging on George's shirt sleeve as if he meant to rip it off. Then the orderly dropped her rag back in the bucket, rose, and turned toward them, and George saw it, too.

"You!" she said.

"Me." George couldn't think of anything else, was struck almost mute himself. The way the world circled around on itself was a constant amazement.

"This is the one," Sarah started to say, but the doctor had already picked it up, seemed in some odd way to have known all along.

"That stole my water" — George just nodded — "and helped bury my wife, and you're the one" — he'd turned to the boy now — "who about stuck a hay fork through the love of my life." But the boy had already gone beet red. Something else he must have learned from Jake: embarrassment. George thought the boy might run to daylight, but Sarah had already wrapped her arms around him. Thirty seconds of that, George thought, and he'll just explode.

"You found a horse?" George asked, enough of a question to get her to leave the boy be.

"You would have, too, if you'd looked hard enough."

"And you got here all right then?"

"Had to shoot up a few more canteens, but I made it." She told it as a joke, laughing like her father. Their wife and mother dead, destruction all around them, that big white place maybe ripped to the ground by now. A joke? There were things about the South he would never understand.

George had nothing more to say that wasn't obvious as dirt. He wanted to take Sarah, hold her in his arms like she had done the boy, rest his head on her shoulder. Not for love — he had a love — just to feel a woman again, to smell one up close, to breathe one in. Eliza, he thought. Soon enough: Eliza.

The boy looked as if he were ready to be smothered again, too. Maybe, George thought, that had never happened to him before. Some people have no mothering at all. He could see a clot of men walking by outside the tent, talking as if they meant whatever they were saying, as if they weren't just making sounds: the Irishmen. Henry was still hanging with them. George wondered if it had to do with pissing himself and blubbering that awful day: The Irishmen wouldn't know about that. Henry came down too hard on himself, whipped himself where even Josephus couldn't.

Sarah, Lorena, whoever she was had picked up her bucket by the time George's mind got back to her, was moving on to the next cot, the next sick man, the next maybe lost cause. He reached down and felt Ephraim's forehead — cooler now, by far.

"What about him, Doc?" he asked. "We got to get Ephraim to Muncie, up in Indiana."

"He's half dead."

"How about the other half?"

The doc ran his eyes over Ephraim, bent over and listened to his lungs, felt his forehead just where George had.

"Maybe. Maybe not. Not much strength left him. He can't take but so many more of those fever spikes."

"I'd appreciate your doing all you can for him." Another minute and George worried that he might be in tears, Henry all over again.

"And I appreciate you digging that hole for my wife and telling Sarah to get out of there. Takes a hornet's nest to move those damn Bevingtons." The doctor was pumping his hand, slapping him on the back as if they'd known each other for years. From out of his pocket he produced a peppermint for the boy, half covered in lint.

War's over for sure, George thought as the doc moved on to the next bed. Now, if we can just survive the peace.

28

Jake's sense of geography was confined in any practical sense to maybe eighty square miles of east-central Indiana — five miles in any direction outside Muncie and every scrap of land within that circumference, plus however many miles he had walked since the summer of '62 always with a weather eye out for his nephews, for Henry, now for the boy, plus that final, defining one-one-thousandth of a square mile at Cahaba, the patch of land and building that when all else faded from memory and his ears were no more than worm holes would still be with him.

Jake knew math, enough geometry and algebra (words he never would have used, words he had never heard) to plumb a wall, calculate the height of a tree, and build a boiler to specifications that no professor could have translated into any functioning reality. He could read and write although he did little of either. He'd learned sufficient history to understand that the war whose actual fighting he had mostly sidestepped was unlikely to be the final word on anything. Four and a half years earlier he had voted without a moment's hesitation for John Bell, the Constitutional Unionist candidate for president, one of 5,306 Hoosiers (out of 272,000-plus total Indiana voters) to do the same. Lincoln meant secession, and secession meant fighting for sure. Breckenridge was beholden to the southern planters. There was something about Douglas he just didn't trust, a sixth sense. Whatever Bell stood for, it had to be better.

On religious matters, Jake liked to say if pressed — and he almost never was — that he stood four-square with Noah: a dry boat always beat a flooded shore. He couldn't have explained at the point of a Bowie knife how that translated theologically, but those three days and nights as watermen had convinced him he was right. That was just overflow, though. Standing on the wharf at Vicksburg was something beyond imagination.

Even in his narrow world, Jake had seen rivers, lakes, ponds that stretched for acres. He'd crossed the Tennessee with a load of half-dead mules. But he had never seen any body of water whose far shore was invisible. Maybe that was just the afternoon haze rising off the river, yet that didn't seem likely. The five of them had slogged, plodded, carried, rode, and otherwise transported and propelled them-selves across one and a half states to get here, and now the Mississippi looked boundless, as if it were China on the far shore, not just sorry Arkansas.

He'd seen plenty of raging currents, too — in the spring run-off, in summer floods — but from their dry perch not many feet overtop the river, this current looked animal. Whole trees bobbed up and down in the flow, got swallowed up and spit back out. A few minutes earlier a pig swollen to bull size had come careening past them, close enough to see its blank pig eyes. Where would it be deposited? New Orleans? Cuba? Some South American coast where giant sloths hung upside down from trees and the forests were live with cannibals dressed in gold? Jake imagined a giant bird pecking at the pig's stomach, letting all that gas loose, and being blown to Kingdom Come.

"It looks a tad fearsome," he was explaining, "but that's the way these big rivers are. The harder they flow, the easier they travel, especially if you're going up the opposite way. Why, the way this river's running along, I don't believe Aladdin himself would have a easier ride on one of them magic carpets."

He'd brought the boy along — talked the Confederate guard back at the camp into letting them pile into the train cars with the soldiers being paroled out and sent north on today's ships. There might have been a full three-dozen men on litters, mostly New Yorkers from Andersonville. They would need carrying on board. Jake and the boy could help with that. The guard could count on their coming back, Jake promised. It was only a four-mile walk, even if they missed the train, and the Muncie men would never leave a one of them behind. He went on more, swore fealty, criss-crossed his heart, vowed that he would rather spend eternity in a hell he didn't fully believe in than break his word a single time even to a damn Confederate, but the Grayback guard could have cared less. This was the tail end of the camp, the last days of a dying dream. This man, the boy, all of them who remained would almost certainly be gone by tomorrow evening. The guard waved them through with barely a glance. Not quite good riddance, but not far from it.

Jake wanted the boy to see water before he had to set foot on a boat that purported to float upon it. He didn't want him shying at the gangplank, but he hadn't counted on this: a torrent.

They must have carried a dozen stretchers on board themselves: men with missing this's and that's, men so pared down that they were light as feather pillows, one of the foot-less soldiers from their first train ride fattened up some now but still pathetic, another man Jake was sure was dead but didn't want to mention. Even the dead deserve to go home.

The *Olive Branch* was, in Jake's estimation and that based on scant experience, a "proper and tightish sort of wooden packet," and he took pains to point out its many virtues to the boy as they trudged back and forth with their melancholic loads. Caulking, oakum, tar — they'd all been applied so thoroughly that not even a ghost could squeeze through. The railings were strong enough to contain a herd of buffalo so long as someone — and here he stared hard at his charge — wasn't fool enough to cut capers along them, ships being known to roll to and fro and careless boys to be thrown from the railings on to the decks below where their heads were dashed into corn mush or into the water from which there was no hope of recovery. As for propulsion to carry them up the river, though the ship was clearly newish (two years old, in fact), the boilers were of the old-fashioned, tried-and-true variety such as he himself had helped construct, and so there was absolutely nothing that even a half-witted boy need worry over.

"Not that that applies here," Jake was quick to add. "You got a brain, for sure, a good one, but it never pays to think you know it all."

And on and on. Jake seemed to be discovering a new caution every few minutes. There was nothing fundamentally wrong with the boy — anyone could see that — but someone so willing to pee on his own fresh-dead father needed, Jake thought, a certain amount of modification before they arrived back home. That wasn't the way things were done in Muncie.

Truth told, Jake liked everything about the *Olive Branch* — the way she sat in the water, the breeze that kicked up across the hurricane deck as he and the boy laid their litters down, the glint here and there of polished brass as they turned the corner at the promenade, the crisp orders raining down from the pilot house at the steamer's crown. At least seven hundred men must have climbed, hobbled, or been carried aboard by the time the captain ordered the ropes thrown off, pulled twice on his whistle, and set off bumpily upriver. Jake and the boy waved after them, but everyone seemed to be looking forward to where they were headed, not back to where they had been.

The two of them sat on a crate, just where the *Olive Branch* had pulled out, chewing away on hardtack that Jake had brought from camp and washing the sawdust down as best they could from a canteen. The haze had lifted off the river while they were working. The Mississippi wasn't limitless after all: Arkansas was almost close enough for cannon fire. Figures, Jake thought: They'd put the city where the river was at its narrowest, not its widest. He'd let his imagination run away from him.

The wharf was a seedy affair: Behind them stretched a gaggle of frame buildings — a two-story warehouse, shacks, half caved-in roofs, not a one of them squared off to anything. Mules and carts tromped this way and that, hauling cargo away, hauling it in, Negroes and whites shouting alike, half of them it seemed in languages Jake couldn't quite make out. The place smelled half a barnyard, half a sewer. But this was freedom — Jake couldn't have enjoyed himself more.

Maybe it was the freedom that got Jake talking, lack of restraint breeding volubility. Or the foreignness of the place — babel of tongues, water slapping against the wharves in front of them when he had been a land man all his life long. Whatever it was, Jake's whole life story came tumbling out of him, and pretty much George and Ephraim's, too, and even what part of Henry's he knew or had heard of. There was no particular logic to it, no chronology that anyone could have followed. Jake jumped from plowed fields to boiler parts, from a favorite dog dead of a rattler bite, to that horrible day standing naked in the yard at Cahaba in the sleet and snow, to a grandmother barely remembered and an upside-down pie she had once baked by accident, her mind all but gone by then, while the boy sat there, his face a perfect mirror of whatever was going on in Jake's face as he talked on.

When Jake got to the part about his true love and her swan's neck broken on that buckboard ride, he looked down at the boy and saw tears in his eyes, and then he realized there were tears in his own, rolling down his cheeks. Strange he thought, I never told that story before and now I've told it twice in two days. Telling George, he now saw, was only rehearsal for this.

The sun was just going down behind the forest across the river — long past time to head back to camp; George would be a fidget — when Jake and the boy looked up from their thoughts to see a side-wheel steamer every bit as big as the *Olive Branch* slide into her berth, with a scattering of passengers staring over the railings. New Orleans, Jake reckoned: That's where something like this would have started from.

While she was tying up, Jake paced her off bow to stern, with the boy matching him every step of the way: 260 feet, and by the looks of her almost new, too. The economy must have boomed during the war, at least for paddle-wheel steamers, which would mean for boilers, too. Jake wondered if Quinn had laid on new help, if he would even have a job left when he returned home. He'd just been assuming until now. The boy pulled on his arm, pointed back to the stern. Fire men were tipping wheelbarrows of red-hot embers into the river, the hiss like a lighted fuse.

They were just about midships along the wharf, by the wheelhouse, studying the huge block letters that spelled out the name in a gold-trimmed black paint — SULTANA — when her captain stepped on shore with a burst of profanity that had Jake practically clapping the boy's ears into his skull.

"No need for that," he said, loud enough to be heard, but there must have been need because the captain kept it up along the rutted, muddy road for a good three or four minutes before he turned into some open door and slammed it behind him. Yet he must have kept on cursing inside because Jake had no sooner let go of the boy's hearing than the captain burst back out the door, screamed "Get it done, goddammit! Get it done!" at the top of his lungs at someone still on board, and slammed the door again.

Jake looked behind him. What seemed to be an engineer, maybe the chief one, was standing on deck, covered almost head to toe in grime and grease, muttering his own set of curses but these under his breath. An improvement, Jake thought, turning back to the boy, but the boy was gone, slipped through his hands like butter.

29

Jake took two quick steps up the road the captain had gone along, thought better of it — the boy wasn't a wraith for all that he could walk through walls; he'd see him for sure — and stepped on board.

"Hey, you!"

It was some other ship's officer, barely a man at all.

"Hey to hell and all!" Jake said, brushing by him. Now I'm doing it, he thought, swearing like a sailor, too. The menace in his voice was enough to convince the officer to go about other duties. The *Sultana* wasn't going anywhere until she was full up again.

Jake threw open the wheelhouse door: nothing but the wheel in there. He raced around the boilers in the engine room, some kind of new configuration he had never seen before, another way the world had changed while he was living in a dirt burrow down in Alabama. The fire room he didn't bother with: Not even the boy would be fool enough to go there.

He ran aft, then fore on the lower deck. Hogsheads of wines stacked everywhere, sacks of sugar, a damn herd of cows, mules, a pen of hogs, every goddamn thing under the sun but what he was looking for. He checked the railings too, thinking I never should have told him not to walk on them because now he's done and gone just that and sunk to the bottom of the river. The water was dark: no hand waving back to him, no frantic arms saying come save me.

Up to the promenade deck, fore, aft, and not a thing there either, except a knot of men standing at the stern, smoking cigars.

"Seen a boy?" Jake asked them. "About this high?" — he held his hand up nearly to his shoulders — "hair like straw?"

"Why?" one of the men asked him.

"Why? Why! Because I'm looking for him!" But they hadn't.

The chandeliers, up close this time, swayed gently back and forth over his head as he barreled down the hallway and threw open the first door he came to. There inside, on a bottom bunk bed covered with a deep red cloth, were a man and woman jaybird naked, wrapped around each other like a pair of snakes. Do they have to do that all the time, Jake wondered as he pulled the door shut behind him? A state-room, they call it, as if that made any difference.

On the steps up to the hurricane deck, he all but trampled a man at least his own age dressed up like he was president of the United States. No point asking him anything, and no one on the hurricane deck either that looked anything like the boy.

He tore up to the Texas deck, his last chance, raced over to the port railing again — no chance of seeing a drowning boy up here — scanned the twin stacks to see if he had climbed them like a goddamn monkey, and was about to start tearing his hair out when he looked down from the fore rail and saw the boy, three decks below him, kneeling down by some sort of wooden cage.

"What in the goddamn," Jake was still saying, forgetting all propriety, when he finally reached the boy, kneeled beside him, had a look at what was so interesting, and all but jumped out of his own skin. Whatever it was had chosen that moment to yawn: gaping jaws, studded with razor teeth. An alligator, Jake realized, all of ten-feet long, and bars or not, this tom-fool half-wit has practically got his head in his mouth.

The boy chose that exact moment to smile up at Jake, a wide beam of a winning grin that couldn't have been more the wrong reaction. Jake thought of grabbing him by the ear but couldn't remember which ear that son of a bitch store-keeper in Meridian had about ripped off. No sense finishing that work for anyone, so he simply took the back of the boy's neck in his mitt of a hand with enough pressure that finger marks would stay there for days, all but lifted him to his feet, and started quick-marching him back to the gangplank. Camp Fisk would be closed and gone by the time they got there.

Jake's anger had cooled enough by the engine room that he thought he might have one last look at the boilers. True, he had a junior monster on his hands, but Jake knew boilers. The camp, the guard, George, Henry, Ephraim, William Tecumseh Sherman, Ulysses S. Grant: the whole lot of them could just plain wait. He was measuring the boilers out with his eye — four of them, maybe four feet in diameter, each as much as eighteen feet long, a single water pipe below tying them all together, brick-and-mortar furnace below that to heat the water to make the steam to drive the paddle wheel, coal stacked by it — when he saw someone studying the far larboard boiler with what looked like a professional eye and dragged the boy back for a consultation. Maybe, he thought, just maybe he could *learn* a little something out of this whole, nearly disastrous, and entirely unnecessary perturbation.

"Something new?" Jake asked, nodding toward the nearest of the boilers.

"You understand 'em?" The man had two wooden tool boxes by his feet.

"Enough," Jake said.

"Well, then, these here *are* new. Been in service about two years now. Twenty-four flues in each boiler, five inches each, instead of the old two flues of a foot or more across. Supposed to heat the water more efficiently."

"Except — "

"Except what?"

"Except when I had a look at that river this afternoon it was mighty silty. Seems to me that silt is going to clog up a five-inch flue a good deal quicker than it could clog up a twelve or sixteen inch one."

The man broke into a broad smile.

"Well, that's just the problem. These boilers were made for up river, where there's nowhere near so much silt. Down here, these modern advancements gum up all the time. Keeps me in a living. Taylor," he said, sticking out his hand. "They call me R.G."

"Jake and this here's the boy," shoving him forward like a loaf of bread. "Looks like this boiler's got worse problems than that."

"Sure does."

Jake could see a bulge along a seam just below the midpoint. Where there was a bulge, there was sure to be a leak. Where there was a leak, there was trouble, for the ship and for the workers. The pressure in a boiler is enormous.

"Well?" A different voice, stronger, just on the edge of a burning anger, what Jake himself had been not long before. He turned and saw the same grease-and-grime-covered man the captain had been shouting at earlier. Seemed he really was the engineer.

"Oh, it can be fixed, Mr. Wintringer," R. G. was telling him. "I'll have to get some boys in here to pull it out, put two new sheets on it, then — "

"No time!" Wintringer was shouting at the mechanic from five feet away. Maybe the boiler room had left him half deaf.

R.G. looked as if he'd expected the answer.

"Well, then, I'll have to pound that bulge back in place. You can't — "

"I said, no time."

"No time? Then just what in the" — he caught himself with a nod at the boy — "heck do you expect me to do. Say the Lord's Prayer over it and go away? Kiss it and make it better?"

"Patch it."

"Patch? Patch without pounding out the bulge first? Patch when I don't even have the same gauge — "

"Patch it and patch it now, or you'll never work for the Merchants and People line again. That's from Captain Mason, not just me. And you" — turning now to Jake and the boy — "what in the h-e-double-l are you doing here? How do I know you're not some damn Reb spy, dropping a torpedo down there in my coal bin? We got rules around here. Security."

"He's — " R. G. started somehow to defend him, but Jake hushed him. Wintringer had a pipe wrench in one hand big enough to knock a steer out, and he didn't look as if he would stop with Jake's head either. Jake put the boy behind him, and the remaining three boilers between himself and the engineer and edged on out of the way. R. G. Taylor, he thought, looked just then like a man who badly needed a friend.

30

t had been a night of frantic dreaming: George of the little ones — Eben and Madeleine. He bursts through the door, home from war at last, and they run screaming from him. "Who is he, Mama?" Madeleine shouts, all a'panic. "Who is that man?" Having rid himself of his own history, Jake spent the late night with that goddamned alligator chewing its way bar by bar out of the cage while the boy sat dreamily staring at it, dinner for sure. The boy dreamt about the alligator, too. He was riding on its back up that churning river, shouting "Yee-haa!" with an upside-down pie balanced tipsy-turvy on his head. Over in the hospital tent, Ephraim all but had the raven-haired orderly, but the doc kept popping up at the most inopportune moments. Half delirious, sure he was living naked in a meadow just a step outside of Muncie, Ephraim ached with want, ached with shame. "Dear God, deliver her. Deliver me."

Henry put complexity into his, as if he were auditioning for one of those head-doctor couches that wouldn't be popular for another sixty years. His mother, Josephus, Henry, the Irishmen were all in it, gabbling back and forth every which way with Josephus's bullwhip whistling overhead while Ephraim — best friend, bosom-buddy of a lifetime — sang a soft lullaby and his mother as always wept tears big enough to fall to the floorboards with a large, hollow "thud." That's what I want, Henry thought, when he finally opened an eye:

not having to go on being me. How to do that? Overhead, the moon was a dull, hazy crescent.

Now it was morning, chicory-coffee time. The boy had foraged some more, down by the river just where he'd gigged his frogs. Henry had worked his usual miracle with nothing but a fistful of greens and roots to coax flavor from. Not quite a feast, but with the hardtack and a pull of jerky, not so far away either. Yet the wind was cold and raw, out of the north, augur of a day ahead best spent indoors by a real fire with a real ham on the table and a real mug of coffee, a glass of whiskey by the side, none of which even in this new, relative luxury was any more possible than a hot soak in a tub, a professional shave, or a trip to Mars. Better wasn't best. Better wasn't even normal.

"They're good boys, good men," Henry was saying, while the others stared morosely into the hot ashes of a campfire that never seemed to catch just right.

"For Irishmen," Jake kicked in, not really following what was being said. "Ain't much of a standard you're setting."

"For anybody!" Henry growled back.

Oh, Lord, George thought. Another spat.

"Anyone seen my brother today?" Anything to change the subject.

"Took him the first mug of this make-believe coffee," Henry said, pouring the last of his out on the ground, "long before any of you sleeping beauties had stirred." That much explained at least. George had figured Henry was wandering off with his new friends again. Without Ephraim around, he seemed unmoored.

"How was he?"

"Hot and bothered."

"Fever."

"Not that kind of hot. Or bothered."

Enough. Even the boy's ears had gone flaming red.

31

Two campfires down some slack-jawed Massachusetts cannoneers were overworking a fiddle, stomping their feet just to stay warm, George supposed. The strings screeched, as if they were made from fence wire. As for the stomping, they might as well have been leveling a hill of red ants as keeping time to anything else. But George recognized the song right off: "Hog-Eye Man," a favorite of Ephraim and Henry's, and little surprise there:

> *Oh, he came to the shack where Sally did dwell,*
> *He knocked on the door, he rung a bell.*
> *Oh, who's been here since I been gone,*
> *Railroad navvy with his sea-boots on.*

Jake had climbed back in his tent and was already asleep — an early afternoon snooze, all this day was good for. His snoring had a roar like a tornado. George could see the boy's head popped up over the embankment, slipping down towards the music men. I should stop him, he thought. "Hog-Eye Man" was likely to be the least of their lyrical offenses. Jake would have already stuffed the boy's ears with mud. But that was Jake, always fretful, a four-by-four mother hen. George had his own fretting to do, not for a living soul anywhere nearby.

He tried counting backwards from 100. When that didn't take, he did it again, first by fives and then by threes.

Tired of numbers, he plotted his Daddy's quarter section: corn here, wheat there, windbreaks, an acre for his mother's kitchen garden. George dug holes, put in an orchard — apples mostly — something they'd never had, why he couldn't imagine. The hard cider alone was worth it, and — Lord! — the vinegar.

He'd been gone now a quarter of Eben's life, so he gave him a quarter more of everything: inches, pounds, brains, common sense. Eben wouldn't run, never, when George finally came through that door. Madeleine might just be another story. Dreams sometimes foretell, but maybe not all of it.

Wary of that box canyon, he backed his way out and turned his mind to the very worst things he had ever seen: the two brothers squeezed into one by a cannonball during that first, disastrous battle back in Kentucky; Henry's back the morning he showed up after Josephus had flayed him; the other flaying, back at Cahaba; Jake's intended with her brains bashed out and that ruined buckboard upended beside her (which, of course, he hadn't seen but might as well have after Jake was through telling it).

"God works in wondrous ways, his miracles to perform," his mother liked to say. And awful ways, too. The war, the prison, it had all been a lesson in that. George found himself wondering if he could ever attend church again. Where was the miracle in what he and Jake, Ephraim and Henry had been through? Where, except maybe the boy? Maybe that. Maybe the boy was what God had sent to make sense of the misery. Was that possible?

Another dead-end. He tried to work his way through the presidents — Washington to Lincoln and back again — but for the life of him, he couldn't fill the hole between Van Buren and Tyler (or Tyler and Van Buren, depending on which direction he was headed). The one who had run his mouth forever in the wintry sleet of his Inauguration and died a month later. Maybe over-talking just came with the job — one problem the boy would never have.

Finally, he gave up and let himself imagine what he had been trying not to imagine all afternoon long — the other, better half of that dream he'd had the night before, the part he hadn't let himself go to. It was past two in the morning when he finally made it home — raw-footed, worn to the bone. He opened the door inch by inch, knew just where the creak was even these three years gone by, babied the hinges past it. The fire had been banked, just embers enough for a quick look around. He could hear the children breathing gently in their bed as he eased past their door and into his own bedroom.

Eliza lay sprawled, half tangled in the bedding. He watched her breasts rise and fall as he worked his boots off, pulled off his shirt, let his pants drop to the floor. And then with a hand placed gently over her mouth — no shouts, no children to come running to or away from him — he slipped in gently beside her, and at last the war was really, truly over.

"14th," he heard. Not Eliza's voice — a man's. Her flesh was pressed against his. He popped open one eye and saw the boy running in from the embankment. Propped open another one, and there was Henry hot-footing back from who knew where. Behind him he could hear Jake rumbling round in his tent.

"14th," the voice said again, a sergeant walking down the line. "Indiana 14th Volunteer Infantry?" A question.

"That's us," George answered, rising to his feet, half surprised not to find himself in his birthday suit.

"Grab your stuff if you got any," the sergeant called out, barely looking his way. "You're shipping out this evening."

Maybe dreams really do foretell, George thought, in good ways, too. Even with all his imagining, bidden and unbidden, home had seemed impossibly far away. Until now.

It took all of five minutes for the lot of them to descend on the hospital tent. The boy was carrying George's packet

— what few things of his own he had could fit in a pocket. Jake had the captain's saddlebags thrown over one shoulder. What good it might do on a Mississippi steamboat, he couldn't imagine. Henry was hauling two loads, his own and Ephraim's. Between the two, they didn't amount to a hill of beans — shirts, a change of trousers, whatever the Sanitary Commission had handed out that hadn't disappeared already.

Ephraim was fever-red, flat out on his back, clutching the raven-haired nurse's one hand as she sponged him with the other. His lips were moving, a song for sure, but for once George couldn't make it out.

"Planning a trip?" It was the doctor, riding wing on his daughter.

"This evening," George answered as the doctor took his elbow and pulled him to the side.

"He could stay here, you know. We'd look after him," nodding to his daughter. "Send him home well."

George shook his head. "We can't go home without him. Will he make it?"

"Maybe," the doctor said, "and maybe not. About the same chances there as here when you get right down to it."

He handed George a twist of paper.

"There's a powder inside. Give him a pinch if he gets delirious, with water if you have it, even from that pestilent river. It'll calm him."

He pulled the blanket off the foot of the cot as well.

"And wrap him in this if he gets the chills."

"And if he gets both at the same time?"

"Pray," the doctor said, "even if you've forgot how."

Henry already had Ephraim on his feet. He took the right shoulder, George the left. The nurse was unlocking his fingers from her hand one by one.

"I'm sending for you, Lorena," Ephraim promised. "I'm sending for you sure. Glory hallelujah."

32

"See that?"

Jake was pointing to the lower foredeck of the *Sultana*, tied up just down river of the *Oliver Ames*.

"See what?" It was Ephraim, rallied again, though not yet ready to stand on his own two feet.

"Why, the top of that crate yonder. Any tomfool can see it. Below the rail, just beyond that pen of hogs."

"I suppose so," Henry chimed in, although no one — not even him, with eyes like a hawk — could see a blessed thing.

"That's where it happened." Jake was getting himself worked up again. "That very spot."

"What happened? Sometimes talking with you is like talking to —" Henry was going to say "a mule" or maybe "ten pounds of mud," but Jake had gone beyond listening.

"Where a boy who ain't got no more sense than a squirrel stew almost got his head bit off by an —"

Jake was reaching down, feeling for some part of the boy that hadn't been too labored before to twist by way of exclamation, when the boy looked right back at him with his mouth opened wider than anyone had ever seen it and his teeth practically leaping out of that maw.

"Alligator," Jake finally concluded, almost blubbery with what he couldn't say. Something he hadn't felt in so long he could hardly remember it. Instead of tweaking the boy, he let his hand fall on the top of his head. He'd take some cleaning up — that was for sure.

"Wish they'd let that gator out for an airing." Henry added. "We could use a little entertainment. Or maybe we could just send the boy up the line here to nip off a few body parts. Might get us on this floating hotel a trifle sooner." And just on cue, as if they'd been rehearsing this act for years, the boy started snapping those huge killer jaws in every direction.

They all thought it then, each in his own way: How could a mouth that big, with all those perfect looking parts inside it, not make a single sound. It didn't stand to reason.

Ahead of them, maybe 100 men were waiting to board the *Oliver Ames*. To their rear, three, four, five times more. There was no reckoning where the end of the column might be. The same held over at the *Sultana* even more so — a tail that rounded a bend on the muddy, rutted road and disappeared from reckoning behind a stand of shanties. Who knew how many others had already boarded both ships: The lame, the halt, the half- and whole men — they were beginning to pile up at the high railings, claiming space for this last troop movement of the war. The worst, the stretcher cases, the barely alive got set aside to carry on last. No sense boarding a man they'd just have to haul off dead before the ship ever left port.

By the time the line ahead had thinned to no more than a few dozen, George had picked out a spot for the five of them, bottom deck and forward. Everyone was scrambling to the upper decks, but below would be breeze enough if Ephraim's fever flared up, and if any docs were to be on board, they'd be just one deck up, in the staterooms.

Jake would be the bull to push their way to where he wanted everyone to settle. George nudged him now, jutted his chin toward where they were headed, but Jake's eyes were fixed downriver. George followed his gaze to the *Sultana* gangplank and an officer — his braid shining in the light — racing down it.

"That's the captain I told you about," Jake said, "the one who was swearing like a saloon full of Irishmen. No offense," he added to Henry, whose hackles were never far from a rise these days.

"And the other one?"

A grease-stained ape was on the captain's tail, lumbering down the gangplank just behind him.

"Wintringer. The engineer. The one with the monkey wrench I didn't fancy having buried in my skull or —" He nodded down toward the boy, his hand still tangled in that rat's nest of blond hair.

A mule-drawn flat-bed wagon sat halfway between the two gangplanks. A desk had been set up on it and half a dozen chairs put around. The captain and Wintringer met there with an officer off the *Oliver Ames* — more braids, a captain himself, they were close enough to see that now. The columns on both sides had stopped moving. A silence had come over everything. Even Ephraim had stopped his gabbling. A lieutenant standing behind the two captains produced a scroll, an ink pot, a writing instrument of some kind to go with it. Scrawls were affixed, handshakes exchanged. Both captains and the engineer were already headed back to their respective steamers when the lieutenant climbed up on the desk itself and shouted "Attention!" — as useless a command as was ever given. The attention by then couldn't have been more absolute.

"By order of Captain Frederic Speed, acting in the absence and with the authority of Lieutenant Colonel Reuben B. Hatch, be it known that further embarkation on the steamer *Oliver Ames* is hereby forbidden. All passengers waiting to board the *Oliver Ames* will be from this point forward received on the *Sultana*. Shift the line to the left, men. Shift to the left and step lively. We're going to *expedite* this service!"

And expedite it they did. Soldiers were practically being run on to the *Sultana* by the time the Muncie men had merged themselves into the other steamer's column.

"I don't like this."

Edging Jake toward the *Sultana* gangplank was like pushing a horse up a hill.

"There's still plenty of space on the *Oliver Ames*. I don't like it at all."

"Look down the wharf, Jake." George had had it with second thoughts. "You see anything else waiting to take us up river, take us north, take us home?" He could still feel Eliza's flesh on his.

"I've been on the *Sultana*. I've seen that boiler. I heard the way they were talking. I told you all that, George."

"Well, hell, Jake, I know that, but we could be waiting a day, two, maybe three more. Who knows?"

His voice dropped into a whisper: "Ephraim, he might —" But Jake had bolted, just like the boy, as if bolting were contagious. R.G. Taylor was leaving the *Sultana*, hauling his two heavy wooden toolboxes up the wharf. Jake all but knocked him into the river by way of greeting.

"Did you fix it?"

"Best I could with a patch that don't match up and no time to set it in right."

"You think this here steamer's going to make it to St. Louis?"

That one was harder. R.G. looked down at his hands, then back at the *Sultana*, then straight on at Jake.

"I think them boilers can make it to St. Louis, all right — if they ain't asked to carry too much of a load, in too high a river." A long pause followed, maybe for effect, more likely because R.G. didn't know what next to say, how far to go. Men were rumbling up the gangplank behind them.

"You had a good look at that river?" the mechanic finally asked. The Mississippi was rushing by just below them, nearly lapping at the boards. "Must have had a lot of snow up ways this winter cause we sure getting the run-off now. I hear the Mississippi is near to four miles wide north of Memphis."

"And the load?" Jake asked, but that question was already answering itself over their heads. The crew was hammering six-by-six uprights in place between the lower and promenade decks and, above that, between promenade and hurricane, and hurricane and Texas.

"This boat's going to need all the shoring it can get with the number of soldiers Captain Mason is planning to take on," R.G. said.

"Why's he doing it?" Jake ventured, ever practical. "Seems he'd want to go light on that boiler you mended for him."

"That one's easy. Five dollars a soldier, ten an officer. Captain Mason and his officers are fixing to make a fortune." R.G. had lifted his toolboxes and was heading wherever he went — home, shop; you never knew where a man put his head. "Hell, for that kind of money, I'd probably do it, too."

"Seems as if we're being herded on like cattle, don't it?" Henry said. They could see Jake fighting his way back toward them, a bull racing through a china shop.

"One difference though" — more nonsense from Ephraim though George was long past discouraging the two of them.

"What's that?"

"Cattle most generally being led to the slaughter."

Henry looked stunned for the moment, then a broad grin spread over him as he pulled his friend of a lifetime into his arm, his chest, his heart: "How the hell could I have forgot that?"

"The boy!" George warned, but too late. The damn fool thing was as grinning moony-eyed as any calf at the teat.

The boy, it turned out, was exactly what Jake had on his mind, too.

"He ain't going."

"What?"

"I said, he ain't going!"

He'd stepped in front of three of them, grabbed the boy, was holding him high over his head while the boy kicked his feet and flailed his arms every which way he could. Why? The question practically jumped out of that quiet mouth. Jake heard it clear as could be.

"Because I said you ain't gone," he answered. "You're staying right here in Vicksburg!"

They'd come to the gangplank now. A small cordon of ship's mates lined it to keep the men from falling in the river as they pushed on board. Jake handed the boy to the officer in charge of them.

"Don't let him on," he roared. "He never fought no one. He ain't worth no ten greenbacks, or five, or a plug goddamn penny to you or your captain, you hear."

"Fine with me," the ship's officer replied. "We're getting a tad full at any rate. Send that boy back down the line. He's taking a good man's place."

By the time George, Ephraim, and Henry had forced their way to the railing, all they could see of the boy was a lone foot waving in the air, sliding back through the sea of men still waiting to board. When even that disappeared, when the boy just vanished, it was like something had been ripped out of them.

"Jake —" Henry started to say, but George grabbed his arm to silence him. George had never seen his uncle so flat out miserable.

33

The boy had taken a vow when Henry handed over that watch to get him out from under the grip of the fat pig of a storekeeper back in Meridian: He would steal no more.

He'd renewed the vow a half day later by that baptismal river even as Jake and the others scrubbed themselves clean with the soap he had filched just before he grabbed the No. 12 Garber Boots and tried to run — the soap that fat pig of a storekeeper had been too stupid to discover.

Before they left that river, he had renewed the vow a third time as he streamed piss on the soon-to-be-rotting corpse of his father: I ain't going to steal. I'm not going to be like him.

The Muncie Men — *his* Muncie men — had showed him another way. They'd taught him about something he'd never known, something his own father didn't have it in him to do: good. That's it, he said to himself, as Jake screamed at him to lay off taking a leak on the gaggle-toothed shell of a human being who had sired him into the world: I'm walking the straight and narrow.

But this was an extraordinary circumstance.

The bucket brigade of soldiers had deposited him where their line finally wore out — back in a warren of ramshackle cabins that he immediately recognized for what they were: places where men and women come together, where they grunt and groan, where there was drink and carelessness, and sometimes knives and guns to settle things. That much about his father had been useful: There wasn't a sorry-ass place on earth — or hell — that the old drunken cheat hadn't dragged him through.

One other thing about the cabins: They were places where men took off their clothes and mostly threw them on the floor, by the door, right where they had come in, and where women never wore much of anything at all.

He tested the first door he came to, found it latched or blocked somehow, and moved on to the next cabin. This door gave when he nudged it. The boy went around to the side, put an ear to the wall, and could hear a man inside panting louder and louder. Just when it sounded as if the man were about to burst wide open, the boy dashed to the door, slipped it a crack wide, grabbed the first thing his hand came to, and raced down the line. A Union forage cap — just what he was hoping for. Now, he would have to be a little more particular.

He settled behind a stack of barrels and watched the soldiers tramp back up the road: fat ones, tall ones, soldiers reeling with whiskey, loud-talking ones, ones who looked like they'd seen a ghost. Then he saw the one he wanted. He was maybe a head taller than the boy and — what? — thirty pounds heavier, but he wasn't all that much more than a boy himself, nervous, fidgeting, pivoting his head this way and that before he ducked down a side lane, came to a cabin door, knocked twice, fished whatever money he had out of his pocket, handed it around the door, and walked on inside.

His uniform shirt didn't even hit the floor before the boy had it and was running full tilt back to the wharves, dressing as he flew.

"That's it!" Captain Speed shouted as the boy arrived pell-mell at the wharf, 22nd New Jersey shirttails trailing behind him. "That's all we're bringing on board." Two armed guards had taken up positions at the gangplank, ferocious-looking men covered in scars and tattoos.

The captain gestured aft, where a clot of orderlies waited. "Bring those stretchers on," he shouted. "Now! Don't bring me no dead ones, either, and make it snappy. We've got to move this pride of the Mississippi out of here."

The boy slipped his way through the grumbling soldiers left on shore to where the orderlies were stirring, grumbling themselves. Twenty-plus stretcher cases waited, and not but three orderlies to haul them on board. He jammed his cap down hard on his head, pulled an eyelid up on one soldier who could have been living or not, saw his eyeball swimming underneath, and bent to grab the back handles.

Soon enough, another orderly came along to grab the front, and they were off. The guards on the gangplank poked the man once hard in the ribs, saw him flinch, and signaled the stretcher through, without so much as a look at who was doing the hauling. A space had been cleared aft, behind the engine room. They laid the man down carefully there — a stink of a place, with no breeze and none likely unless the *Sultana* decided to turn around and chug up-river backwards — and while the orderly on the front duty raced back to bring another stretcher on board, the boy did what he did the very best of all: disappeared. Poof. Gone.

34

The Sultana, Texas deck

At ten on the night of April 24, 1865, the *Sultana* cast off from the wharves at Vicksburg, gave a blast of its whistle, and turned out to beat its way upstream into the surging river. On board, the men let out a deafening roar. "Home!" they shouted. "My God in heaven, home!" The soldiers who still had caps tossed them in the air. The ones who didn't caught the caps that fell and tossed them up again. Most had survived two wars —the fighting and their own confinement. A forage cap was nothing by comparison.

It wasn't long before singing filled the steamer, on every deck. Johnny really was marching home again. Hurrah! Hooray! Who could blame a man for letting his thoughts wander to the big parade in town — and the ladies who would all turn out to fill with joy the warrior's heart? Even down among the stretcher cases, in that still space behind the engine room, the feeble chords of song could be heard.

The gayety, though, was not universal. Up high, along the rail at the aft end of the Texas deck, Ephraim, who might have been leading the song, who might even have forced his way back below to comfort the stretcher men with a song of his own, half sat, half lay with his head on George's shoulder. Henry had gone off with a fistful of rags in search of a water barrel — something to cool his friend down. Jake, for his part, was cursing a blue streak, his ban on such outbursts having been lifted for what seemed all time and eternity.

"Goddamn it all to hell. Goddamn it all to hell!"

His legs were stretched out in front of him, his hands lay useless in his lap. Captain Downey's hand-tooled saddle-bags, the inexplicable burden of so many hours, was wedged between his back and the bottom rail. A blubber of snot dripped from his nose.

"All to hell — you hear me?" But Jake wasn't talking to anyone other than himself, and no one answered.

Though he was 34 years old, a father twice over, a man who only a few years earlier could hitch himself to a plow if need be and clear a field in a day, George wished at that moment that his mother was with them. It was her shoulder Ephraim should be leaning into, her hand that should be comforting his brow, her voice that should be whispering the reassuring words that George simply could not find.

His mother would know what to say to her brother, too — Jake, another love of her life. She could lift the pain from him. George couldn't do that either, or anything like it. His pain was George's pain, all their pain for that matter, only (George thought) so much worse for Jake whose love (he saw it now) had been the cause of his own desolation.

"You reckon Henry has gotten himself lost?" George asked, mostly to break their silence.

"Or found them Irishmen."

"Irish — " Ephraim tried to chime in, but whatever he was gone to say was lost before it got out of his mouth.

The humanity around them was crushing — man piled against man like Cahaba at its worst. The bottom deck had been full of freight and livestock; the hurricane deck already claimed fore, aft, port, and starboard. They'd had to race another gaggle of Hoosiers to this last rail space on the Texas deck, Jake blocking the competition while George and Henry dragged Ephraim across the finish line. Now, there was no running room left, and no order to it either. Two steps in any direction was a challenge. Crossing the deck was an ordeal akin to weaving through a herd of stampeding buffalo, one reason they'd sent Henry with the water rags: Henry could track a rabbit through a briar patch.

"You'd think," Jake was saying, "you would damn well think."

He'd gotten himself worked up again.

"Think what, Jake?"

"What? What! I don't know why I bother! You would just goddamn think — "

He was pounding his fists into the deck as he ranted — *Bam! Bam! Bam!* — when a Union forage cap dropped into his lap as if it had been floating up there all this time, wafted up on some kind of providential breeze ever since the captain had tooted his horn and started beating north.

Except it wasn't that at all.

George and Jake looked over their heads at the same moment. The boy was perched there on the top rail, as if standing on that thin balustrade of wood were the most natural act in the world, not the terrible, perilous thing that Jake had warned him about only a little more than a day earlier.

"Are you damned crazy?" The boat was lurching in the current. "Are you —?"

But the boy was already floating like a bird into Jake's arms.

35

The boy was propped up on both elbows, staring right in his eye, when Jake first tested the early morning light. He'd slept with his head cradled in the captain's saddlebags, relief for an aching back. Now his neck felt as if someone had locked it in a vise and was jabbing needles in it left and right. On the whole, he couldn't have been happier.

East, the sun had barely cleared the shoreline, impossibly far in the distance. To their west, a row of cottonwoods lined the banks. Jake could see mule carts moving along a road behind the trees, smoke rising from the chimneys of shacks at the other side of a wide, plowed field. This was one of those cold mornings when you could already feel the heat building up. By mid-day they'd have a scorcher on their hands. Below the Muncie Men's perch on the Texas deck, the river seemed almost tame.

"Let's have a look at them boilers again," Jake whispered to the boy, but the boy was already on his feet, ready to lead the way through the tangle of sleeping men that littered the deck.

"Don't be racing," Jake cautioned. Give the boy half a chance, and he'd run a fox to its hole. Racing, though, wasn't at all what the boy had in mind. He reached back, took Jake's hand, and led him almost in a beeline to the small enclosure at the center of the deck, under the pilot house, where the officers were quartered. From there, the two tip-toed along the wall and around the corner to the stairway, the boy finding foot-holes even for Jake's Garber No.12s where it didn't seem any deck at all could be seen.

It was yet another of his miracles of conjuring — something where nothing was — and the boy repeated it down three flights of stairs, themselves filled with sprawling men, just beginning to stir, past a brace of dozing guards and a gaggle of Christian ladies readying hymnals and crackers for the day's mission work, and straight to the engine-room door. Inside, he pulled Jake into the deep shadows, behind the patched boiler, reading his mind as if Jake's skull was made of glass and all his thoughts written in giant letters inside.

Jake put his finger to his lips — "shhhh" — and then realized just how foolish he was being. Telling a mute boy to be quiet? It was enough to bring on another of those ear-to-ear grins the boy seemed to be newly specializing in. Does he understand why I wouldn't let him on board, Jake wondered? Does he forgive me if he does? Mysteries compounded on mysteries, never to be answered in this world.

In the fire room, black men, stripped to their wastes, shoveled coal into the hungry, gaping furnace maw. Their backs ran with sweat. Muscles bulged overtop of muscles. Jake bent over and whispered in the boy's ear. "That's got to be one of the worst jobs in the world." He meant it as a lesson: Set your sights high, get your learning, don't be any man's slave. And the boy seemed to take it that way, for he nodded in solemn agreement.

As if to punctuate the point, Wintringer chose that moment to scream into the hellhole: "Shovel, goddammit, you lazy nigger sons of a bitch — I want these boilers full throttle when we pull back into the river!"

For once, Jake didn't clap his hands over the boy's ears. Cursing, he supposed, was an education, too. You had to learn what not to do in this world, along with what was right.

R. G. Taylor's patch glowed a slight pinkish red against the flat gray metal of the rest of the boiler. "Lighter gauge," Jake whispered to the boy. "Easier to work with. See them rivets that hold it on?" Did he understand a word of this?

Jake stepped out to take a closer look at the mechanic's handiwork just as the *Sultana* began listing sharply to port. A chair, a crate, shovels went tumbling past him. The boy, too. Jake reached out his right arm and caught the boy seconds before he went face-first into the boiler itself, burned to death for sure.

"What in the hell?" Wintringer was shouting as Jake threw the boy under his arm and half crawled his way back to the starboard door and out it.

"What in the hell!"

On deck, everything was sliding to the port side. Jake and the boy slid with them — they had no choice. At the port rail, they finally learned what the commotion was all about. A photographer had set up on shore, preparing to capture the steamboat as it muddled on by. Just as the phosphorous ignited into a flash, there was a moment when Jake felt certain that they had passed the tipping point, that the steamer was going over for sure, but then — as he would later learn from George — Capt. Mason and his officers had come racing out of the pilot house with pistols raised.

"Get back from that rail!" they were shouting. "Back to mid-ships! Move over to starboard!" If the shouting didn't get attention, the pistol shots did. There wasn't a man among them who hadn't learned first hand what a bullet was made to do. Slowly, the *Sultana* righted itself and moved on.

The photograph — taken at Helena, Arkansas, on April 25, 1865, at just about 7 a.m., 33 hours after leaving Vicksburg — is the sole surviving image of the *Sultana's* final voyage.

36

"George?"

"Right here, Ephraim."

The listing boat had jolted them both awake, and the mass of men sliding their way, nearly crushed them. George was soaking hardtack in his makeshift tin-cup of water, softening it up, then breaking it into tiny pieces so his brother could gum some down. He'd seen songbirds with bigger appetites.

"What color are Daddy's eyes?"

"Color? Why they're—" But what color were they? Hazel? Brown? Grey? Not blue. That was out.

"Truth is, I'm not sure." He'd looked his father in the eye all the time — he'd insisted on it. No staring at the ground when you talked to him. How had he missed that?

"Henry will know," Ephraim said.

"Why Henry?"

"Remember that time Daddy told Henry he was heading off to kill Josephus?"

"Course. What's that got to do with it?"

"Concentrates your attention, George. When someone says a thing like that, you remember everything around it."

Henry, though, had wandered away as soon as the boat righted itself and hadn't been seen since. The Irishmen — that's always where he was when he wasn't with them.

"Maybe Jake then. Will you ask Jake for me?"

"Why do you need to know?"

"Seems important, that's all." But Ephraim was already back asleep, worn out from nothing more than thinking on his father's eyes.

Besides, Jake was too occupied to bother. He had decided that the Texas deck of a jammed-to-the-rafters steamboat was the perfect place to teach the boy how to tread water.

"This ain't the easiest thing to show on land," he was explaining, "or in these cramped conditions." He was glowering, to no effect, on the Vermont clot hard by them. "But you've got to learn sometime. First, see, you keep your hands flat on the water. Just move 'em in easy circles like this."

He looks like he's rubbing breasts, George thought, but kept it to himself. The boy was rubbing them, too, a perfect imitation.

"Then, your legs. They got to be like a pair of scissors."

Jake balanced on one leg, began scissoring with the other, tipped south, and almost hurled himself over the rail.

The boy wisely skipped the balancing part. Instead, he leapt in the air, scissoring his legs back and forth like the world's greatest ballet star. The Deadman's Dance, George remembered — the boy could imitate anything physical. Jake recalled it, too. For someone who had nearly scissor-kicked himself into the roiling Mississippi, he was laughing like a raging fool.

"Time we moved on to swimming itself. You'd already know to do this if you'd spent more time watching frogs and less time gigging them."

He was drawing his hands together in front of his chest, reaching them up towards the sky, drawing one knee up (to stand for both legs) and spreading the leg out as wide as space and common sense allowed when a commotion that had been building for minutes finally found its way to the stern.

"Ain't got no room here," George heard someone saying.

"Move on."

"This space ain't for you."

By the time he looked up, a black soldier was standing in front of him, his face a haggard mess.

"Name's Albert. Been standing since Vicksburg," he said. "I'd welcome a chance to sit down."

George wanted to say no. His brother was half in his arms, half living, half dead. Ephraim's best friend would be back sometime. Jake and the boy took up more room sitting and lying than they did standing by the rail. What looked like a sliver of space wasn't that at all. But, my God, he thought: We've all been through this. We're not the only ones hanging on by a thread to what we've got, what we want, where we need to get.

"You ever been to Muncie?" The question was half a challenge, half an invitation.

"Not if it ain't in Massachusetts."

"Well, let's say you were to go to Muncie, what would you expect to find?"

The black soldier pondered the question for a careful minute before answering.

"Muncie? Wherever it is, I would find the streets paved with gold just like the heavenly city."

"Then let me ask you one more question," George went on, the catechism growing. "What do you expect the story is with this gentleman over here?"

He was gesturing toward Jake, who was bent over with his hands on the rail, flailing first one foot out wide, then the other, and drawing them back in again.

"Why, I expect he's a Muncie gandy dancer."

"Gandy dancer!" George all but shouted. "Hell, I figured you for a Muncie man straight away. Have a seat. How'd you end up in this sorry war?"

As Albert lowered himself to the deck, a tattered Bible tumbled from his shirt.

37

"Schooling, too," Jake was saying.

The boy had Albert's Bible spread open on his legs, lit by a beam of moonlight as if ordered up by Higher Authority. A flying pig couldn't have amazed him more.

"It ain't enough in this world to be a championship water treader. You got to know how to read and write as well."

He was about to give the boy a first run through the alphabet — A is for "apple," B is for "boiler" — when Ephraim broke gently into song in that beautiful tenor:

The years creep slowly by, Lorena.
The snow is on the grass again.
The sun's low down the sky, Lorena ...

Henry picked up the song there with him, and George a few lines later.

A hundred months have passed, Lorena,
Since last I held that hand in mine ...

By the third stanza, Albert had added a fine, resonant bass, and Jake his best scratchy croak. Soon the boy was moving his own lips, a mute soprano to complete the sextet.

It matters little now, Lorena.
The past is in the eternal past.
Our hearts will soon lie low, Lorena
Life's tide is ebbing out so fast.

It was the boy who noticed first. His eyes led the rest of them there. Ephraim had gone a near bright red — he was burning up. George took the twist of paper the doctor had given him, tipped half the powder that was left in his tin cup, added some water from his canteen, and held it to his brother's lips. No sooner had he coaxed him into drinking, then the shakes came on, uncontrollable.

Prayer time, the Doc had said. George got to it while he wrapped Ephraim in the blanket.

"Dear God. Dear God in heaven." Forgive my brother his sins? Hold him in your blessed arms? He was still struggling for the right words an hour and a half later, cradling Ephraim in his arms, when he felt a hand weakly squeeze his wrist.

"Coal black," Ephraim said. "Black as coal."

"What's black as coal?"

"Daddy's eyes. I just seen 'em."

"Seen 'em?"

"I'm home, ain't I, George? I'm home. Momma! Momma! I'm home."

George had just put his lips to his brother's cheek when he felt the life lift right out of him.

38

They waited until the next morning to bid Ephraim goodbye. The night was cool. It seemed right to sit with him a little longer. Besides, he wasn't going anywhere. Jake awoke determined to talk to the boy about death before whatever George had in mind to do. Death was part of life, going home as Ephraim himself had put it, all that, but he abandoned it before the first word got out. However old he was, the boy had seen plenty of dying already, seen his own father plugged like a mad dog (which maybe he was) and some things a man might consider worse. Jake couldn't get those footless prisoners from Andersonville out of his mind. How could he have complained so about his bowing ankle? At least there was something below it.

Also, there was this: Ephraim wasn't the first man tipped into the Mississippi from those steamboat decks, and unless the boat somehow became a magic flying machine and sped to Cairo like a hawk to its prey, he was certain not to be the last. Just a few yards over from where they were wrapping Ephraim in his blanket, a redhead no older than him was coughing his lifeblood away. By the looks of the crowd around him, they might just toss the redhead overboard in advance of the inevitable and be done with it.

Family mattered, Jake thought — in war, in life, in everything. What would he tell his sister? And yet there was, after all, the boy.

It was Henry who produced the missing piece of the puzzle this time — two lengths of twine to tie off the blanket at either end. He and the boy stood back as Jake and George hoisted Ephraim to the rail. A half circle of men had formed behind them — three, four, five deep; quiet as could be, hushing the soldiers behind them, blocked off from view. Respect must be paid.

The Muncie men had come into contact with thousands of others at Cahaba, had cooked beside them, stood with them in that flood, become fellow watermen, been stripped naked with them in the sleet and freezing rain — had been slammed up against them cheek to jowl in every way that men could be pressed against each other, same as they were now. Yet there wasn't a face among this crowd that looked familiar to George, a face that even called back a name, a memory, an anything. But why should there be? As much as it seemed like yesterday, Cahaba also felt like another place in another country in another time — a place never to be visited again, in thought or deed, if George could help it.

And now there was this: his own brother, wrapped in a blanket, propped on the top rail, waiting to be committed to all eternity. George thought for a moment that he might just jump in after him.

"Would you like to read something?"

Albert had pulled the worn Bible out from inside his shirt.

"There's a marker at Isaiah 41:10."

"How about if you read?" George asked. "Be good to have a Bible man say the words."

"I don't know but a few of them," Albert said, shaking his head. "I just got the numbers down."

"Henry? Can you —"

George motioned for Henry to come take his end of the blanket, but Henry was rooted to the deck, no more able to move than if a boulder had been strapped to his back. The boy stepped forward instead and grabbed hold of the blanket for dear life as George took Albert's Bible and began to read aloud:

"Fear thou not; for I am with thee: be not dismayed; for I am thy God."

He nodded at Jake and the boy then, and as he read on, they tipped blanket and body over the rail:

"I will strengthen thee; yea, I will help thee; yea, I will uphold thee with the right hand of my righteousness."

Behind them, Ephraim's body bobbed once in the ship's wake, then sank under, food for catfish and gars.

There is a future, oh, thank God!
Of life this is so small a part.

George wheeled around, thinking maybe his brother had somehow escaped death and returned as a specter, a voice that would float forever beside them. But it was only Henry, standing stock still, eyes riveted to the deck, finishing the song his bosom friend had been singing for half his life.

'Tis dust to dust beneath the sod,
But there, up there, 'tis heart to heart.

How am I going to get word to the doctor, George wondered. How will Lorena ever know?

39

"Tie it off! Tie it off dammit all! You understand nothing other than voodoo talk?" The ship's officer had pushed and bullied his way from the pilot house to the aft rail of the Texas deck, not more than five feet from where the Muncie men had camped. Now he was shouting down to the wharf where a black man held a limp hawser in his hand.

"Tie it off where, boss?" he called back.

"Where? To your goddamn neck!"

George could feel Albert going stiff beside him. Life was a thousand insults — a thousand times a thousand times a thousand times more, numbers incalculable. George had never thought about that before, but he could see it now.

"This Memphis?" he asked when the officer paused to catch his breath.

"Sure as hell ain't St. Louis."

"And you sure as hell ain't fit to be around no boy."

Jake was on his feet now, blocking the way. The man thought once about trying to push Jake out of the way, gauged the task, and decided he had made more than enough progress along the rail.

"Tie it to that mooring right beside your foot!" he yelled back to the wharf — "that is, if you know what a foot is."

"Why are we tying up?" Jake's insistence tended to grow with the occasion.

"Why? You want us to just throw the freight over? The passengers? Them hogs? Got an opera troupe to offload here. They'd make a fine sight jumping for the wharf, wouldn't they? Got sugar. Got wine. You name it. Always stop in Memphis. Always have. Always will. Not that it's any of your damn business."

"How about repairs? You got some repairs to make? Or maybe a repair on a repair that had already been made?" Jake had him boxed now against the rail. One hard shove from him, and the officer would be water-borne, just like Ephraim.

"How in the hell would I know? I ain't the engineer."

"Maybe it's a repair on a repair on a repair." Henry had decided to chime in. "Or a repair on a repair on a repair on a repair. You want me to go on? You got my drift, Jake?"

The two, Jake and Henry, had been sniping at each other all day long, ever since Ephraim went under off the stern. This time, George thought, it might get serious.

"I get your drift, Henry." Jake had his back to Henry, still had the ship's officer pinned against the rail although he seemed to have forgotten that he was there. The tendons were standing out on his neck. "I get it all."

"Well, now, ain't that something, George. Jake gets it all!"

That's it, George thought. They're going to jump each other like two dogs in a pit, and for no other reason than they can't say what's really tearing them apart: a nephew, a best friend lost forever.

George got between them just as Jake spun around on his one good ankle, ready to charge. The boy must have sensed it, too, because he slid in beside George, a skinny pile of rags to hold off two storms rushing at each other. And that's when the idea hit George.

"How long are we gone to be tied up here?" he called to the officer, who'd made his escape and was putting all the distance he could in those jam-packed circumstances between himself, Jake, and Henry.

"Captain says two hours, but I wouldn't count on nothing. He wants to get this load to St. Louis fast as he can."

"Well, that about does it," George said as the officer disappeared into the crowd.

"Does what?" Jake was still steaming, but George could feel the rage leaving off him.

"The boy," George answered. "We can't introduce him to society in Muncie looking all tatterdemalion like that. He needs some clothes appropriate to his new station in life."

"And what are you going to pay for them clothes with?" Henry had eased off, too — found someone else to ride for a while. "I don't recall them giving away outfits, even for young gentleman."

"Captain Downey," George answered.

"Captain Downey? Back in Cahaba? Hell, he's long gone."

"Sure," George said, "but his bequest isn't."

George threw the saddlebags over his shoulder, took a quick eyeball measure of the boy — shoulders, pants length, waist — and started for the stairs down to the main deck.

"Time I'm through with him," he called over his shoulder, "he's going to look like Bonnie Prince Charles."

40

For a man who only that afternoon had seen his dead brother consumed by the mighty Mississippi, George was almost glowing as he returned to the flood-shaken Memphis wharves. Not only had he found a merchant with shelves inexplicably stacked with the goods he sought; the merchant had also appreciated the hand-tooled quality and supple leather of the saddlebags George had to trade if they were to bring the boy properly into Muncie society, or what there was of it.

What might have taken two hours had taken less than one. Deals had been struck in utter amity. They'd drunk a toast to celebrate: The war was gone. We were one nation again. They had clinked cups a second time, pledged everlasting fealty — although to what would remain unclear — and George was on his way, filled as so rarely in recent years with the milk of human kindness. My natural state, George thought. War had reamed it out of me. Now corn whiskey was encouraging it back.

He had two packets under his right arm and one under his left, all carefully bound with string, when he rounded the Custom shed, heard the *Sultana* ring its hurricane-deck bell, and watched the guards herding maybe two dozen caterwauling drunk soldiers toward the gangplank while a pen of hogs grunted from the wharf, happy for the entertainment and glad to be land-bound again.

Just behind him rose a bigger racket still. George turned to see four guards hauling a familiar giant, two on each arm, toward the ship. Turns out, he did know someone on board.

"Big Tennessee!" George yelled, his own ear-to-ear grin playing across his face. But Big Tennessee was beyond pain, beyond sense, beyond recognizing even (George supposed) his own mother.

"Ha-Ya!" he kept roaring. "Ha-Ya!"

"Let's leave him," one of the guards said. "This one ain't worth it." The others were about to agree when George laid his packages carefully on a packing crate, fell in behind the raging giant, and started pushing for all he was worth. Big Tennessee had been full of good deeds. He deserved one of his own, and it worked. Slowly, forward momentum built. By the time George turned back for his packages, Big Tennessee and his escort were barreling pell-mell for the gangplank.

Paid in full, George thought, as he cradled his packages in his arms, turned again, and saw the gangplank draw up and the *Sultana* begin to pull away into the broadening river.

"Wait!" he yelled, running to the wharf's edge. "Wait dammit!"

"Already gone." The explanation came from a dark-browed man tying his up own steam-powered tender where the *Sultana* just vacated.

"But why? I was just ...."

"Captain has no time to waste. He's burning too much coal. Got to go cross river to the yard at Hopefield and load up with another 50 tons or so if he wants to make it up to St. Louis."

"Any chance you could catch it for me?"

The boatman gave George a good hard gaze, turned around to his immediate tasks, then looked up at him again.

"Depends on what you got in those packages."

"How's that?"

"Well," the boatsman said, "even I'm not likely to mistake you for one of those fine officer-gentlemen Captain Mason got crammed into his staterooms, so I'm guessing that whatever you got to pay me with, you just spent."

George untied one package and held up a linen-colored shirt, so spanking new it didn't seem real.

"Mighty handsome," the man said. "Ought to fit my boy just about right. What else?"

A pair of pants came out of the next package, too big by inches but something to grow into. Didn't make any sense to buy something just for the moment. Ephraim was gone, but the boy was a weed, and the rest of them were in it for the long haul.

"Britches! Hell's bells, Beauregard's got an outfit!"

The boatman lifted a pair of heavy burlap sacks from the wharves and dropped them by his feet.

"Climb in," he said to George, "I got to run back over to Hopefield anyways."

41

Selma, back in Alabama, had looked like it had been trampled by elephants and set on fire with dragon's breath when George and the other Muncie men disembarked there a few weeks earlier, in the infancy of their liberation. But at least they had ruins in front of their eyes to suggest what once had stood there before Selma's Confederate defenders had lit their own stores on fire and the Federals had set about finishing the job for them. Hopefield couldn't even claim that.

Founded by a Dutchman just before the end of 18th century in what was then Spanish territory and conveyed to American hands by the Louisiana Purchase — thus Campo de la Esperanza became Hopefield — the town had prospered at the conjunction of river and rail, and despite the constant threat of flooding. Mighty Memphis, after all, was directly across the way, reason to dream, but Memphis was also Hopefield's Achilles Heel.

Early in the war, a Confederate armory was established at Hopefield, another feather in its gritty cap. Then in June 1862, Memphis fell into Union hands, and Hopefield became such a rear-guard burr in the saddle of the Northern occupiers that the following February, Major General Stephen Hurlburt ordered the place burned to the ground, just to shut it up, and so it was. By the time George stepped off the tender with his one surviving package, the place was nothing but a rickety rank of piers and a small mountain of coal, Hopefield's last reason for being, the one useful artifact of its past that remained of the place.

"Step lively," the tender captain told George as he heaved the two burlap sacks on shore. A woman and two men were waiting. One of the men picked up the sacks as if they were filled with feathers and swung them beside him as he headed for a wagon waiting by the road. As George clambered out, the remaining man and woman lowered themselves into the steamer and took his place. A rough, hand-painted sign was nailed to the piling the captain had tied up to: "Memphis-Hopefield Ferry. 50¢. We don't *never* stop running."

George turned to curse the boatman, but he was already pulling away with a merry wave. River life was confounding, no matter which shore you landed on.

The *Sultana* was tied up at the other end of the wharf, taking on sacks of coal — hundreds upon hundreds of them by the looks of it. George was almost up to the wheelhouse when he saw a cluster of men slipping down the gangplank and heading for a stand of willows. The walk of one of them, his hunch, the round of his shoulders was as familiar to George as the back of his own hand.

"Henry?"

The shadow stopped, turned.

"I couldn't do it, George. You got to do it for me."

"Do what?"

"Tell them goodbye. Jake. The boy."

The Irishmen had stopped maybe ten feet ahead and turned themselves.

"Gotta get going. Wagon's waiting," one of them said.

"Goodbye?"

"You heard about the railroad?"

"Can't say I have, Henry. What about it?"

"They're building one. Clear across the country. All the way to the Pacific Ocean."

"And?"

"And we're going to help them build it. These boys" —
the Irishmen were shuffling their feet, impatience leaking
out all over them — "been recruited. I'm going with them."

"But Henry —" He'd known Henry all his life, known
him when he was a baby, known him through the best and
worst. You didn't just up and leave something like that.

Henry put a hand on his shoulder, looked George
straight in the eye, something he hadn't been constituted
to do. George could see dead Ephraim in his eyes, Henry's
suffering mother, everything about his brother's best friend
— Josephus, too. Josephus most of all.

"I'm just going to kill him, George, or he's going to kill
me. That ain't much to go home to."

Henry turned, caught up with the Irishmen, then turned
once more.

"I'll send for my mother, George. I promise that. I'll send
for her." And then Henry, too, was gone — the Muncie Men
pared to three.

42

Muncie, Indiana,
1:30 a.m., April 27, 1865

At first, she thought it was a bird pecking on the rough-hewn siding George had managed to hammer over the log walls in those hurried weeks before he and Ephraim, Henry and Jake had marched off to war. Spring was on, sap rising. Except what sort of bird would be rat-tat-tatting in the deep dark of night?

Could it be one of the children — a nervous thrumming? Mice scavenging? The hard beating of her own blood and heart, always worse when she woke up alone in the still hours long before morning?

The door, she finally thought. A knocking. Gentle but insistent. What in heaven's name?

Eliza found a robe long ignored to slip over her nightdress, lit a candle from the embers of the fire so carefully banked by Little George — hardly "Little," his split wood, almost a man now — and started for the door.

She could hear it now — "Eliza," whispered so as not to wake the children, not the voice she wanted to hear, home from war now that the war they said was over, but a voice she would have recognized anywhere all the same.

"Doctor Sitterson!" His buckboard waited just behind him, the horse all but asleep in its traces. Even in the weak candlelight, she could see the dark rings around his eyes. "The Raccoon" everyone called him, perpetually overworked.

"So sorry to wake you at this hour, Eliza, but I was coming out this way to see Peyton Bursk — he sent word he'd broken his hip again — and Miss Aggie asked me to carry this letter out to you."

"Letter?"

"I would have had it here sooner, but Peyton's made a mess of it this time."

"From George?"

"I've been out there half the night trying to get him settled down."

"The letter, Doctor Sitterson, is it from George?"

"Well sure, I reckon so. Looks like it's come a long way. That's why I wanted to get it here. I figured there wasn't any acceptable reason to delay."

"Oh, thank you. Thank you! Don't you want to sit a second, before you head back into town? I could put some water on."

The doctor shook his head, tipped his hat, and turned to go. "I've done about all the sitting I can stand tonight. I'm hoping it's good news, and I suspect you want to start reading."

Eliza was latching the door when she heard coughing behind her. George and Eben stood by the fireplace, rubbing sleep out of their eyes. Madeleine was wandering toward her mother with a thumb stuck in her mouth.

"It's your Daddy," Eliza said, holding the letter up. "Boys, you get that fire going. It's always colder in the dark. Madeleine, pull in some blankets."

The Sultana, *Texas deck*

"Let me get this straight." Jake picked up the flap hanging from the long-johns the boy was holding up and let it drop again. "Let me just understand. You took them hand-tooled saddlebags and hornswoggled those poor rubes in Memphis, Tennessee, into trading them for a brand new Union suit."

"Jake — "

"I swear, George, I just sometimes don't know how you do it."

"Jake, please."

"Why, when I think of the figure this here boy is going to cut walking down Division Street with us, wearing his brand spanking damn new Union suit, it just makes me feel I don't know how inside. Robbery, George. That's what you're guilty of. Just plain robbery."

"Jake, I never meant for everything to turn out so bad."

There was a hitch in George's voice, something wrecked. Tears had started to stream down his cheeks. The boy didn't know which was more amazing — George's crying or something he'd never had before, never thought of having: a new piece of something to wear. Miracles kept piling on miracles as Jake stepped toward his nephew and wrapped him in his brawny arms.

"You couldn't a done nothing," he said in a whisper, his mouth no higher than George's neck. "Listen to your old useless uncle: You couldn't a done a thing."

"But I said I'd bring him home."

"And you're bringing the boy home, instead. And you gave a helping hand to Albert here when no one else would make space for him."

"This war ain't changed things *that* much, it seems," Albert added, worried himself. "I was about out on my feet."

"Things have purposes, George," Jake said. "There's a plan. Ephraim's gone. Henry's lit out for California, just the way he should'a. And the boy's coming with us. Out of death, life. Out of absence, presence. Don't the Bible say that?"

George shook his head. Try as he could, he couldn't stop a smile. "I don't know. I never heard you quote the Bible, Jake."

"Well, I'm not so sure I ever did afore, and I doubt I just did then. Hear that?"

A fiddle and a banjo had started up on the backside of the pilot house. Men were clapping. Boots and bare feet stomped the boards. The boy had already scurried to the top of the aft rail, Union suit held high, flapping like a regimental banner in the night breeze. Below him, the *Sultana* was winding its way through a maze of here-today gone-tomorrow islands known as Paddy's Hen and Chickens.

No one dared join the boy that high, but as the crowd cleared out in front of them and migrated toward the music, they could make out in the light shining down from the pilot house a circle at the center of the din and dancers jumping into it as the music played on.

"George" — Jake put his nephew at arm's length and turned him toward the music — "ain't it true no one jumps like a Muncie man?"

"It's a given fact."

"Me and the boy and Albert here, we're gonna have a look from the rail. I'm getting a little old for this business, and Albert and the boy are still kind of new to Muncie ways. Why don't you go show them left-footed clodhoppers what dancing really is."

Muncie, Indiana

The fire had burst into flame in no time. Madeleine curled in Eliza's lap; George and Eben were pressed in on either side of her.

"My dearest Eliza," she began to read. "What I would give to be back in Muncie with you and the children just now — the stars, the moon, everything I might ever own.

I've dreamed so many times that I'm waking up in our bed. I can hear little George shuffling around in the kitchen, getting the fire going. Eben is trailing behind him. Madeleine, God bless her, barely makes a sound in her crib. And your body …"

Eliza went silent, read briefly ahead. "Some of this you don't need to hear," she finally said. By then, Little George had blushed a beet-red.

The Sultana, *engine room*

Wintringer was screaming into the fire room.

"Stoke it, you lazy nigger sonsuvabitches. Stoke it! That coal ain't going into the furnace on its goddamn own!"

He could feel the ship slowing, yawing in the current. He thought for a moment about climbing down into the hold, taking the huge monkey wrench hanging from his left hand to every last one of them. Instead, he spun around, and there, face unto him, was the jerry-rigged boiler patch, two feet long, a foot wide, glowing an angry crimson against the flat gray of the rest of the boiler. The patch seemed to be almost pulsating with a life of its own.

"Shit," Wintringer said, half aloud. "Fucking Holy Jesus shit." His mother, he knew, would die again if she could have heard him.

Muncie, Indiana

"We all look out for each other," Eliza was reading. "Why this stationery I'm writing you on was giving to me by Capt. Downey. He's about the only officer in here." Madeleine was almost asleep again. Eben yawned and leaned in heavily on his mother's breast. Only George was fully awake — like a raptor, Eliza thought, circling hungry over every word. "The captain said just this morning that he was going to give me his saddlebags when we finally get free. He said he wouldn't have hands enough left to carry all the things he wanted to take with him. I like the life out of him."

The Sultana, Texas deck

George took two or three steps to fall in rhythm with the musicians, pulled off his shirt and threw it aside, and jumped into the circle. My God, Jake thought, George is alive again. What in the Hell *did* the Bible have to say about that?

Muncie, Indiana

"Ephraim hit a rough patch a few weeks back, but he gets a little stronger every day. You tell Mama and Papa that Jake and me are doing everything we can to keep him and Henry out of trouble down here. ... We're going to bring Ephraim home safe and sound. Mama and Papa can count on that."

The Sultana, Texas deck

One by one, the other dancers dropped out until George was alone in the circle, bending with the music, moving to it, testing the limits of his own ability. *Ars longa, vita brevis.* The Latin came to him from nowhere and everywhere — another favorite of his always-surprising mother. Art is long, life short. He dropped into a crouch, coiled his legs. The whole center of the deck was riveted on his performance. What was art? What you did? What you wanted? What you dreamed might one day be? Maybe it was simple: one perfect thing.

Muncie, Indiana

"O, Eliza, hug the children for me. Don't ever let them go." She reached out, pulled them all to her. Even Little George, reluctant to be a child any longer, leaned in for all he was worth. "Listen to this. Listen children," she read. "My darling, my darling. We just heard. We're free. Free! Henry, Jake, Ephraim, and me — we're Muncie bound!"

Through the shouts of the children, Eliza could barely hear the clock on the mantle strike two chimes.

The Sultana, *Texas deck,*
2 a.m., April 27, 1865

The musicians, the clappers, the foot stompers — they had all hit the peak of a crescendo and George had gone leaping into the air with them when the first of the four boilers exploded, followed instantaneously by two others, the force driving up through the center of the steamer in a rapid succession of energy waves, heat, and flames. Already launched, George was caught in the uplift and continued to rise into the night sky.

At the aft rail, Jake and the boy watched in amazement, then horror as a wall of fire raced out toward them from the center of the deck.

"Jump!" It was Albert, turned to them now. "Jump!"

But in the end, they had no choice. Whatever it was pushing out from the center of that doomed vessel launched Jake and the boy on their own ascension, this one bound by the immutable laws of gravity. The last thing they saw as they hurtled into the dark was Albert consumed by flames, air-borne with them.

43

The Mississippi

"Boy! Boy! Boy!"

Somewhere in mid-flight they had become separated — the boy, Jake thought, soaring off like a sparrow, and no better able to swim than one, lessons notwithstanding.

"Boy!"

He struggled to keep his head above water in the surging current, was pulled down in eddies, hurled up again, thrashed this way and that, those prize Garber No. 12s like deadweights now, impossible to pull off. Jake was trying to will night vision or something like it when he finally thought of Moses — if it was Moses — parting the Sea.

"BOY!"

And then, as had so often happened before, there was the boy magically beside him, clinging to a short piece of driftwood, beckoning Jake to join him.

Jake had just gotten his own, half-secure grip when there was a second explosion behind them — the final boiler gone — and the *Sultana* blossomed anew with flame. Looking back over their shoulders, they could see men leaping into the water by the hundreds upon hundreds — the new leapers, Jake supposed (and maybe the boy, too), landing on top of old ones and all of them being dragged down by each other, a mat of despairing humanity.

The steamer itself had begun to disintegrate. In the glow of the fire, they could see whole sections of the deck and superstructure breaking off and plunging into the river below.

No more than fifteen feet from them now, a chunk of bench drifted by with three charred and hollow-eyed soldiers sitting upright in it. That was followed by a terrifying braying to their other side. Jake and the boy turned in unison to see a soldier and mule fighting each other for a six-foot-square section of deck. Beyond that, its door yawning open, the alligator cage tumbled in the current.

The boy's eyes had flown wide open with that — An alligator? Where was it? — when their driftwood perch caught another eddy, was sucked down, and then shot back out so hard that Jake cracked his head on a passing piece of ship's timber. The boy lunged and grabbed Jake by his shirt just as he was about to let go. Blood was pouring over his forehead now, maybe one of those scalp wounds that bleeds out of all proportion to injury, maybe something worse.

"This ain't gone to work, boy." Jake said, washing the blood from his eyes. "We need us something more seaworthy."

As if providential, a mass of some sort was coming toward them. Jake reached out to grab it, saw it was a body, and let it pass. Two more followed, hurtled along on what seemed a special current reserved for the dead. Jake wanted to cover the boy's eyes, but what good would it do? And then, distracted, he nearly got his head stove in again by yet another section of decking that seemed to have been tailor-cut by some benevolent god to the boy's exact dimensions.

"Climb on it! Climb on! Now!"

The boy hesitated, looked pleadingly at Jake, and then with one more "Now!" roared in his ear, let the driftwood slip from his hands and scrambled aboard.

"You hold on, boy," Jake said to him, eyes locked on his. "You hold on to this thing with every bit of strength you got."

No! The boy was shaking his head No! No! No!

"It ain't big enough, boy. Don't you see that? Not but one of us can ride this. Hold on!"

Jake was drifting off with the current now. Behind the boy, the *Sultana* glowed red on the horizon.

"Don't let go. Son."

"Jake!"

Had he actually said it? For one last time, Jake's eyes filled with wonder, and love. And then he gave himself over to the river for good and left the world behind.

"Jake! Jake! Jake!"

Afterword

The *Sultana* left Vicksburg at 10 p.m. on April 24, 1865, carrying as many as 2,500 people, on a ship with a listed capacity of 376 passengers. Perhaps 2,300 of the passengers were soldiers — no exact count was made at boarding — and of those the vast majority had been recently released from the Confederate prisons at Andersonville, Georgia, and Cahaba, near Selma, Alabama.

Army Capt. Frederic Speed, who oversaw the loading of the *Sultana*, was court-martialed, but a Navy commission of inquiry largely exonerated Speed and his court-martial was eventually overturned. Capt. Speed and the *Sultana's* chief mechanic, Nathan Wintringer, were the only ones officially sanctioned for their parts in the disaster. J. Cass Mason, the *Sultana's* captain, died in the explosion.

The neglect brought on by the Civil War had left the dikes and levees along the Mississippi unprepared for the spring thaw of 1865. The best estimates are that the river stretched four miles across where the *Sultana* went down. A southbound steamer, the *Bostonia II*, happened upon the wreckage about 3 a.m. and managed to rescue hundreds of soldiers, but many of them died later of burns and other injuries, or simply of exposure. Water temperature was in the range of 60 degrees, and these were damaged men to begin with.

The first meeting of the Sultana Association was held in April 1885 in Fostoria, Ohio. On April 27, 1930, the association met for the last time. Present was a lone 84-year-old veteran named Pleasant Keeble. The last known survivor of the *Sultana*, Charles Eldridge, died in 1941, at age 96, in Dennison, Texas.

Because no exact count was made of the passengers who boarded the *Sultana*, the number of dead in the aftermath can only be estimated. Some say 1,800; others go as high as 2,200. Whatever figure is used, low or high, the explosion resulted in the greatest loss of life ever in U.S. waters. Only four battles of the Civil War claimed more Union soldiers: The Wilderness, Spotsylvania, Gettysburg, and Antietam. Ironically, because such a disproportionate number of the *Sultana's* passengers had come from Cahaba, that relatively unknown prison ended up having a higher effective death rate than the famous chamber of horrors known as Andersonville.

On June 27, 1999, at the Beech Grove Cemetery in Muncie, Indiana, a marker was placed in commemoration of those who died on the *Sultana*. This novel is dedicated to their memories and to the survivors forced to live with what they saw and experienced that early morning of April 27, 1865 — when peace was finally on the land and hope filled hearts so long despairing.

About the Author

Howard Means is a former senior editor at *Washingtonian*. He is the author or co-author of eleven books, including, most recently, *67 Shots: Kent State and the End of American Innocence* and *Splash! 10,000 Years of Swimming*. He and his wife, Candy, live in Millwood, Virginia, in the Northern Shenandoah Valley.

About the Publisher

The Sager Group was founded in 1984. In 2012 it was chartered as a multimedia content brand, with the intent of empowering those who create art—an umbrella beneath which makers can pursue, and profit from, their craft directly, without gatekeepers. TSG publishes books; ministers to artists and provides modest grants; and produces documentary, feature, and commercial films. By harnessing the means of production, The Sager Group helps artists help themselves. For more information, please see TheSagerGroup.net.

More Books from The Sager Group

Chains of Nobility: Brotherhood of the Mamluks (Books 1-3)
by Brad Graft

The Deadliest Man Alive: Count Dante, The Mob and the War for American Martial Arts by Benji Feldheim

Death Came Swiftly: A Novel About the Tay Bridge Disaster of 1879
by Bill Abrams

Sing Sing Follies (A Maximum-Security Comedy): And Other True Stories
by John H. Richardson

Going Home to Die No More: A True Kentucky Story about a Train Robbery and a Hanging after the Civil War
by Russ Witcher

Who She Was: My Search for My Mother's Life
by Samuel G. Freedman

On the Run with Mad Bombers, Outlaw Lovers & Movie Stars: True Stories
by Daniel Voll

Lifeboat No. 8: Surviving the Titanic by Elizabeth Kaye

Hunting Marlon Brando: A True Story by Mike Sager

Miss Haviland: A Novel by Gay Daly

Saloon Man: A German Immigrant Battles the Limits of Liberty, 1870 to 1915 by Robert Mugge

See our entire library at TheSagerGroup.net

THE SAGER GROUP
Artifex Te Adiuva